Atlantis Rising

Atlantis Rising

Gloria Craw

Entangled Publishing, LLC
2614 South Timberline Road
Suite 109
Fort Collins, CO 80525

Entangled Teen is an imprint of Entangled Publishing, LLC.

Visit our website at www.entangledpublishing.com.

Edited by Liz Pelletier
Cover by Liz Pelletier
Interior design by Jeremy Howland

Hardcover ISBN 978-1-62266-519-8
Paperback ISBN: 978-1-63375-305-1
Ebook ISBN 978-1-62266-524-2

Manufactured in the United States of America

First Edition January 2016

10 9 8 7 6 5 4 3 2 1

To my sister, Jennifer, who believed in me and this project from the beginning, and to my husband, Mark, who believed until the last.

Prologue

This is all I know about my real mother. Her hair was white, and her eyes were gray, like the sea on a stormy day. She was one of the last of her clan and powerful for someone so young. She fought a great evil and almost won the battle. She was twenty-six years old when she died. I was a baby then. Not old enough to form a memory of her face, how she smelled…or even how her voice sounded.

Chapter One

I left my house the first day of my senior year thinking I had everything under control. Fillmore High, better known as Feel-Me-More High, wasn't a complicated place to navigate. I'd spent the last few years observing my classmates with a kind of hungry curiosity, so the social network wasn't difficult to steer through. The plan for this year was to get decent grades, keep my head down, and stay out of trouble. I didn't like my life in the shadows, but lives depended on me staying as invisible as I could.

The problem was, my mom stopped at the main entrance of my school rather than the side entrance like she'd promised, and we were in her candy-apple-red Porsche Carrera. Several kids had gathered in groups on the lawn. They all turned to see who would get out of such an obnoxiously expensive car in front of a run-down public school in a sketchy part of town. It was a valid question. I'd attended a nicer school closer to our house until my sophomore year, when I'd begged my parents to transfer me out of district. I'd wanted a new start where no one knew me. To be honest, I'd come to like the crumbling monstrosity that was Fillmore High School. People tended to mind their own business and there was a certain charm to the old architecture in the area.

Cursing my luck and my adoptive mom's insistence that I be chauffeured around like a twelve-year-old, I grabbed my backpack to get out. Mom gripped my arm, stopping me. "I've got to teach a yoga class this afternoon," she said. "You can catch the bus to work, right?"

I rolled my eyes. "Why didn't you just let me drive myself? I have my own car. I'm ridiculously responsible. I even pay for my own car insurance."

Mom patted my knee. "Don't be mad, Alison," she said, looking reminiscent. "I wanted to drive you one last time."

She could be aggravating, but then, I'd heard most parents could be. A ride to school on the first day was a family tradition, and not much topped tradition when it came to my mom. Catching the bus to work would be a major pain, but it was impossible to stay angry with her. I smiled. "Sure," I said. "I'll manage somehow."

As she pulled away in her flashy car, the stares of a least ten kids zoomed in on me. I formed a thought—*The flag is on fire*—and pushed it into their minds. Expressions of shock and astonishment crossed their faces and their heads turned quickly toward the flagpole in front of the school.

I sighed in relief. The results of my thought transference were mixed. Sometimes it worked like a charm; other times I had a hard time making it stick. Fortunately, it worked this time, and no one gave a crap about me as I continued on.

I switched my backpack to the other shoulder while the sun's heat beat down on my back like a death ray. It was seven thirty in the morning and already eighty-five degrees. That's how August in Las Vegas was. You accepted it after a while, but you never got used to it.

I opened the heavy glass doors at the front of the school, and a gush of cool air hit me. Fillmore might be a crumbling pile of bricks, but the air-conditioning was top-notch. It had to be, or the student body would die of heatstroke. Several people watched me come in, so I kept my expression bland, and their eyes glazed over with a lack of interest.

Dressed in my usual camouflage—jeans and a nondescript T-shirt—I wasn't much to look at. I wore thick-rimmed glasses and no makeup. I also pulled my dark hair into a bun at the back of my neck, which added greatly to the blah factor. I'd designed my style to look like paint on the wall—there but rarely noticed.

Putting my earphones in, I turned up the volume on my iPod and stepped into the crowd. The place reeked of cheap cologne, drenched on the boys with reckless abandon. People were wearing their best, which in Vegas was usually a new pair of shorts and an overpriced T-shirt. Everyone was trying to impress but appear casual at the same time. Not many managed it. I watched the smiles and conversations around me, feeling the familiar bubblings of envy.

I didn't have friends at Fillmore High, not a single one. I wasn't friendless in the sense that I couldn't make them. I practiced good personal hygiene and could carry a conversation. I'd been a sociable and outgoing girl once, but that version of me had gone into storage years ago. I kept things as impersonal as possible now.

I pushed and dodged my way through groups of talking kids until things started to thin out around the north hall. Only a few people had gathered there, and most of them stood alone, working the dials on their lockers.

Skirting around a janitor wielding a mop and bucket, I tried not to gag on the pungent odor of industrial cleaning supplies. The north hall always smelled funny because it was home to maintenance and supply closets. It was long and dark, too, giving it a creepy feel. It wasn't anyone's first choice for a locker assignment. Except for me. I'd wanted one there because the majority of the metal boxes around it would stay empty for the year.

I found my locker and flipped the dial back and forth. I didn't need a written reminder of the alpha sequences… or anything else, for that matter. One of the benefits of being like me was perfect recall. Since my eighth birthday, everything I'd seen or heard had been stored away in a neat filing system in my brain. The lock clicked under my fingers, and I stacked some notebooks on the bottom shelf. Then I stuck a mirror and a picture of my dog to the inside of the door. The result wasn't homey, but it appeared occupied and that was good enough for me. I would open it a couple of times each day, but I would never leave anything I actually used inside it. One of the rules I lived by was keeping my personal things with me at all times.

Halfway down the stairs to my first class, a gangly boy and a girl who was round in all the right places were putting the Feel-Me-More back into Fillmore High. It was impossible to get around them, so I cleared my throat loudly. When they didn't look up, I tapped the boy on the shoulder. He mumbled something like "Go away" but didn't shift. I focused and then sent "*Move*" into both of their minds.

The girl backed against the wall and the boy quickly shifted to resume his Velcro stance against her. I squeezed by them.

I faded into the darkness below with a big smile on my face.

I was the first to arrive for AP English. The room was typical of most in the building, boxlike, bars on the windows, and white walls with brown carpet on the floor and up the kickboard. The only thing missing was a straitjacket.

The desks had been arranged to form a tight semicircle at the front of the room. I was going to have a neighbor on at least one side no matter where I sat, so I chose the chair farthest from the door. Unzipping my backpack, I got out the supplies I would need. I'd turned getting ready for class into an art form. I could stretch getting my stuff organized on my desk out for two minutes. Those who lived in the shadows learned to look busy even when we weren't. As usual, I kept my head down while the class filled up fast around me. When a warm body slid into the chair next to mine, I looked through my lashes to see who it was.

Connor McKenzie was cute and always dressed to perfection. He even ironed his shorts. He was also notoriously talkative. Opening my notebook, I began doodling, hoping he'd see the illusion I worked to create…a silent uninteresting girl.

I cursed internally when he cleared his throat in preparation for conversation. It wasn't that I didn't want to talk to him. It was that I shouldn't. Knowing what was coming, I formed the thought *Talk to the girl on your right.*

The girl on his right was the female half of the kissing couple from the stairwell. The boy half was sitting next to her, and they were still exchanging saliva. Connor wasn't ballsy enough to intrude on that type of conversation, and I couldn't say I blamed him. He turned back to me instead. "You're Alison, right?" he asked.

I nodded.

"You're a senior."

I nodded again and sent the thought *You don't want to talk to this girl* into his mind.

My transference would sometimes short-circuit if the target was really fixed on something specific. Talking was as necessary to Connor as breathing was to the rest of us, so he continued, "We're all seniors then. Except for him." He gestured toward a really cute blond boy sitting across the room next to a girl with curly hair. "That's Ian and Brandy Palmer. They're new. I think they're cousins or something."

I nodded a third time, hoping my silence would discourage him. I should have known better. Nothing discourages a talker when they're in the mood.

"So, what's your last name?" Connor asked. "I know your first name is Alison because we had trig together last year. Mr. Yardley called on you sometimes. You always got the answers right."

Rather than let Connor draw attention to us by looking like he was talking to himself, I gave in. "My last name is McKye," I said.

"Hey, that's Scottish. I'm in a Scottish heritage group online. I'll give you the site. You should join. It's—"

"I don't have Scottish heritage," I replied, cutting him off. "I'm...adopted."

Mrs. Waters, our teacher, walked in, putting an end to Connor's talking. Which was good because he seemed the type that wouldn't hesitate to pry into someone's adoption, and I really didn't want to go into how I'd been passed around in foster care for five years before the McKyes came along and rescued me.

Calling for our attention, Mrs. Waters started handing books around. In a no-nonsense tone, she told us to open our poetry text to William Blake's *The Tyger*. Then she asked Melissa, of the make-out pair, to read it aloud.

I followed along with half my brain while Melissa read. The other half of my brain retrieved a picture of the room and everyone in it. With the exception of the hot guy and his cousin across the room, I knew all of my classmates. There were only eleven of us in the room. I hadn't anticipated so few. Such a small group would be difficult to hide in, and it worried me. My stomach was doing nervous flip-flops when I glanced up and met the eyes of Ian Palmer.

He held my gaze and the corners of his mouth tipped up in a slow smile. It was a nice smile…warm and friendly. I was tempted to smile back, but studied my book instead. Melissa finished the last two lines of Blake's *The Tyger*: "What immortal hand or eye / Dare frame thy fearful symmetry?"

Ian would be another complication. I'd known before Connor pointed him out that we had AP lit together. I'd stood in the registration line with him last week. He was blond, about my height, with a long, strung-out build that told me he was growing upward faster than outward. My younger brother was going through the same kind of growth thing. Ian's eyes were an unusual color. From across the room, they appeared to be light blue. But up close, there were flecks of green, like the turquoise stone in a Navajo bracelet my mother owned.

Judging from the way he'd smiled at me, Ian remembered me from registration, too. And it didn't give me a warm fuzzy feeling.

"You will all be expected to read material in class when called on," Mrs. Waters continued, "and you will be assigned two in-class presentations each quarter."

More bad news. In-class presentations didn't fit with my plan to stay invisible. Mrs. Waters picked up some Post-it notes from off her desk. "I have the names of five poets in my hand," she continued. "You will each pick a slip of paper and partner with whoever gets the same poet as you."

My stomach churned as I took my paper and unfolded it. "Lord Byron" was spelled out in dark print. Stomach problems stayed with me for the rest of class and got worse when everyone started searching for their presentation partners afterward. I overheard Connor's exclamation of happiness when he found out he had Keats, the same as Nate Hopkins. Whether Nate was as delighted as Connor, I couldn't tell. Ian's cousin, Brandy, was standing close to Michael Larson, their eyes locked on the Post-it note in her hand. Evidently they were partners, too.

I repacked my things, trying to figure out how I was going to handle the situation. Nervous energy made me drop my class schedule, and it fluttered to the floor. Annoyed, I bent to get it and then started walking without looking up. It came as a complete surprise when I walked into a soft cotton shirt and the surprisingly strong chest beneath it.

Finally, physics class had taught me something I could reference. *When two objects collide, the lighter one gets knocked farthest off course.* I was the lighter object, and I felt myself careening off balance with no hope of correction.

My last thoughts were that my head was in line to collide with the edge of the desk where Connor had been sitting, and that the chest responsible for my imminent pain belonged to Ian Palmer.

Chapter Two

I fell to the side, my head hit the desk, and I crumpled to the floor like a wet noodle. The impact didn't knock me out, but it stunned me so much I couldn't remember where I was for a moment.

"Alison, are you all right?" Mrs. Waters asked. Concern showed on her face as she looked at the warm liquid running down the side of my neck.

I reached up to touch it and searing pain shot through my head. Squeezing my eyes closed, I swallowed hard. The last thing I wanted was to cry in front of people I wanted to remain a stranger to. "I think I'm okay," I managed to say.

Mrs. Waters took my hands and helped me sit up. The room went fuzzy and came into focus again. As I looked at the people around me, the seriousness of my situation registered. Not only was I hurt, but I'd given the people in room seventeen a reason and the opportunity to mark me in their memories. If any of them had a stronger than normal interest in my fall, I wouldn't be able to make them forget about it now. I wouldn't be invisible to them anymore.

Closing my eyes, I formed the thought *nothing to remember* and pushed it into all the minds around me. A wash of crushing pain and then fatigue followed. I'd never felt pain or weakness in connection with transference before, which made me fear some real damage had been done to the inside of my head.

I opened my eyes to see if my efforts had any success. The results were mixed. Connor, Ian, Brandy, and Mrs. Waters continued to stare at me, but the others didn't seem interested anymore. "I think she's going to be okay," Mrs. Waters said to the people who cared. "You'd better get to your next class, everyone. The second bell will ring shortly."

Six of my classmates filed out the door without glancing back. The others stood in a semicircle around me. Ian got to his knees, his attention focused on the bleeding gash on the side of my face.

"I'm really sorry," he said. "I shouldn't have been standing so close to you. I didn't expect you to turn around that fast."

"Really," his cousin, stated. "I thought that was your plan. Knocking people down is the best way to make friends at a new school."

Her sarcasm didn't faze Ian. He asked Mrs. Waters to hand him the box of tissue on her desk and then he handed one to me. I applied gentle pressure over the cut with it. Ian was too close for comfort, so I shifted to put more distance between us. When I pulled the tissue away, it was saturated with blood. "I think I'm going to need more tissues," I muttered.

"You need to see the nurse," Connor said. "I'll help you get up."

He took my arm with enthusiasm and pulled. Not much happened. At almost six feet, I was four inches taller than him. He couldn't get enough leverage to raise me from the floor. I tried to help by getting get my feet under myself, but my legs weren't taking orders from my brain the way they should. Connor kept pulling even after I gave up.

Ian's eyes were lit with amusement. "I got it," he said, waving Connor off.

A second later, I was lifted off the floor and onto my feet. Ian steadied me with his arm around my back. When I came to my senses enough to realize it, I jerked away from him. Ian noticed my reaction and backed away, too. I hadn't meant to offend him after he helped me, but I'd been avoiding anything more than a handshake for so long his arm along my back almost burned.

Mrs. Waters checked me over and gave a quick nod. "I'll take you to the nurse now. We have to hurry, though. I've got tenth-grade English in two minutes."

"I can make it to the nurse's station on my own," I assured her.

"I don't know..." Mrs. Waters replied, with an expression that said *I seriously doubt it.*

As if on cue, Ian and Connor said, "I'll take her."

"You take her, Ian," Mrs. Waters said. "I'll call the office and explain what happened."

"Where's your next class?" Connor asked, trying to be useful. "I can tell your teacher."

I had enough presence of mind to look around for my class schedule before answering. Ian picked up the crumpled paper from under my desk and handed it to me. I glanced at it. "Trig with Mr. Armstrong in room one ten."

"My next class is in room one oh nine," Brandy chimed in. "I'll tell Mr. Armstrong for you."

"Thanks," I replied.

Connor's face squished into a pouty expression. He'd tried and failed in three attempts to help me. Spending so much time alone, I'd fallen out of the habit of sympathizing with people, but I did feel bad for him. He was trying to be nice. "Thanks for the help, Connor," I said with a small smile.

That was all the encouragement he needed. His light brown eyes met mine and the twinkle in them returned. "Sure. I'll look for you at lunch…to check on you, okay?"

I managed to choke out something like "Super" before he left with Brandy. Mrs. Waters was right behind them.

"I'm Ian," my companion said.

"Alison," I replied.

He smiled at me and then reached for my bag. "Are you ready to go?"

"Really, I can go by myself. You don't need to come."

I followed up with thoughts in rapid succession: *The girl*

is fine. She wants to go to the nurse by herself. You shouldn't miss your next class. Raw pain shot through the side of my head and down my jaw. I had to sit on one of the desks to keep from falling over. Exhausted, I put my head in my hands. The worst part was that none of my thoughts worked. When I lifted my head, Ian was even more concerned than before. My transference was definitely messed up.

"Maybe we should stay here for a few more minutes," he suggested.

I considered it, but the only thing worse than feeling like crap was feeling like crap with him around. The sooner I got to the nurse, the sooner he would leave me alone. "No, let's just get this over with," I replied.

I took a breath and stood up. Then I held my hand out for my backpack. I got hold of a strap, but Ian didn't let it go. It turned into a weak game of tug-of-war. "I can carry my stuff," I insisted.

He tipped his head to the side, then let go. "If you say so, but you'll have to stay on the floor if the weight knocks you down again. I don't think I've got the strength to pick you up again."

It was a backhanded way of implying I was enormous when I was just tall. The remark would have offended me if his mouth hadn't quirked up at the corners, suggesting he was teasing.

"Don't worry," I said dryly. "I don't plan to fall down again."

He shook his head and sighed dramatically. "Well, we'll see what happens in the next few minutes."

He followed me out of the room and took up a position near my side. Every now and then he would check to see if I was doing okay. Halfway to the stairs he laughed. It was a great laugh, rich and full, a perfect complement to his smile. I glanced at him, wondering what he found so funny. "Don't take offense to this," he said, "but you look kind of…drunk."

I didn't understand what he meant at first, but then realized I was walking in jerky steps that veered to the left. "I never get headaches," I said, trying to explain something I didn't understand myself. "The pain is messing with my motor control."

"Sure, blame it on a headache," he said with more laughter in his voice. "I'm going to help you along a bit, so don't jump out of your skin when I touch you, okay?"

Even with a warning, I flinched when his arm went around my waist. It was worth it, though, because with his help, I managed a much straighter course. When we started up the stairs, he commented, "You look like you've been in a bar fight. You'll probably get sent home for the rest of the day."

"I hope not," I muttered.

He gave me a questioning look. "Missing school is generally thought of as a good thing."

"Not when your mom is Deborah McKye."

"Why is that?"

"You'd have to know her to understand."

I climbed the stairs and felt much better at the top. My healing ability was starting to kick in. Thank goodness. Thinking I didn't need Ian anymore, I pulled away from him. Then I formed the thoughts *The girl will be fine, go to your next class* and pushed them into his mind.

Like before, pain and a wash of fatigue rippled over me. I fell sideways against the wall. Ian caught me before I could slide down it. "Wow," he said, steadying me, "Maybe I should carry you."

I pushed his hands away, leaned my head against the wall, and closed my eyes. I'd gone from feeling better to feeling worse in a few seconds. If I wanted to stay upright, I was going to have to give thought transference a rest for a while.

"I just need a minute," I said. "You can move back now."

He shook his head like he was coming out of a dream. "Sorry. I'm just a little freaked out, I guess."

I had to push back a laugh. "You're freaked out. Try being me."

"When you hit the floor after class, I thought I'd killed you," he said. "Lying there on the floor with your eyes wide-open and blood pooling around your head…well, it scared the crap out of me. I don't want a repeat performance, so if you feel like you're going to faint, tell me now."

"I'm not going to faint," I assured him. "But just so you know, I thought you might have killed me, too."

He gave me a sympathetic laugh, and my eyes widened at the realization I'd just made a joke. It was a lame joke, but it was an attempt on my part to make another person laugh. I couldn't deny it felt good, but there was a reason I hadn't done it in a very long time. I didn't want to come off as amusing to anyone. I wanted to come off as boring. The blond boy next to me had breached some of my defensive walls, and by the light in his eyes, I assumed he liked doing it.

He was only a little taller than me, so when he smiled and ducked his chin, it looked endearing. Then a lock of gold hair fell low over his forehead, and the look turned into something else entirely. Something devilish and hot.

"I'm really sorry," he said.

I swallowed hard. The third apology wasn't an apology. It was just something to say. He shifted closer to me and tipped his head to the side. I could feel his exhale on my cheek. The quirk of his lips told me he knew exactly what he was doing, and I wasn't the first girl he'd tried it on. Maybe I should have been flattered, but it just irritated me.

"Are you kidding me?" I asked. "Are flirting with me right now?"

His expression changed abruptly. If I had to guess, I'd say he was as surprised as I was by what he'd tried. "That obvious, huh?" he asked.

"Try your smolder on a different girl. One without blood in her hair. I'm not in the mood."

Instead of being embarrassed or shamed by my rebuff, he seemed intrigued. Tan clothes and thick glasses notwithstanding, I'd become a challenge to him. And Ian Palmer was the kind that liked a challenge. What a disaster.

I pushed myself away from the wall and took a step to test my legs. They felt good, so I continued on. "I think we're partners for the poetry presentation," Ian said. "Everyone in class has already paired up."

Of course I would get him as a partner. He was already too interested in me. "Who did you get?" I asked.

"Lord Byron."

"We are partners," I admitted. "Yay for us."

"Yay for us," he repeated.

The nurse's station was empty when we got there. I was the first casualty of the day, because all three cots where still nicely made up with a paper sheets and thin cotton blankets. Nurse Paula came through the back door and, seeing me, hurried forward. Taking my hands in hers, she checked my face. The damage was bad enough that she immediately lead me to one of the cots and helped me sit down.

"Lie down, dear," she directed with a gentle push. I complied and then watched her bustle around collecting things from cupboards in the sterile white room.

Everything about Nurse Paula, from her ultra-short hair to her white slip-on shoes, spoke efficiency. She was back at my side in seconds. "This might sting a little," she said, waving a bottle of something and a cotton ball in my direction.

It did sting…bad enough to bring tears to my eyes. I almost whimpered as she applied the second coat.

"Sorry," Ian said with a sympathetic wince of his own.

It was the sting, not the apology, that irritated me, but I took it out on him anyway. "You've said sorry like…four times now," I growled. "Stop repeating yourself."

"Sorry," he replied automatically.

When the absurdity of his fifth apology occurred to me, I couldn't hold the laughter back. It burst out of me and rang off the walls. Ian joined in. That's when I saw the full force of his smile coupled with a laugh, and my breath caught in my throat. It was beautiful. He was beautiful.

"I don't see what you two think is so funny," Paula interjected. "You're going to be bruised like a ripe banana tomorrow."

"I'm a fast healer," I replied, turning my head away from Ian.

She snorted her disbelief and dabbed at me with the stinging stuff again. That's when I noticed I wasn't wearing my glasses. "Oh, no. I think my glasses fell off in the classroom," I said.

"No problem," Ian replied. "I'll go get them."

Paula continued her evil work after he left. "The cut isn't deep enough to need stitches," she said, peering closely at it. "You should remove the bandage and apply more antiseptic tonight. The right side of your face is going to be sore for a while. Aside from that, you should be fine."

I accepted her warning, but I hadn't been lying when I said I was a fast healer. My bruises faded and my cuts closed long before they should. The common cold lasted only a few hours in me, and like I'd told Ian, I never got headaches. Not until today, anyway.

She checked her handiwork one last time and appeared pleased. "I'll leave it up to you whether you go home or stay the rest of the day."

I didn't want Mom to come and get me. She'd spend the rest of the day fussing over me and driving me crazy. "I'll stay," I replied.

She pointed to a sink and mirror in the corner of the room. "You'll probably want to fix your hair. And stay here until the third-hour bell. That will give you some time to collect yourself. I'll be in the next room filling out your paperwork if you need anything."

I checked my watch. I had thirty minutes before my next class.

Sitting up slowly, I checked my balance. It was good enough so I could walk to the sink and look in the mirror. My dark hair had fallen out of its bun and was hanging in a crazy tangled mess around my shoulders. Paula had cleaned the blood off the side of my face and put a bandage over the cut, but the hair above my ear was matted with blood.

I turned the water on and let it run over my hands while it warmed. The heat reddened my skin, making the two faint blue lines in my palm, which I'd had for as long as I could remember, stand out. Seeing them like that reminded me of how I'd learned their significance.

At fourteen I'd met a man who changed my life forever. It was a hot day at the park where my younger brother, Alex, and I were splashing around in some sprinklers to cool off. When he sprayed me in the face with one of the hoses, I practiced a little sisterly retribution by putting *You just rolled in poison ivy* into his mind. He started to scratch his neck and arms like crazy. The effects of my thought only lasted a few seconds, just long enough for me to feel I'd gotten proper revenge.

Happy with myself, I walked to the grass and sat down to dry off in the sun.

"You did that, didn't you?" a deep voice asked from behind me.

I didn't think the question was directed at me, so I didn't answer.

"You did that, didn't you?" the voice asked again.

Curious, I looked around to see who was talking. A sandy-haired thirty-something man was staring at me. I moved to get up, and he repeated the question for the third time. "You did that, didn't you?"

I'd been through about a hundred stranger-danger lectures and I knew I should run, but I didn't. Something deep inside told me told me stay. "Did what?" I asked warily.

"You made your brother think he was itchy."

Since discovering my thought-transferring ability at the age of eight, I'd intuitively known not to tell anyone about it. Yet somehow this man *knew*.

"I do it sometimes," I replied.

"Have you ever tried to make someone think they were more than itchy?"

"No…it probably wouldn't work."

"That boy is my son," he said, nodding toward a little boy on the swings. He said it as though it should mean something to me. Then, nodding in the direction of my mom and dad, he added, "Those aren't your parents, are they?"

"Not my biological parents…how did you know?"

"Your parents would be our kind. They would have known it was you making the boy scratch himself like that." He paused a moment before continuing. "If I told you there were others like you, others who could do things with their minds, would you believe me?" My answer was *no* and *yes* at the same time. He didn't wait for an answer. "You probably never get sick," he continued. "You likely remember all sorts of things most people don't. I'll bet you're in the accelerated-learning program at your school, aren't you? Your parents and everyone else probably call you gifted."

"Yes," I said amazed that he knew so much.

"Humans think we're brilliant, but it's normal for our kind to remember, learn, and understand faster than they do."

"Our…kind," I repeated.

His eyes met and held mine while he raised his left hand so his palm faced me. Through the space that separated us, I saw the familiar outline of the letter *V* in his palm. The lines were faint in my hand, barely noticeable unless you saw them every day. The lines in his hand were a deeper blue, but the shape was a perfect match.

"There's not much difference between humans and us," he said. "Human medicine hasn't advanced enough to see the difference between our species. But make no mistake, the children of Atlantis are a separate people."

At this point, a normal girl would have concluded the man was delusional. But I wasn't normal. "The children of Atlantis?" I asked.

"We call ourselves the dewing," he continued. "It's an inside joke. Like dew on the grass in the morning, our elements are always present but seldom visible to humankind. We all have certain…abilities. I can join a mind to see emotions as clearly as words on page. This ability is fairly common. Yours is not, which makes you valuable."

I snorted at the idea that my itchy thoughts were valuable to anyone.

"You don't know what you're capable of," he insisted.

My mind whirled. A part of me wanted this conversation to be a figment of my imagination. Another part of me couldn't deny he knew way too much about me to be accidental.

"Alison, it's time to go," my dad yelled from across the park.

"I have to go," I said, getting up. "Can we talk again, though?"

"I'm afraid that's impossible. I'm only vacationing here. We leave tomorrow."

"Who else can I talk to?"

"No one," he replied sternly. "I shouldn't have spoken to you…it's just, you look so much like her."

"I look like who?"

The man called for his son and swung the child onto his shoulders. "A woman I owe my life to." There was both compassion and apprehension in his expression when he turned to me. When his eyes darted to the parking lot, I realized he was expecting someone and didn't want to be caught talking to me. "I'll leave you with some advice. You are one of us, but do your best to hide it. If you're lucky, that will shield you."

He turned to leave. Gripped by dread that I'd learn nothing else about myself and the mysterious dewing, I ran around to face him. "Explain what that means…please."

He nodded once, a concise movement, indicating what

was coming wouldn't be pleasant. "We are in the middle of a war. A struggle for power. As an unprotected thoughtmaker, you are valuable. There is someone who, if he knew you existed, would stop at nothing to control your power. If you love your human family, never use thoughtmaking for amusement. Use it to hide yourself. Use it to become as invisible as you can. It's the only way to protect yourself and them."

"Protect them from what?"

"He would hurt your humans in order to control you, and when he finished with you he'd kill you all."

I stood still, feeling the weight of the world shift and then settle onto my fourteen-year-old shoulders. I loved my adoptive family more than anything else in the world, and I knew in that moment, with surety I found devastating, he was telling the truth. My family was in mortal danger because of me.

He walked around me with a final warning. "Become invisible to protect your humans, thoughtmaker."

Now, three years later, I was standing in the sickroom, trying to get blood out of my hair and wondering what use I would be to anyone, dewing or otherwise. My thought transference was weak, unreliable, and limited.

I was twisting my hair into a bun when Ian came in with my glasses. He gave me a teasing smile as he held them out to me and then pulled them back. He was good-looking and he knew it. His hair was bright like sunshine and his eyes were fascinating. In a plain white T-shirt and worn jeans, he looked amazing. I could probably get around those attractions. It was his smile that could get me into trouble. I reminded myself to be on guard with him. I put my hand out for my glasses, and he handed them to me.

"I won't apologize again," he said, "but is there anything I can do…to make amends?"

I didn't intend to say anything, but for a moment my headache made things hazy and the words came tumbling out. "You could give me a ride to work," I said.

"Okay. I'm parked by the tennis courts. We can discuss our poetry presentation on the way."

He turned and walked out of the room. "Why did I say that out loud?" I muttered to myself.

Chapter Three

My last class of the day was Art Appreciation. It was popular, which should have made it easy for me to maintain a low profile. Except Brandy was in it, too. My calculus class had run late, so when I got to the room, most of the desks were already taken. Brandy saw me looking over people's heads for a place to sit and motioned toward the one next to her. There weren't that many options left, and I didn't have it in me to pretend I hadn't seen her, so I reluctantly went to sit down.

"Hey, how are you feeling?" she asked with a bright smile.

"I've still got a headache, but other than that I'm good."

"You look a lot better than the last time I saw you. Honestly, I didn't think you'd stay for the rest of the day."

"The nurse gave me the option of going home," I admitted, "but I'd feel the same way there as I do here."

She reached out and rested her hand on my arm, not seeming to notice how I froze at her touch. "You should take some ibuprofen," she suggested sympathetically. "A lot of it."

She went on to say something about one of her earlier classes. I would have liked to talk with her, but I couldn't let myself. Instead, I let my gaze wander and kept quiet while she chatted away. I could have been a potted plant for all she cared. She was one of those people that felt perfectly fine carrying on a one-sided conversation. Much like Connor. I rolled my eyes when she wasn't looking. Two talkers in one day was really bad luck.

Aside from the constant babble, she seemed nice. She was quite pretty, too. Her hair was dark brown and curly. Her eyes were so dark they were almost black. She was fortunate to have a skin tone that would always look tanned. "You and Ian have Byron for the presentation, right?" she asked. Without giving me the time to answer, she moved on to another subject.

As the minutes passed, it became more difficult to be withdrawn with her. Even though she didn't expect me to contribute much to the conversation, she had a dry wit that drew me in. When she said something funny about Connor trying to help me up from the floor that morning, I laughed. A glance in her direction showed she'd welcome more of it. Like Ian, she wanted to get to know me. I focused my attention on my pencil after that.

When our teacher, Mr. Dawson, walked to the front of the class and asked for our attention, I settled in for another boring first day lecture. I got a surprise instead. Mr. Dawson was middle-aged, short, and rounded, like a garden gnome. He must have been a fan of color, because he was wearing every shade in the rainbow somewhere on his squat frame. The introduction he gave was impressive, largely because he was passionate about the subject matter. He wasn't just teaching an art curriculum—he was teaching something he loved.

As he paced animatedly back and forth at the front of the room, I began to feel the stirrings of my own excitement. Since transferring to Fillmore, I'd slowed down academically. It was a dodge to avoid accelerated-learning programs where someone might look for me. The excitement I felt as Mr. Dawson talked was because I had no artistic talent whatsoever. The history part of the class would be easy for me, but the subjective aspects were going to be difficult. At least one of my classes would be a challenge, for a change. Like friendship, that was something I missed.

When the bell rang, I packed up and left class as quickly as possible. I thought I'd ditched Brandy, but she came up behind me when I stopped at my locker. "You left this on the floor," she said, handing me my class schedule.

The stupid thing had caused me nothing but trouble all day. "Thanks," I replied, stuffing it deep in my pocket.

"So…Ian is driving you to work today," she said.

"Yep. We're going to talk about our poetry presentation."

"He looked for you at lunch. Where did you go?"

I'd just met her and my eating habits were none of her business. My response was stony silence, but it didn't faze her. She stood there smiling like she was my best friend. Sighing, I replied, "I usually bring something from home and eat by my locker or in my car."

"That sounds lonely. You should eat with us tomorrow. There's a lot of something in the cafeteria."

"I don't like the something they serve."

She tried to form an argument in favor of the cafeteria's food, but it was a hard task. I decided to let her off the hook. "I'll think about it," I assured her. "Thanks for the offer."

That satisfied her and she ambled off, humming some tune I didn't recognize. Opening my locker, I straightened the mirror on the door and looked at the side of my face. As I'd expected, it was healing quickly. The swelling was entirely gone, but in its place was a multicolored bruise. The bruise wouldn't last long, either. It was the pounding in my head that concerned me most. It hadn't let up at all.

I squeezed out the school doors with the rest of the crowd and squinted in the bright sunlight. Putting my hand up to shield my eyes from the glare coming off the pavement, I mentally kicked myself for asking Ian to take me to work. I still didn't understand how it had happened. It was like some unseen force had pulled the thought out of my brain and sent it straight out of my mouth.

Ian and Brandy had become complications that I needed to get rid of. I understood that they were new at school and trying to make connections. I'd just been in the wrong place at the wrong time. With my head injury, I hadn't been able to use transference to get rid of them. Now I was left with only my own charming personality to work with. I didn't doubt I could be repellent, but I needed to strike just the right balance. I needed something that would be off-putting without being cruel. Cruel people were the most difficult to forget.

I was a sweaty mess when Ian came toward me. "Been waiting long?" he asked.

He stood with his backpack slung over his shoulder and a couple of books under his arm. The sun lit his eyes and glinted off his hair. I reminded myself not to be impressed. "Yeah," I replied.

"I didn't mean to keep you waiting. I had to talk to my physics teacher. I think the class isn't advanced enough for me, so he's letting me switch to the honors class tomorrow."

I nodded, deciding the best thing to do was come off as dull as dirt while we were together.

"Brandy said she has sixth period with you," he continued. "Art history, right?"

"Yep."

"That's a great elective."

"I guess so."

He gave me a fleeting glance, probably wondering if I'd lost brain function since leaving the sickroom that morning.

We got in his navy-blue Audi, and he turned the key in the ignition. The speakers banged to life with Daft Punk. It made the thumping in my head intensify.

"Sorry about that," he said, turning the volume down.

The car was sweltering, so he turned the air-conditioning

on full blast. It worked a lot better in his nice car than it did in my junker. I was a little jealous.

"Where am I taking you?" he asked, running his hands through his hair. It stood in little spikes when he finished.

"The new-and-used bookstore off of Vine."

"The Shadow Box?"

"Yes," I replied, surprised that he knew the place.

"That's not far from where I live. I've been in a few times, but the only person I've *ever* seen there is the angry-looking old woman behind the counter."

"That would be Lillian. She's not angry, she's just... Lillian."

He raised an eyebrow.

Figuring a discussion about Lillian was neutral territory, I went on. "She owns the Shadow Box. It doesn't attract a lot of customers, but that's okay because she really doesn't need the money. She makes a boatload of cash as a rare-book dealer."

"Why does she keep a place like that going if she doesn't need to?"

"She says she likes the smell of books around her while she works."

He glanced sideways at me. "The inside of that store smells like feet. Do you like working in the dark, cramped, stinky little space?"

"I like it well enough," I replied. "The hours are good, and I can usually finish my homework before I leave. The big bonus is that Lillian lets me take anything I want out of the used section as long as I return it. And just so you know, the smell is aged paper. According to Lillian, it's like the bouquet of a fine wine."

He chuckled. "So you have a passion for books, like Lillian?"

The conversation had taken a personal turn. "Not for smelling them, but I like reading them," I replied in monotone.

From that point on, I kept my gaze focused out the side window and refused to say more than three words at a time. Ian got the message and turned the conversation to the business of our Byron presentation. As the minutes passed, it became clear he loved books as much as I did. We would have no trouble giving our presentation on George Gordon Byron, because Ian was one of his biggest fans.

I caught him looking over at me a couple of times as we talked. I tried not to read too much into it, but it was surprising that he found anything interesting to look at where I was concerned. I thought I'd done an awesome job guarding against male interest. I certainly hadn't inspired any boys' attention before, which was good and bad.

Boys had been a complication since I'd taken my vow of invisibility. At first, I'd been frustrated by the necessity of keeping my distance from them, but the idea of a romantic relationship lost a lot of its appeal when I realized how much power I'd have over a boyfriend. There were limits to what I could do, but a hormonal teenage boy would be like putty in my hands. I could have my mental way with him, and he'd never know it.

There was also the fact that I didn't know how the

interspecies thing worked. Maybe I'd turn green and sprout horns if I kissed a human boy. I'd had my share of crushes, but knowing the risk factors, I'd grudgingly come to terms with remaining a single undefined species.

Whether I understood why or not, I had registered on Ian's radar. It made me nervous. Fortunately, I had a natural preference for tall, dark, and handsome types. Ian was too Captain America for my taste.

When he pulled the Audi in front of the Shadow Box, he asked, "How are you going to get home after work?"

"I'll take the bus," I said.

"I could come around and get you. This place closes at seven, right?"

"Yes, but I'm taking the bus home tonight. Thanks for the ride to work."

Lillian was sitting at her messy desk behind the counter when I went in. She watched with disapproval as Ian's car drove away. "Who was that?" she asked.

"Ian Palmer from school."

"I've never seen him before. Why did he drive you here?"

I pulled my dark green work apron off its hook, wondering who the stranger inhabiting my boss's body was. Lillian never asked me questions about my personal life. It was one of the things I liked best about her.

"My mom insisted on driving me to school this morning," I explained. "Then she couldn't pick me up. Ian physically assaulted me after first period, so he drove me here as penance."

She got up and came toward me. "He did what?"

I chuckled a little. "Don't worry. It was an accident. He knocked me off balance, and I hit my head on the corner of a desk. I'm fine."

She looked at the bandage on the side of my face and didn't appear convinced. I couldn't blame her. The bruise was pretty nasty looking.

"I was planning to run errands," she said, "but maybe I should stay."

"Go on. This is what you pay me to do."

She paused for a moment and then started looking for her car keys. Lillian was constantly misplacing important things. It was easy enough to do in the messes she created. I spotted her keys poking out from under the cash register and pointed toward them.

"Thanks," she said. "I'll be back around seven."

The bells above the door jingled as she left.

As usual, haphazard stacks of books had been piled on the floors, on the chairs, and behind the counter. Reshelving the tripping hazards was a big part of my job, so I started sorting through the piles. I found a copy of *Dragonsong* at the bottom of one of them. There were some powerful memories attached to the title, because it was the first book I'd bought when I found the Shadow Box.

After I met the dewing man in the park, my life had sunk to a new and depressing low. Detaching and then isolating myself from my friends left me bored and miserable. I'd started reading everything I could get my hands on so I wouldn't dwell on my own misery. The only downside to my new hobby was the price. My money went farther when I got books from the used section at the Shadow Box, and the dim, cramped space was comforting rather than repellent to me. There was the added benefit that not many people shopped there. Though it was a bus ride away, the store quickly became my favorite haunt.

I'd been a weekly regular for over a year when Lillian had approached me and asked if I was sixteen. She'd followed that question with, "Do you want to work here?"

Those were the longest sentences she'd ever said, and it had totally freaked me out. I'd scooted out the door as fast as I could, but I thought it through that night and accepted the job the next day. It was the best decision I could have made. My job was perfect. I was able to save money and get out of the house, and Lillian practically ignored my existence.

I only had one customer come in during my shift, and she didn't buy anything. By six thirty, I'd straightened the store and finished my homework. Bored, I walked back to the used section to check for new arrivals. There weren't any, but there was an unopened box stuck under the bottom of the bookcase. Assuming it was an order I needed to check in, I pushed the package out with my foot. Then I felt in my apron pocket for the utility knife I kept there.

When the bells above the door jingled, I glanced up to see a heavyset man wearing a dark fedora standing at the counter. "I'll be with you in just a minute," I said, finishing a cut on the box.

"Actually, that might be what I'm looking for," he replied

in a thick voice. "A package meant for me was left here by mistake today."

There was no shipping address on it, which was strange. Still, I wasn't going to hand it over to him without checking to make sure it wasn't for the store. I started to open the cardboard flaps, but his huge hand closed over my wrist. Jumping to my feet, I stepped away from him. "Yes, this is it," he said.

"I can't let you have it," I replied shakily. "You need to come back when my boss is here and check with her."

The man wasn't listening to me, or he simply didn't care, because he picked the box up and turned away. I knew what I was supposed to do under the circumstances. Lillian had made me promise never to put the money in the register or a book before my personal safety. I should have let the guy take the package, but for some reason, I *really* didn't want him to have it.

Gripping the utility knife tight, I shouted the thought *Put the box down* at him. Just as before, my head throbbed from the effort and it didn't work.

I ran up behind the man and grabbed a corner of the box. It surprised him enough that he loosened his grip. The box fell to the floor, bursting open. A large book spilled out of it. I didn't need Lillian around to tell me it was old and valuable. The leather binding had darkened with age, the cover was embossed, and the pages were gilded with gold.

I was quicker than the bulky man, and I got ahold of the book before he did. I held my utility knife out to look as threatening as I could. The man wasn't intimidated, though.

He slammed his fist into the side of my face, and I went flying backward, landing next to a bookcase. The fall completely winded me, but I hadn't let go of the book.

I struggled to catch my breath while he stood looking down at me. My headache intensified, and a cruel joy spread over his face. I kicked out, hoping to connect with his feet. He dodged, laughed, and then kicked me in the ribs. I had no strength left to hold on as he wrenched the book out of my hand.

The bells above the door jingled when he left.

A few seconds later, they jingled again.

Chapter Four

Figuring the man had come back, I played dead.

"You've got to be kidding me," Ian said from somewhere above me, in voice full of worry.

I opened an eye to find him staring down at me. "What happened this time?" he asked, kneeling next to me.

"Ugh," I replied.

My hair had come out of its bun and was splayed everywhere. He pushed it back from my face to assess the damage. His nose wrinkled in sympathy. "The cut has opened up again. There's a lot of blood. Where's the bathroom?"

I pointed.

His light eyes met mine. "Don't move until I get back," he said.

The last thing I wanted to do was to move, but lying on

the hard floor wasn't helping my aching ribs. Using a nearby bookshelf, I hauled myself to a sitting position. Then I sat there in a miserable heap with a blood-soaked bandage hanging loosely from the side of my face.

Ian came back carrying a roll of paper towels. He pulled the useless bandage off and gently blotted away blood. I hissed when he applied pressure over the wound. "I don't think you're going to need stitches," he said in the same tone Nurse Paula had used, "but you should go to the hospital and get checked out anyway."

Hospitals always meant tests, and though the dewing man in the park had said the differences between humans and us couldn't be detected, I never wanted to take the chance. "No, I don't want to go to the hospital."

Our eyes locked and a few seconds passed before he agreed. "All right, no hospital. Tell me what happened."

I was trying to decide where to begin the story when Lillian came in. The look of horror on her face when she saw me slumped on the floor would have made me laugh if my ribs hadn't hurt so much. Turning a suspicious look on the boy next to me, she retrieved something from the enormous black bag she was carrying. With a determined expression, she marched toward Ian, pointing a bottle of pepper spray at him.

"No, Lillian!" I shouted. "Don't spray him."

She blinked and then stopped with the bottle still raised. "What's going on here?" she asked.

I took a deep breath and explained as steadily as I could. "Some guy came in here and stole a book. I tried to stop him, but he hit me…then he kicked me. The important thing is Ian came in after he left." Lillian's grip on the bottle of pepper spray tightened instead of loosening. "I promise he's not hurting me. He's trying to help me."

Ian's eyes were fixed on the bottle. "I found her bleeding on the floor," he reaffirmed.

Finally she put the weapon back in her bag. "You know better, Alison," she said accusingly. "Never try to stop a thief. Whatever he took can't have been worth the risk."

I hadn't expected a thank-you card, but acknowledgment that I'd suffered bodily harm to protect her property would have been nice. I tried to straighten my back to ease out the pinch in my side. "It was one of your rare books," I grumbled.

"I don't keep my rare things here, you know that."

"I found it on the floor," I insisted. "It was packaged and taped up tight."

"Taped up tight," she repeated. "Did it have an address on it?"

"No."

She let out a long breath. "That package wasn't for me. It was for you. Someone came in this morning, handed it to me and asked me to give it to the dark-haired girl who worked here. I was going to put it away someplace safe, but I got distracted by a customer."

I searched my mind for anyone who would have left a book for me. There was absolutely no one. "They got the wrong store and the wrong girl," I said firmly. "I wasn't expecting a book."

Ian seemed to ignore what I said. "If this was a robbery,

we should call the police," he suggested.

I glared at him. "No hospitals or police."

Ian glanced at Lillian, hoping for backup, but she was undecided. "Technically, it was Alison's book. I suppose she should make the decision."

"It wasn't my book, so no police," I insisted. "The package was delivered here by mistake, and the guy came to get what was his."

"He hit you," Ian said. "That's reason enough to call the police."

"It was probably just his reaction to the box cutter I was waving under his nose."

Both Lillian and Ian turned a surprised look at me. "What a stupid thing to do," Lillian stated. "He could have grabbed the knife from you and slit your throat."

I had acted recklessly, but I couldn't change any of it now. "Maybe it was a dumb move on my part," I said, "but I'm fine, so there's no need to call the police."

Lillian nodded to indicate I'd gotten my way. Then she extended a hand in Ian's direction. "You must be the boy who knocked Alison out today. I apologize for pointing pepper spray at you."

I could see the wheels in his head turning as he associated *the boy who knocked Alison out* with himself. Like most people, he was dazed by her frankness. "Apology accepted," he said.

While Lillian took her turn admiring the damage above my ear, I looked around for my glasses. They'd fallen off again, and I couldn't find them anywhere. Giving up, I smoothed my shirt down. The adrenaline rush had started to wear off, leaving me sore and exhausted. "Can we sit in a chair instead of on the floor?" I asked tiredly.

"Perhaps the sitting area near the window would be good," Lillian suggested.

Just like before, Ian put an arm behind me and lifted me to my feet. I tried not to let on how badly my ribs hurt as he guided me to a chair. Lillian started to sit, too, but then changed her mind. "I'll make sure the back door is locked," she said, heading that way.

Ian sat across from me. His face was flushed from his own adrenaline rush. "So, you ended up on the floor twice today," he said. "Is that normal for you?"

I let out a long breath. "No, fortunately it isn't."

"What a relief. My heart can't take another scare like that."

I couldn't hold back a smile. "It's all about you now?"

"I didn't say that…exactly."

"Why did you come back here?" I asked.

"I thought maybe we could get some dinner and talk about our presentation some more."

I appreciated his help, and I was even coming to like him, but he wasn't taking the hints I'd been throwing at him. Brutal honesty was required under the circumstances. "I appreciate the offer, but I'm not interested in going to dinner with you."

I expected some backtracking and awkwardness on his end, but he just leaned back in the chair and stretched his long leg out. Then he smiled one of his big smiles. "Sooner or later you'll accept the invitation," he said confidently. "Everyone does."

I rolled my eyes.

"Hey, I'm just being honest," he said with a wink.

"And because I like honesty, I'm telling you straight up that I won't go to dinner with you…ever."

My words were brutal, but he just stretched back a bit more. "Wanna bet on that? Fifty dollars says you have dinner with me within the month."

I was tempted to take the bet, if only to wipe the smug smile off his face. There was a problem, though. If things worked out the way I wanted, he wouldn't remember who I was in a week, let alone a month. I wouldn't get the satisfaction of collecting my winnings.

"I'll pass," I said, checking my watch, "but I'll accept that ride home if the offer is still open. I missed the last bus ten minutes ago."

"Sure, no problem."

"The back is locked up," Lillian said, coming to sit with us. "I'll set the alarm after the two of you leave."

That was Lillianspeak for *get the heck out*, but Ian didn't know that.

"Hey," Ian said conversationally. "What did the person who left the package for Alison look like? If they come back, she should at least ask about it."

"There was nothing remarkable about him," Lillian replied. "I think he was in his thirties. He was shorter than the two of you…light brown hair and eyes. I noticed a tattoo about halfway up his arm. It looked like vines or some kind of calligraphy. There were small flowers running through it. I thought it was an odd tattoo to see on a man."

Ian's eyes widened and his head swiveled toward me.

"What?" I asked.

He shook his head. "Uh...nothing. Just sounds like a weird tattoo. I'd better get you home before your parents start to worry."

"They won't start to wonder where I am for another half hour, and I don't want to freak them by out walking into the house looking fresh from a fight. Can you wait while I wash up?"

I could see he wasn't really comfortable with the idea of being left alone with Lillian. Not many people were. I gave him props for courage, though. "Sure," he replied with false enthusiasm.

I went to the bathroom and ran some water in the small sink. As I washed away my blood, I wondered what strange property in it helped me heal so quickly. After my adoption by the McKyes was finalized, my dad had ordered a complete medical workup for me. Being a doctor himself, he'd wanted to be sure any dangers to my health were dealt with immediately. He was a plastic surgeon, not a pediatrician, but he was certainly educated enough to spot any abnormalities in the test results. Neither he nor my pediatrician had found anything to worry about.

Whatever helped me heal, I was grateful for it, because the pinch in my ribs was starting to ease up. If only it would work on the headache, too.

When I got back to the front of the store, Lillian was

staring at Ian, and Ian was staring at the floor. He had more confidence than most guys, but Lillian couldn't be charmed. He'd met his match.

"Ready to go?" I asked, trying not to let my amusement show.

Ian jumped up. "Yes."

I gave him directions to my house and then sat in the passenger seat like a wilted flower. The day's events had taken their toll. All I wanted to do was to curl up in bed and sleep. He was sympathetic enough not to make me talk during the drive.

When we got to the gates of my community, I handed him my electronic swipe card. He used it, and the imposing set of wrought-iron gates in front of us opened up. "Nice neighborhood," he commented. "You're not inside the boundaries for Fillmore High, are you?"

"I waived in," I said with a shrug.

"Brandy and I did, too," he commented.

We drove straight two blocks and then I pointed to my house. "It's that one."

He turned the car onto the circular driveway in front of our two-story Spanish-style home. I moved to open the door but stopped when my headache suddenly got a lot worse. My eyes began to water, and I groaned, putting my hands to my head.

Ian rested a comforting hand on my knee. His voice sounded far away when he said, "Alison, I know you've had a hard day, but I need to make sure I understand things. Are you sure the book at the Shadow Box wasn't meant for you?"

I wanted to get away from him, but I couldn't move or stop my response. "I'm positive it wasn't for me," I said in agony.

"And the guy who left it? You've never met anyone like that?"

The pain in my head kicked up another notch. I struggled to breathe normally. "Of course I have. There have to be a million guys like that around here, but none of them would give me a book."

"What about the tattoo?" he pushed. "Have you ever met anyone with a vine tattoo like the one Lillian told us about?"

"No," I panted. "Why are you asking me all these questions?"

"I guess I need to be sure we did the right thing keeping the police out of this."

I took a deep breath as the pain eased off a little. "We did," I said.

He nodded and then raised his hand from my knee to run a gentle finger along the side of my face. "The nurse was right," he said. "You're bruised like a ripe banana."

I pushed his hand away. "Thanks for the ride," I said, getting out.

I heard him honk once as he left the driveway, but I didn't turn around to wave good-bye.

The smell of lasagna greeted me when I walked through the front door. It was Monday, Mom's night to cook, and universally dreaded in the McKye household. She'd recently gone vegetarian and was trying to convert the rest of us. Which meant we ate whatever she cooked, or we went hungry. Regardless of how good the lasagna smelled, it was guaranteed to taste awful.

Everyone was at the table. My brother was chewing his food with revulsion on his face while Mom spooned runny casserole onto a plate for me. My dad was doing a better job hiding his disgust, but I could tell he was holding his breath until he swallowed. When I sat down next to him, he noticed the bandage on the side of my face.

"What happened there?" he asked, pointing to it.

His tone alarmed Mom and she got up to check me out. "I just got a little banged up," I said.

"You better look at it, Bob," Mom said.

He leaned in, peeled the bandage away, and gave the wound a professional once-over. "It's nothing serious," he said. "The bruising should be gone in a couple of days. If it had been anything to really worry about, there would have been signs of it by now."

My mother was still concerned. "Are you sure?" she asked. "Maybe we should take her to the ER to get checked."

"After thirty years of practicing medicine, I assure you, she's fine," he replied. Then with the look of a condemned man, he added, "Anyway, I've got to finish this food before it starts to congeal."

Mom scowled at him and then asked how I'd gotten hurt. I told her how I'd hit my head on a desk during first period. I left out the bookstore fiasco. She would have had a major freak over that.

Alex was sneaky. While her attention was on me, he fed the rest of his lasagna to our dog. I wondered if poor old Tsar would survive the digestion process.

I finished my story, and Alex wiped his mouth with a napkin then rubbed his stomach theatrically. "That was great, Mom," he said.

Before she could offer him more, he hustled out of the kitchen. I admired his acting skills and his speed.

For the next ten minutes or so, I made small talk with my parents and gagged down runny lasagna. Mom wanted to know about my first day of school. I answered her questions, embellished when necessary and did my very best to leave her with the impression my life was great.

It was my night to load the dishwasher and wipe down the table, so I was left alone in the kitchen when everyone finished eating. I did my chores and then hunted in the cupboards for some kind of medicine to help my headache. It took a while, but I found a box in the cabinet above the refrigerator. Most everything in it was homeopathic. I wasn't sure what to choose, but remembering Brandy's suggestion that I take some ibuprofen, I opened a bottle of Advil and chased a double dose down with some water.

I took the stairs to my room two at a time and heaved a sigh of relief as I opened the door. The space was a weird sanctuary. Mom had done the decor in Pepto-Bismol pink and floral patterns. Nauseating on bright days, the space was nevertheless mine, and that was what mattered most. In a tired haze, I showered and dressed in a pair of jogging shorts and a worn shirt. Then I set the alarm on my phone and collapsed onto my big four-poster.

Turning my lamp off, I looked up at the ceiling. It appeared to be rotating in a circle. Regardless of whether the results proved successful or not, the ceiling always seemed to spin at the end of days when I did a lot of thought transference. The process required a kind of energy that wasn't physical but not entirely mental, either. I didn't understand how it worked, but I'd come to expect the spinning-ceiling thing as a side effect.

What happened at the Shadow Box had shaken me more than I wanted Lillian or Ian to know. But in truth, there were probably hundreds of dark-haired girls working in bookstores around Las Vegas. Only Lillian wouldn't ask questions, figuring I was the only one. The package had been left at the wrong store for the wrong girl, and fedora man had come to get what was his. That was the logical conclusion to make.

Closing my eyes, I replayed in my mind what had happened at the store. I pushed the pause button when the old book spilled out of the box and hit the floor. The embossing on the cover resembled a circle of leaves with flowers running through it. Much like the tattoo Lillian said she'd seen on the arm of the man who left it.

Before the heavy hand of sleep dragged me under, I wondered what about the book connected tattoo man to fedora man. Whatever it was, I hoped I wouldn't get caught between them again.

Chapter Five

I got out of bed the next morning feeling a whole lot better than when I'd gone to sleep. The ache in my head and in my ribs was gone. I hoped the problem with my thought transference was fixed, too.

Mom sipped a cup of tea while I ate a bowl of organic whole grain cereal, aka cardboard. "Why do you always wear such drab colors?" she asked with her nose wrinkled like they smelled bad as well.

"I like this outfit," I said, glancing down at my white shirt and jeans.

Mom shook her head in disbelief. She wasn't a vain person, but she put effort into maintaining her health and appearance. With her light brown hair in a high ponytail, she was wearing a pink tank top and a pair of dark yoga pants.

She looked like she was in her midthirties, not fifty-two. I knew it frustrated her that I didn't make the most of my assets the way she did. I couldn't very well tell her I picked my super-bland clothes to protect her, so I usually ignored her comments about them.

"Maybe I'll get you a pretty dress at the mall today," she said with a wink at me.

"Nice offer, Mom, but I don't do any pretty-dress activities. It would just sit in my closet and collect dust."

"You *should* do pretty-dress activities," she insisted. "You're a beautiful seventeen-year-old girl. You could be out with friends enjoying life. Instead you spend every Friday night playing video games with your brother. Don't get me wrong, I'm glad you love your brother, but you should have more of a social life."

"I appreciate your concern, Mom. I really do, but I'm happy with how things are. The day will come when I need a nice dress, and I promise you'll be the first person I tell, okay?"

"I'd better be," she muttered before sipping her tea again.

I took my bowl to the sink and then scooped my backpack off the floor. "Gotta go," I said, heading for the garage.

My old car, with its squeaky doors and rust spots, waited for me in the garage. Our housing development had labeled it an eyesore and ordered us to park it in the garage or risk a fine. Mom hated the car more than she hated my old jeans, and I'd caught her staring at it a few times like it might give her posh car some horrible disease. To me the dents were character. My car had tinted windows and a good stereo, and it blended in a lot better at Fillmore than my mom's Porsche.

I got to school early. The north halls were even more deserted than they had been the day before. I opened my locker and moved things around, keeping the illusion as consistent as possible. There were no kissing couples to get around in the stairwell, so I made it to room seventeen in excellent time. That's where my stellar morning ended.

Brandy and Ian flashed smiles of welcome as I entered the classroom.

I'd spent a good part of the drive to school trying to decide how I was going to deal with them. There was nothing special about our interaction yesterday. We only knew the basics about each other. I'd decided to be pleasantly withdrawn with them. Over the next few days, they would likely find more exciting people to hang out with, and then I would fade into the background.

Doing it that way would be easier on them than on me. Exposure to the normal world would make me want more of it. I'd had a social life before, and I craved friendship like a drug. A little taste of it would drive me crazy for more, so I would have to keep strong in my resolve to remain invisible.

Giving the Palmers a small smile, I headed for the desk I'd been sitting at yesterday. Brandy was out of her seat and had a grip on my arm before I could put my backpack down. "Hey," she said, pushing me toward an empty chair next to Ian. "We saved you a seat."

I tried to move away from her, but for such a thin person, she was remarkably strong. She maneuvered me into the correct position and pushed me down into the chair. It was a shock to the system to be manhandled like that. I turned, wide-eyed, to Ian. He was chuckling. "You get used to it after a while," he whispered.

"Ouch," Brandy said, pointing to the bandage on the side of my face. "That looks painful."

In reality, the edges of my cut had come together seamlessly, and the bruise had faded to a barely noticeable shade of gray. I'd darkened it with a deep mauve blush from my mom's cosmetics case that morning. "It's not too bad," I said, adding a wince.

"Ian and I were just talking about you," she continued. "I was saying how nice it would be to get to know you better. We're kind of new here. I mean, we've been here for a few weeks, but we don't really know that many people. And, well, I'm bored. Not that Ian isn't great company, but he's not a girl. You know what I mean?"

Ian rolled his eyes and smiled. "I can't pretend to be interested in everything she says every second of every day. She lives with us, so I've gotten pretty good at tuning her out entirely."

She pushed his shoulder, pretending to be offended. "Anyway, I think it's time for us to branch out," she said, "and I was wondering if you have plans for this Saturday."

I was prepared to be pleasant with the Palmers, but I wasn't going to hang out with them. "Um...ugh," I replied inarticulately.

"We're inviting a few people over," she continued. "Ian's parents are going to be out of town, so we'll have the place to ourselves. It won't be anything crazy. We just want to get to know some people better."

Feeling a rise of desperation, I formed the thought *You don't want this girl to come* and pushed it into Brandy's mind. She was already fixed on the idea and my thought didn't take hold. She kept staring at me expectantly. The only thing worse than accepting her invitation would be a drawn-out discussion about why I couldn't.

"Okay, sounds good," I said, vowing to come up with a good excuse as to why I had to miss it.

Brandy did a little bounce and clapped her hands like a child. A couple people had come in and were watching us. Fortunately, Connor arrived, and like sunshine, her attention turned to him. Within fifteen seconds, their mutual excitement had them talking over each other, and no one noticed I was in the room anymore. Except for Ian.

He tapped his pencil on my desk, and asked, "Feeling all right?"

"Better than yesterday," I admitted.

"Good, because I worked on our script for the Byron presentation last night, and I was hoping you could take a look at it."

When he bent over to search for it in his backpack, I smelled the clean scent of soap and noticed the hair behind his ears was still wet from a shower. I stared a little longer than I should have. Pulling my eyes away, I repeated *I'm not interested in Ian Palmer* ten times in my mind.

He sat up and handed me a stack of papers. I did a quick look through them and found he'd done a good job of compiling a history of Lord Byron and various examples of his work. "This is great," I admitted. "I didn't expect you to do so much of it without me."

"I hope you're not offended," he said, running a hand through his damp hair. "You can change anything you want. I couldn't sleep last night, and working on the presentation was better than tossing and turning for hours."

I found that ironic. I was the one who'd been assaulted and robbed, but I'd slept like a baby.

"Oh, and I picked up your glasses at the store last night, too," he added. He laid the mangled things on my desk and one of the lenses popped out. "That's tragic," he said, shaking his head in mock sympathy.

"No worries," I said, pointing to the pair I was wearing. "I have a spare."

"Why do you even wear them? The lenses aren't pre-scription."

I pretended not to hear him and turned to ask Brandy what time she wanted me to come over Saturday.

I planned to go to my car to eat lunch, so feeling like a fish swimming upstream, I steered and dodged through groups of people going the other way toward the cafeteria. Wyatt Smith, a particularly burly football player, was a difficult obstacle to get around, and he accidentally pushed me sideways as we passed. I careened into a group of giggling girls. They weren't happy about it, and one of them, Nikki Cole, yelled, "Watch it!"

"Sorry," I said to the group as a whole.

"I guess we'll have to forgive you," Nikki said with a cunning smile. "If we had feet as big as *yours*, we'd probably be clumsy, too."

The girls around her laughed.

I knew more about Nikki Cole than I wanted to. She was tiny, barely five feet tall. Her hair shone an unusual reddish-blond color, and her wide eyes were a striking cornflower blue. She was cruel but about as popular as a girl could get at Fillmore High. "Watch it next time, Sasquatch," she said, turning her back on me.

I paused long enough to form the thought *nothing to remember* and pushed it into the minds of the girls in the group. Their expressions cleared and they went back to ignoring me like nothing had happened.

I breathed a sigh of relief. My thought transference was working again.

Brandy waved to me when I walked into sixth period. Remembering my resolve to be pleasant, I took my seat next to her. She leaned over to give me a hug. I held still as a statue until she let me go. She seemed to like physical contact with strange people as much as I hated it. "Why didn't you come eat lunch with us today?" she asked.

"I had an errand to run," I lied.

"Well, Ian went looking for you when you didn't show up. I think he was worried. Maybe because of what happened at the bookstore last night."

"He told you about that?"

"I knew something was bothering him when he came

home, and I bugged him until he told me. Are you mad?"

"No. I guess not."

"It is weird, isn't it?" she continued. "That some guy would leave a package for you and another guy would steal it on the same day. I wonder what was in it."

"A book," I said, seeing my mental picture of it all over again.

Mr. Dawson cleared his throat noisily in our direction, indicating we were to stop talking. With apologetic smiles, we focused our attention on his lecture.

She stuck by my side after class and followed me all the way to my locker, where Ian was leaning with his shoulder against the wall. His pose was casual, but he looked kind of sweaty and his face was flushed.

"Something wrong?" Brandy asked, eyeing him up and down.

He made a go-away gesture with his head. "I'll see you at the house, okay?" he said.

"Sure, I guess," she replied. "I'll see you tomorrow, Alison."

"You look like you've been running," I said, going around him to my locker.

"If you only knew," he said irritably. "Where were you at lunch?"

We weren't on a level where that was any of his business, and I was taken aback that he'd ask in such a harsh way. "I had an errand to run," I said.

"What kind of errand?"

I turned to look at him full-on. "What's it to you?"

"Some guy smacked you upside the head yesterday and left with a package that didn't belong to him. Then you just disappeared at lunch, and I thought… It doesn't matter what I thought. I guess the whole thing bothers me more than it bothers you."

So much for being pleasantly withdrawn with the Palmers. Ian was pushing all my buttons. "It *does* bother me," I said grumpily, "but I doubt the guy will come all the way out here to knock me around some more. I find it really hard to believe you're worried about that, either, so what exactly is the problem?"

We were both in nasty moods and standing nose to nose like a pair of boxers before a fight. I opened my locker to block him out of sight. He pushed it closed. "I can't explain why," he said, "but when you didn't show up for lunch, I thought something bad happened. The feeling was strong enough to make me drive around looking for you while I fried half to death in the heat. Believe me, I didn't want to."

I narrowed my eyes at him. "I'm not your responsibility," I hissed, "and I don't want you checking up on me. I can take care of myself." I did my locker thing, closed the door, and walked away.

He caught up. I heard him exhale a long sigh before he spoke again. "Like I told you last night, I saw you lying flat out in a pool of blood twice. Both times you looked dead. Admittedly, I don't know you that well, but seeing that took a toll."

He had a point. If I'd found someone beaten and bloodied, not once but twice in the same day, it would have messed me up a little, too. I was still mad, though.

At the parking lot he touched my arm. "Listen, Alison," he said more gently. "Obviously, where you go and what you do is your business. I was just really worried." He ducked his head, letting the gold hair fall across his forehead and shade his eyes. "I'm sorry," he said with half a smile. "Forgive me?"

I wanted to stay angry, but my heart had twisted in all sorts of ways. "Okay. Just...give me some space, will you?"

He nodded and more hair fell across his forehead.

Crap, crap, crap.

"I'll give you space, if you promise to watch your back."

It was a strange request for him to make, but I agreed. "I always do," I said, getting into my car.

Lillian was back to her usual self that afternoon. She spoke only three sentences to me, made eye contact twice, and never smiled once as we worked. While she searched the internet for treasures, I organized the store and inventoried a new order of books. By six o' clock I'd finished everything including my homework. I pulled out the Byron script and started reading it over.

Byron himself had supplied plenty of fascinating anecdotes, but Ian wrote with a flair that made everything more interesting. According to the script, Byron had been an attractive man for his time, meaning he had a chin. He'd lived extravagantly and partied with flamboyant company. He was also depressed and antisocial sometimes. He treated most people in his life, especially the women he seduced, terribly. All these nasty character traits combined to make him a celebrity in his generation.

On the whole, I couldn't like him. But it was impossible not to love words strung together like, "She walks in beauty, like the night," or "There's not a joy the world can give like that it takes away."

I added a few of my own thoughts to the script and then put it away to discuss with Ian later.

At six thirty, Lillian told me to hang up my apron because I was done for the day. I had thirty minutes left of my shift, so I worried I'd done something wrong. Then I caught her watching me with a concerned expression. Ian wasn't the only one who thought the man from last night would come back and....do what, I wasn't sure.

Chapter Six

I noticed it at a stoplight...a black BMW parked along the curb a few blocks down. The windows were tinted, it had a sunroof, and there was a long horizontal crack across the front windshield. The cracked glass made the car stand out in my memory. I'd seen it twice before that day. It was hard to believe seeing it a third time was coincidence. Weirder things had happened, but still, it sent chills of alarm up my spine.

I checked my rearview mirror. The BMW's windows were so darkly tinted I couldn't tell if anyone was in it until it pulled onto the street a few cars behind me. My first instinct was to bury my foot in the accelerator and get away as fast as possible, but that would have brought a lot of attention or a traffic ticket. I didn't want either, so I pulled forward at a conservative pace when the light turned green. The dark car fell back a bit, but it was still there behind a Subaru and a Nissan. I took a left at the next light to see what would happen. The Subaru followed and so did the black car. Five blocks farther down the Subaru peeled off, leaving just me and the black car. I took another random turn hoping to shed it, but it kept coming.

Feeling the pricklings of panic, I made a right turn and headed for the Vegas Strip. Traffic would be slow there, but there would also be a lot of people to get lost in if I ditched my car and ran. It was vital that I lose the guy. I couldn't let myself fall into the wrong hands. Not so close to my family.

I pulled over near one of the larger casinos, shut the car off, and climbed into the passenger seat. Thankfully, it was a busy night. The tourists were thick and noisy under the brightly colored lights. I waited for the black car to show itself, planning to throw open the door and bolt into the crowd if it did.

After fifteen of the longest minutes of my life, I hadn't seen it. Still, my mind wasn't at ease. I drove home, keeping a sharp eye out for the BMW. I even did two circuits around my neighborhood before driving through my community's gates.

It was a miserable night for me. I tossed and turned, having thrown logic to the wind. If it was a choice between logic and a possible threat to my family, I had to go with the threat. I wasn't 100 percent certain I'd been followed after work, but getting attacked by a book robber and then tailed by a dark car the next day were occurrences too bizarre to ignore. I didn't see an immediate connection between them, but that didn't mean it wasn't there.

Huddled in a pathetical ball of hopelessness under my covers, I made myself face a harsh reality. Whether I understood what was going on or not, if one more bizarre thing happened to me, I would have to leave Vegas for good. It was the only way to be sure the McKyes were safe.

I was late getting up the next morning, and no one was home when I went downstairs. Feeling utterly depressed, I grabbed a handful of granola and headed for the garage. Getting in my car, I leaned over to the passenger seat and felt under the dashboard. I kept an envelope with all my savings taped under it. I pulled the envelope off and opened it to recount the money I had. There was enough to get away, change my appearance, and buy new IDs, but it wouldn't last very long after that. Short of robbing a bank it was the best I could do. I stuck the envelope back in its place and backed out of the garage. I'd pack a few clothes in the trunk after school, and I'd be ready to run if I had to.

My morning was gloomy but uneventful until Connor caught up with me just outside of fourth period. "You headed for the cafeteria?" he asked hopefully.

It was nice of him to offer, but I'd made up my mind to eat in my car again. "Nope. I've got something to do," I replied, sending the same thought at him.

He paused for a second. "Maybe tomorrow, then?"

"Doubtful," I replied, turning away.

I got about three steps before Ian and Brandy showed up. "Let's go, I'm hungry," Brandy said, hooking her arm in mine.

"I'm just on my way out."

"You have to eat with us," she cajoled. "You've given me too many excuses already."

Connor grabbed my free hand and started pulling. "Yeah, you've given her too many excuses. Let's go."

Ian didn't say anything as I let myself get pulled down the hallway. He watched me closely, though. I could feel it. When we were about halfway there, Connor and Brandy let go of me. They'd fallen into such deep conversation they didn't notice when I peeled off and turned back to go to my locker. Ian wasn't so easy to shed.

"Go away," I said. "I'm in a terrible mood."

He gave me a side glance. "You should be grateful they're making you eat in the cafeteria. It's dangerous to drive around in heat like this. And after my experience yesterday, I should know. I'll bet it's ten times worse in your car because the air-conditioning doesn't work. You could die of heatstroke."

"My air-conditioning works," I replied defensively.

"But not very well. Am I right?" I opened my locker and stowed my backpack. "A bit of friendly advice," he said. "If you pretend it's no big deal and stop acting like you're going to your own execution, you'll blend in better."

My nerves were stretched to the limit; I was sleep deprived and on the verge of leaving my entire life behind. I was in no shape to hear anyone critique how I did things. Closing the locker door, I spun the lock and moved away from him.

"At first, I thought you were just shy," he continued, catching up with me. "I thought that's why you kept to yourself. Now I'm pretty sure it's something else. I think you're trying to hide yourself in the crowd, but you're going about it all wrong."

That's when my brain processed the implications in his first comment, and I stumbled forward. He caught me by the elbow before I could fall on my face. "If you want to stand out less," he whispered in my ear, "you should get more involved. Everyone around here thinks you're standoffish and they wonder why."

"They wonder why" echoed loud in my mind until the world around me started to spin. He was right. There had to have been a few kids I missed when I did thought transference. It would only take a couple of them saying, "What's with that Alison girl?" and an undercurrent of feeling would be created. Good or bad, that undercurrent generated curiosity about me. By trying so hard to stay in the shadows at Fillmore High, I'd put myself on the radar.

"I don't know why you've tried so hard to erase yourself," Ian continued quietly, "but if it makes you feel any better, I believe you *thought* you had a good reason."

Still holding my elbow, he steered me toward the cafeteria. When we got there, he handed me a plastic tray. I wasn't hungry, but like a robot, I put things on my tray and carried it to where Brandy and Connor were sitting. Brandy glanced at me questioningly, but Ian shook his head at her, so she didn't say anything.

I was quiet as the others ate and continued in a numb

haze after dumping my uneaten food in the trash. Ian stayed by my side until we got to the north hall. Then he reached over, squeezed my hand, and drifted away.

I walked down the hall on autopilot and froze when I got to my locker. My fingers and toes started to tingle as the blood drained from them in a fight-or-flight reaction. The door was standing open. Someone had gotten into my stuff while I was at lunch. My mind whirled as I took my backpack out and searched through it to see if anything was missing.

A few pages had been torn out of one of my notebooks. I knew they were gone because the ragged pieces were still attached to the spine. I had OCD about removing those bits. Taking long, slow breaths, I reviewed my memory and saw the pages weren't that important. On one I'd written a list of cities I might go to when I left Vegas. Unless the thief knew my plans, the list wouldn't mean anything to them. On the other pages, I'd drawn doodles of my family members, but they could be interpreted as doodles of almost anyone.

That should have calmed me, but it didn't. Someone had searched my things, and this was the third bizarre event I'd been dreading. Three anomalies in three days couldn't be ignored. I'd leave Vegas.

I was numb during the last two periods of the day, but when I found Ian waiting at my locker after the final bell, tears welled in my eyes. I pushed them back.

"What's up?" he asked conversationally.

Where should I start? "My life has spun completely out of control," or "Someone broke into my locker during lunch and took some of my stuff," or better yet, "Surprise, I'm not human."

I leaned my back against my locker, closed my eyes, and slid down the length of it to the floor. A second later I felt Ian next to me. He didn't touch me or say anything comforting. Which, in my messed-up state, I took as a sweet gesture. I was so overrun with dread and fear that I started to shake. I wrapped my arms tight over my chest and fought to pull myself together.

"Are you okay?" he asked.

"It's just been a really bad day," I replied.

"Looks like more than just a bad day."

"I shouldn't be freaking out," I said. "It's really not that serious. Someone went through my locker while we were at lunch. You were right earlier when you said I was hiding. I'm a private person, and I don't like that someone poked around in my things."

I expected his reaction to be a shrug or some reassurance that it had been a harmless prank. Instead, he took a deep breath and looked me straight in the eye. "I think someone has been following you," he stated.

That startled me. Could he really know about the black car that tailed me last night? I couldn't see how. I tried to play it off by laughing. "Why would someone follow me?" I asked.

"Maybe it's the guy who stole your book." I started to object, but he stopped me. "It's okay, Alison. You're not in this alone."

I wasn't sure what he meant by that, but I wanted to get

away from him and his concern as quickly as possible. I tried to get up, but he put a hand on my shoulder and held me back. "There's a lot I need to tell you," he continued, "but not here."

"You have a lot to tell me about what?" I asked lightly.

He bent his head to meet my gaze straight on. "You can trust me," he whispered. "I'm not here to hurt you."

I shook my head at the absurdity of it all. It sounded like he was repeating words from a movie. Was this really my life? I didn't think Ian was a bad guy. Since I met him a few days ago, he'd been nothing but helpful. Annoying but helpful.

I took a shaky breath and smoothed my hair back. "I need to get to the Shadow Box," I said. "I'm late."

He stood up and pulled me to my feet. "I'll walk you to your car. We can talk when you're done at work. Call your parents. Tell them you'll be home late."

He made it sound like I didn't have a choice.

Chapter Seven

The Shadow Box was actually doing some business when I got there. Lillian looked up from the line at the register long enough to say, "You're late."

"Sorry, I got held up at school," I replied.

The store stayed busy for most of the afternoon. Lillian manned the register while I directed people to the books they were interested in buying. I did it on autopilot. In my mind, I was busily formulating an escape route.

I'd decided to go to Alaska. Cooler weather would be a welcome change, and it was about as far away from Vegas as I could get and still be in the US. I would ditch my car a few miles out of town, so it would be harder for the police to track me. My thought transference would come in handy when hitching rides, and if I met up with any weirdos, I'd kick them with my size-ten shoes and spray them with my can of bear-strength pepper spray. I could work my mind magic on the border guards to get through Canada, too. I'd aim for the Anchorage area.

It would help that Fillmore was notoriously late reporting absences. I'd start the ball rolling first thing in the morning. My parents wouldn't know I had been reported absent until after noon. By the time they figured out I was missing, I hoped to have a good cushion of distance between myself and the people I loved.

At a quarter to seven, I saw Ian's light hair over the top of a bookshelf. "You almost ready to go?" he asked, coming around the corner to me.

I'd decided I didn't want to waste time talking with him when I could be spending it with my family, so I had an excuse ready. "My stomach hurts, and I'm getting a headache. I'm going home tonight. We can talk some other time."

He crossed his arms over his chest and tipped his head to the side. "Sometimes you suck at lying."

"I'm not lying. I don't—"

He cut me off. "I just want to talk to you for a few minutes. It won't take long. Please."

He had been nice to me that day. Weird but nice. I supposed I could give him a few minutes. "Fine," I said. "Half an hour."

"Thanks," he replied.

Lillian came around the corner. "Take the trash out, will you, Ian?" she said. "I left it by the back door."

He blinked at her presumptuousness, but agreed to it

with a nod. "Where's the back door?" he asked.

"Through the storage room there," I said, pointing.

He left, and I slid into the bathroom to call home. Alex's thirteen-year-old voice broke as he said, "Hello."

"Hey. Is Mom around?" I asked.

"She went to the gym."

"Will you let her know I'm going to be late getting home? I have to talk to someone about a school project."

"It's your night to cook," he said in bored tones.

"Crap, I forgot. Will you switch with me?"

"For twenty bucks."

"Fine. Don't forget to tell Mom. I don't want her to worry."

"I'm not stupid, Alison."

"I know," I said, and then added, "I love you, Alex."

There was silence on the line for a moment. Then he said, "You still have to pay me twenty bucks."

Lillian had done the locking up when I went back out. She and Ian were deep in conversation near the cash register. It surprised me that they'd gone from awkward silence to rapid discussion in two days' time, but I didn't care that much. I would be miles away from both of them tomorrow.

"I'm almost finished up," Lillian said. "The two of you can leave through the back door."

Hanging my apron on its hook, I listened to the coins drop as she counted the money in the till. Other than Alex, she'd been the closest thing I had to a friend during the last three years. There had never been a lot of warmth between us, but I would miss her constant presence. I tried to think of something appropriate to say in the way of good-bye. I settled on, "See ya."

In her typical style, she looked the other way.

"Stay on my bumper," Ian instructed as we left the store. "Like I told you, I don't live far from here."

I followed him through a neighborhood I'd been to before. Instead of being a gated community like mine, the individual lots were gated. Which made sense since the houses and yards behind them were huge. One set of imposing gates opened as we approached, and Ian drove through them. His house, if you could call it that, was a modern cubist style, complete with hundreds of sharp angles and sand-colored stucco. My parents lived in a nice neighborhood, but this house was owned by someone of an entirely different class—the obscenely rich.

Instead of parking in the garage at the front, Ian turned down an unpaved path that circled behind the house. I followed and pulled in beside him, trying not to feel uncomfortable about my shabby little car parked next to his new Audi.

"Welcome to our humble abode," he said sarcastically. "This place looks like a compound, doesn't it?"

"Don't you like it?"

"Can anyone really like a place that looks as cold as this?" he asked with disgust. "I would have parked in the front, but I can't find the garage door opener. It's lost somewhere inside that maze."

"Can't you just scan your eyeball to open it?"

He looked at me like I'd lost my mind.

"That's how Batman does it, and he's super rich, too."

Ian shook his head and laughed. "That's a good idea. I'll tell my dad."

I walked with him across a rockwork deck, and Brandy opened the back door. She came toward us, holding her hands out, palms up in a welcoming gesture. That's when I saw it.

They weren't faint blue like mine. Hers were more like the white lines of an old scar, but they formed a *V* in the palm of her hand. Just like they did in mine. She'd always kept her fingers slightly curled in, so I'd never noticed it before. I glanced at Ian's hand. Consciously or not, he was curling his fingers in a bit, too. All the pieces came together at lightning speed. The Palmers had been interested in me from the start. I'd assumed they were just looking for new friends and that they'd crossed some sort of barrier when my thought transference was short-circuited. But it had been more than that.

With Brandy standing at the door, and Ian next to my shoulder, I felt trapped. As if reading my mind, Ian grabbed my hand. A part of me wondered what good it would do to run. One look at him, and I knew he was faster than me. The other part of me, the fighter part, wasn't going to go quietly.

I yanked free of him and turned back the way we'd come. In two strides I was running at top speed. Behind me, I heard Ian yell, "Jeez, Brandy, could you be less subtle!"

My best option was a flat-out run for the safety of onlookers. Hot desert air filled my lungs as I ran full tilt toward the gates we'd come through. I had no idea how I was going to get over them before Ian caught me. I only knew I was going to give it everything I had.

Halfway there, I tried to throw him off by cutting sharply between a cactus and a wiry bush. He let me make it just far enough so that we were shielded from the view of traffic. Then he tackled me.

"Get off," I yelled when I found myself pinned to the rocky ground.

"It's not what you think," he said. "We're not the bad guys. We want to help you."

I punched him in the mouth. He swore but didn't let me go.

"I don't believe you," I yelled, winding up for another punch.

He pinned my free arm down. "Think about it, Alison. Either you trust us, or you face the dewing who's been following you for three days on your own. I'm sure you're strong, given who your mother was, but you won't last long against him."

I stopped struggling, partly because I feared he was right and partly because he'd mentioned my mother. "Get off!" I yelled again.

He complied but sat near enough to throw me down again if necessary. When he touched his lip, his fingers came away bloody. "You hit hard."

"Good," I replied. Then I sat up and scooted a couple of inches away from him.

"Come on, Alison. You can try running again, but I

think we both know how that will end. All I want is for you to listen to me. Just hear what I have to say, and then you're free to go if you want."

He stood and offered me a hand. I continued to sit in the rocks, unsure of what I should do. I decided to stall. "You said given who my mother *was*. Does that mean she's dead?"

His response wasn't immediate. He looked back the way we'd come, like he was trying to decide what to say.

"Is she dead?" I repeated.

"Yes," he replied quietly.

Over the years, I'd felt anger, resentment, and longing for my biological parents. Most of the time I chose to think they'd died. It was better than thinking they'd abandoned me. But deep down I'd always harbored a small hope they were okay and would eventually come for me. Confirmation that my biological mother was dead was another blow on an already awful day.

"You're not in this alone, Alison," he said. "I want to help you."

I turned my head to watch a car go past the gate. I understood that going with him would be making a choice of some kind. Unfortunately, I didn't have a clear picture of what that was. I thought I heard a faraway voice say, *Trust him*. I attributed it to auditory hallucination but gave in anyway. Things in my life had taken a turn for the terrible. I needed help, and the possibility that Ian and Brandy might offer some tipped the scale in their favor.

Reaching up to take his hand, I let him pull me to my feet. Then I dusted off the back of my shorts and checked my legs for blood. There were only a few scratches. "If I didn't know better," I said grumpily, "I'd think my butt would be black-and-blue with bruises tomorrow."

Ian laughed and pointed to the bandage near my ear. "You could always darken some places with makeup," he suggested. "Just an observation, but you aren't very good at applying that stuff."

I rolled my eyes. "I don't use it much."

Ian chuckled. "Are you hungry?"

"Not really."

"You will be when you calm down," he assured me. "You didn't eat anything at lunch."

"You kept track of what I ate? Where did you go to stalker school?"

He smiled over at me. "I notice a lot of things most people don't. I'm sure you do, too."

We walked in the front door, through an airy foyer and into a large open space that was both living room and dining room. A gourmet kitchen opened up in one of the back corners. The space looked modern and completely unoccupied. There wasn't a single picture on any of the putty-colored walls in the living room, not one rug on the dark tile floor and no table under the dining room chandelier. The only signs of habitation were the few dirty dishes I saw peeking up from the sink.

Footsteps echoed through the empty space and Brandy came out of one of the darkened hallways. She'd pulled her curly hair into a short ponytail. "I'm sorry, Alison," she said, coming forward. "We greet our own kind with our palms up.

I've been thinking of you as one of us, so it seemed natural to welcome you that way. I didn't mean to startle you."

She'd scared the heck out of me, but whatever. "So when you say one of us, you mean the children of Atlantis?" I asked her.

"Of course," she replied, coming to give me a hug. She laughed when I pulled back. "What's with you?" she asked. "You're so prickly all the time."

I didn't know how to answer that question without going into a very long, convoluted story about hiding my identity, so I just shrugged. Maybe later I'd get into it.

"I'm going out," she said. "It would be best for Ian to fill you in on some stuff before your real education begins, anyway. He's good at explaining things in simple, uncomplicated terms."

It was meant as an insult, but Ian didn't seem to mind it. "Thanks for that," he responded.

With a smile at me, Brandy said, "I'm going to find out where your follower has gone to."

"Shouldn't I come along as bait or something?" I asked.

"I won't need bait," she replied, walking away. "Don't worry. I won't be gone long."

I was left standing in the empty room with Ian, feeling ridiculous. He nodded toward a sofa. "Have a seat," he suggested.

What choice did I have, really? If I tried to run, he'd just tackle me. So I sat while he disappeared down another of the dark hallways.

The windows at the far side of the room looked over

the city. It was a beautiful view. The bright casino lights were just coming on, turning an ordinary desert town into a painted fairyland. I'd always thought of Vegas as a two-faced friend. On the one hand, she was a city of families and hardworking people who were trying to make a decent life for themselves. On the other, she was a city of illusion, living like a parasite off human greed and lust.

Ian came back quietly. I don't know how long he stood behind me before I noticed him. He was perfectly at ease in his frayed denim jeans and faded T-shirt. He'd washed the blood from his mouth, but he was going to have a fat lip. It was weird to think I'd done that to him. I'd never hit anyone before.

I took a deep breath and dove in with a question. "There aren't any adults living here, are there?" I asked.

"That depends on your definition of an adult," he replied with an Australian accent.

"Wow. You're Australian?" I asked.

He shrugged. "Is that a problem?"

"No. Just a surprise."

"Using an American accent when I enrolled at Fillmore simplified things," he explained.

"What sort of alien-species business brings you here?"

He laughed. "We came looking for a young thoughtmaker who was being raised by humans."

"And you think that's me?"

He reached over and turned my hand. Tracing the faint lines in my palm with his index finger, he said, "I'm pretty sure it is."

I didn't deny it further. "Why have you been looking for me?"

"Because we need your help."

It was my turn to laugh. "In what way could I possibly help you? As you so insightfully point out, I've been raised by humans. I know almost nothing about...whatever we are."

"Dewing," he said.

"Right. As if 'children of Atlantis' wasn't creepy enough."

Smiling he collapsed onto the sofa next to me. "I'm not sure if it was naïveté or just hope," he said, "but I didn't expect to find you so...human. I stood next to you in line at registration last week and thought you were just another human girl. Even when I helped you up after your fall at school, I never suspected you were dewing. When I used my joining on you in the sickroom and then again that night in the car, it worked. It shouldn't have. Not on another dewing. Of course, I sensed Lillian the first time I walked into the Shadow Box, but she didn't confirm my suspicion about you until last night."

I felt like I'd been punched in the stomach. "Lillian is a dewing?" I asked in a whisper.

"Yes, but she's an odd one. She's gone rogue. She doesn't interact with others of our kind on a regular basis. She's even stopped going to her clan gatherings. She's chosen to isolate herself, so she's become less sensitive to our clan affiliations. She took you for a human at first, same as Brandy and I did, but when she tried to read your emotions, like she would any other human, she couldn't get a clear picture of them."

"Why didn't she say anything to me?"

"Your skittish behavior made that difficult. She didn't know how or why you ended up with a human family, but she sensed you were afraid of someone discovering you were dewing. She determined later that you were a thoughtmaker like her sister. Maybe because of that, she felt a connection with you. She helped you in the only ways she could, by keeping you close and not asking questions."

I was newly grateful for Lillian's silent presence at the Shadow Box.

"I've been dying to ask," Ian continued. "How did you come to live with a human family in the first place?"

"I wish I could tell you. All I know is that I was left at a state hospital when I was three. I bounced around between foster homes after that. I'd been in system for five years when the McKyes came along and adopted me."

He pondered that and then asked, "And you haven't interacted with any dewing for all these years?"

"Only one. I met a guy three years ago who told me he *saw* human emotions. He was the one who warned me."

Ian leaned back. "What exactly did he warn you about?"

"He said I was valuable to a powerful man and that man would want me to do thought transference for him. He told me to use my ability to become invisible in order to protect my family."

"Did you the two of you talk a lot?"

I laughed ruefully. "We had one conversation that lasted less than ten minutes. I was like a disease he didn't want to catch. He practically ran from me. Basically he messed up my entire life and left me alone to deal with it."

"Considering the tension among us, he could have gotten into a lot of trouble if he'd been caught talking to you."

That tidbit was less than comforting. I sighed. "You can't know how worried I've been. The idea that someone would hurt my family in order to get to me has been my constant companion for the past three years."

"So you turned yourself inside out and tried to stop existing in order to protect them."

"After what you said today, I realize I took it too far, but at the time, I thought I was doing the right thing."

Ian nodded. "I won't sugarcoat it," he said. "The reader told you the truth. As a thoughtmaker you are valuable, especially now that so many others with your ability have been killed. You are right to fear for your family, too. They could be used as a means to control your thoughtmaking."

"That's another problem," I replied. "Even when I want to do thought transference, it only takes a minor roadblock to stop me. I would probably have to watch my whole family suffer and die before anybody realized I can't do stuff the way other dewing can."

"That's only because you haven't been taught," he said.

"Well, I can't endanger my family any longer," I said, pinching the bridge of my nose. "I have to leave Vegas tomorrow."

He put a reassuring hand on my shoulder, and I tried not to flinch. Without success.

"What's with all the touching?" I asked. "Is that like a

genetic thing? If so, I'm missing that gene."

He laughed. "Maybe we are a little more affectionate than the average human. It's because there are so few of us. We have to draw strength from each other."

"At the moment, I don't have much strength for you to draw from, and I'm better able to think when no one touches me."

He moved his hand away. "It's kind of sad that it bothers you so much, but it's not the only thing that's different about you. You don't have a vibration."

"I have no idea what you're talking about."

"We feel a kind of energy, or vibration, coming off of each other. Except you don't vibrate at all. You feel completely human."

"But something about me made you curious anyway?"

"It had more to do with how you acted than anything else. If you hadn't been so edgy, I probably wouldn't have given you a second thought."

It was a good segue into the most important question I had. "If you knew enough to come looking for me, and I've got someone following me, are others coming for me, too?"

"I'm not sure. Only a few of us believe you really exist. I didn't believe it myself until my mom told me. And it wasn't easy to find you. I did months of research and still would have come up empty if it weren't for…a friend who pointed me in the right direction."

"What friend?"

"Just someone who suggested I look for you in Vegas. We got lucky when we started school at Fillmore. If it weren't for that, I'd still be looking."

"That's some pretty amazing luck."

"Call it destiny, then."

"Either way, you found me. If you did it, someone else could, too. I could spend the rest of my life running and never be able to hide well enough to ensure the McKyes are safe."

"Except that other than us, there's only one man who wants to find you. Which brings us back to the original plan. When I started searching for you, I assumed there would be things you didn't know or understand about us. I was prepared to teach you, but now that I know how human you think, I realize the learning curve would be really steep."

His words were like a bright ray of light breaking through the clouds of my miserable day. "So there are things you can teach me," I said. "Things that would help me keep my family safe."

"It would be easier to leave the McKyes and relocate somewhere else, like you planned. My dad has connections. He can arrange a place for you to stay while you figure out what you want to do next."

Leaving would be so much easier with help, but I could see complications now. When I was reported as a missing person, the McKyes would be all over the news asking for the public's help finding me. If anyone suspected who I was, my ties to them would be public knowledge and…so much for hiding in the shadows. Not to mention that I'd wondered for years what I'd be able to do with my abilities if someone explained how they worked. It was an opportunity I didn't want to miss. I didn't want to live in fear and vulnerability forever. I needed to be strong for myself and for my family.

"I'm a fast learner," I assured him. "You said you needed my help. If you teach me, I'll do anything you want me to."

He was softening but not fully convinced teaching me was the best option. "I can help you understand how to use your joining better," he relented, "and how to fight and defend yourself in our particular way, but I *would* have to ask for something in return later."

"Anything," I repeated.

He let out a long breath. "You won't like it, but I won't ask you to give anything I haven't already committed to give myself."

I didn't know how to respond to that, so I kept quiet while he considered what to do. Various emotions played across his face, but I knew the moment his decision was made. "Okay, Brandy and I will teach you. How much do you know about the dewing?"

"Not much," I admitted.

He smiled. "Are you up for a dewing history lesson, then?"

"History is my best subject," I replied with an internal sigh of relief.

Chapter Eight

Ian sat back into the sofa for what I hoped would be an informative lecture. Instead, I got silence and a look of disbelief. "The history lesson will have to wait," he said. "We've got company."

Seconds later, three men and two women entered the room. They'd been talking loudly, but catching sight of me, their conversation died away. Ian got to his feet and said, "Hi, Dad."

I respectfully got up from the sofa. The only light in the room came from the wall of windows and the sunset outside. The low light cast strange shadows across the faces of the people in front of me. As my eyes adjusted, I could see the tallest man in the group looked a lot like Ian. He was likely the one Ian had referred to as Dad.

The woman standing next to him was striking. Her hair was a deep nut brown, her skin a light creamy tone, and her green eyes turned up at the outside corners. She came forward to embrace Ian. "What are you doing here, Mom?" he asked.

"We had an unexpected layover, so we decided to have dinner with some friends in town," she replied.

"I mean, what are you doing here at the house?" Ian clarified. "You called me from the airport an hour ago. I told you everything was fine."

It was strange that Ian seemed so irritated with his parents, but I figured he must have had a reason. The lovely woman brushed this comment aside. "You're being rude. You should introduce us to your friend."

Ian glanced my way. "Alison McKye, this is my mom, Katherine Thane." Then he nodded toward the man who looked so much like him. "Spencer Thane, my father. Bruce and Amelia Dawning and Luke Stentorian."

By the way they watched me, I could tell the people in the room knew more about me than my name, which made me uncomfortable.

"Let's sit so we can get to know each other," Spencer suggested.

"Yes," Katherine agreed. "Have a seat, everyone."

Their language was more formal that I was used to, but it was charming in a way. Kind of old-fashioned.

There were only the two sofas in the room, so Luke sat next to me. He was a thin man, so thin that his Adam's apple stood out, and I could see the blood pulsing in the veins of his neck. There were dark circles under his eyes and he kept sniffing and clearing his throat like he had a cold. Hoping I wouldn't catch whatever he had, I scooted a few centimeters away from him.

"You're in the presence of greatness," Ian commented cynically. "My father and mother are the Thane clan chiefs. Bruce and Amelia are the Dawning clan chiefs and Luke heads the Stentorian clan. He hasn't found his life partner yet."

"Clan chief" wasn't a term used in everyday conversation, so I assumed it was a dewing term and that everyone in the room was a fellow nonhuman.

Ian read my train of thought. "Yes, we're all dewing."

"So, you're not Ian Palmer," I said. "You're Ian Thane, and your parents are just dropping in?"

"This is our house," Katherine replied before Ian could. "We bought it a couple of months ago, but we've never actually stayed here for more than a few hours."

"My parents travel a lot for business, so they have houses all over the world," Ian explained.

"You don't mind that two teenagers live here alone?" I asked.

Maybe the question wasn't as politely formed as it could have been, but Katherine wasn't offended. "Brandy is older than she looks," she replied.

Amelia's eyes narrowed. "It's obvious who your mother was, but I can't feel a single vibration coming off you."

As an introduction to a painful subject, it wasn't tactful. As a conversation starter, it worked. "You knew my mother?" I asked her.

"We all did," Katherine acknowledged. "She did our families a great service once."

In that one sentence, I learned more about the woman who'd given birth to me than I'd ever known before.

For years, I'd been haunted by the fact that I couldn't remember anything about my biological parents when I could remember even the most minute detail of everything else. I'd spent many dark nights searching my memory for a lingering shadow of them. I'd yet to find a single one. "I was three when I was placed in the foster-care system," I replied. "I have no memory of anything before that."

Clearing his throat and shifting his posture, Luke said, "That's normal. Our recall develops slowly. It isn't fully functional until we're about eight."

I gave the awkward man a smile. I was grateful for the explanation, and the small degree of guilt it freed me from.

"She doesn't know much about our kind at all," Ian admitted. "I was just about to give her a history lesson when I felt you guys coming in."

"We're just in time, then," Spencer said enthusiastically. "I can fill in anything you miss."

Ian was annoyed. Maybe because his father was set on taking over the conversation. "You love this sort of thing, Dad," he said. "Go ahead and tell it all. Knock yourself out."

"We'll all tell it," Katherine interjected. With a nod toward Spencer, she said, "You can start, but don't monopolize the conversation."

That was all the okay Spencer needed. He stood up and

posed like a professor teaching a class. "We are what's left of the people that lived on the island of Atlantis," he began. "Our race, if that's what you want to call it, has been around since before the first human civilization. We were reading, writing, calculating math formulas, and curing diseases while humans still existed as hunter-gatherers. What they know about Atlantis in this day and age is mostly fiction, but the island was never a myth. Plato was the first to record what he knew of us, and he got some parts right. Atlantis did disappear into the ocean. What he didn't know was that our ancestors made it disappear."

I gave a short laugh. "Are you telling me, people living thousands of years ago had the know-how to sink an entire island?"

"As crazy as it must seem to you, they did," Spencer answered, pacing a bit. "Eleven thousand years ago, the original inhabitant of Atlantis divided into two separate groups, the Rorelent and the Tenebros. These two groups formed because of opposing political views. The Rorelent, which in our ancient language means 'the dew,' lived by a highly ethical standard. They respected the rights of the weaker species, humankind, to exist undisturbed. The Tenebros were led by Tenebrosus, a power-hungry and greedy man. He campaigned for the people of Atlantis to use their mind abilities on humans. He wanted to turn them into a slave race.

"Tenebrosus convinced many that his idea was the better and more humane approach. According to him, human suffering would be alleviated if they existed only to do the will of our people. Of course, humankind would have lost their free will, too, but he and his followers didn't see that as a problem. Eventually, he gained enough support to put his idea to a vote in government. The vote came back against him, but he wouldn't accept defeat. He continued to campaign for human enslavement, breaking all sorts of rules along the way."

"He was smart about it," Ian interjected. "He never broke a rule until he'd gained enough supporters to make it worth his while."

"Yes," Spencer said. "As the number of Tenebrosus's supporters increased, they began attacking northern African countries, even going into Egypt. They killed and enslaved people along the way."

"You mean they went around reading human emotions and making thought suggestions to them?" I asked in confusion.

Next to me, Luke chuckled.

"It's good that you know something of our joining," Spencer answered with a smile. "I believe you are referring to the abilities of a reader and a thoughtmaker. We call these abilities 'joinings.' There are many different kinds."

"There are sensationmakers like me," Amelia chimed in with pride. "I can join a human mind and make them feel almost anything, both pleasant and unpleasant."

"And there are healers like me, who can fix and rewire problems in the human brain," Spencer explained. "There are futuretellers, like Katherine, who get glimpses of what's to come through the minds of humans. And thoughtseers, like Bruce, who can see human thoughts when two or more of them talk with each other. Then there's Luke. He's rather unique, but we've nicknamed him the Eraser. His joining can remove specific human memories."

Something about that ability disturbed me, but no one else was bothered by it, so I just nodded that I understood.

The only joining left to introduce was Ian's. "Confidant," he stated under the weight of my stare. "I can get a person to tell me just about anything, from their deepest fears to their greatest desires. I can get them to admit past indiscretions and fantasies of future indiscretions. So if you ever want to blackmail one of your human buddies, I'm your man."

"That's what you did to me in the sickroom," I said. "You asked if there was anything you could do to make amends and I told you I needed a ride to work. I said it even though I didn't want to." Ian scrunched his nose, looking apologetic. "Why did it work on me if it wasn't supposed to?"

"I think it's because your thought patterns mimic human ones," he said. "Your mind functions as a human's mind does, so it's possible for another dewing to join to it. That would also explain why you don't register as a dewing to our senses."

I thought of fedora man at the bookstore, and a chill ran up my backbone. "Was the man at the bookstore, the one who took the book, a dewing, too?"

"Brandy and I think he's the dewing who's been following you," Ian admitted.

"There was something really off about that guy," I said. "It was like he enjoyed hurting me. Really enjoyed it. Like he didn't want to stop until I was dead."

Spencer nodded gravely. "Do you know what the people in the jungles of India call tigers?" When I shook my head, he explained, "They call them man-eaters. Dewing tigers are also man-eaters, in a way. Their joining completely destroys the human mind."

"Tigers," I repeated. "So he could have killed me with his mind?"

"Yes," Ian affirmed.

I allowed that shocking piece of information to sit for a moment and then said, "I understand how a tiger could threaten humankind, but other than just messing with them, what damage could the other types of joinings do?"

"Imagine a world leader with a child who suffers from mental disability," Spencer said, "and then someone like me comes along and cures them. It would seem like some kind of magic. What secrets might that leader tell me out of gratitude? Imagine someone like Amelia, who can make a human feel euphoric to a degree that no drug can. What might a human pay or do to get more of that feeling?"

Bruce Dawning spoke for the first time. "There are all sorts of ways we can use our joining to manipulate the human realm," he added. "I see the thoughts behind the words during a human conversation. I see their greed and plans for betrayal, their lusts. I see things no one else would consider asking. Dewing with joining like mine can use this information to manipulate humans into any number of situations."

Spencer continued, "The real damage is done when a group of us work together for a common purpose. That's what made Tenebrosus and his followers so dangerous. They combined their joinings to take secrets, money, power, and the lives of humans. And that was just the beginning. Our kind has always been far ahead of human technology. With the ability to undermine human social structures and our advanced weaponry, he planned to bring humankind to its knees.

"The Rorelent couldn't let that happen. It was against all they stood for. So, they went to war against Tenebrosus. Plato wrote that the Athenians fought the Atlanteans, and that is true. Tenebrosus admired the Athenians' bravery and skill in battle. They were the first civilization he targeted. On his command, they killed thousands of the Rorelent who lived outside Atlantis as protectors. When their numbers decreased enough, Atlantis was vulnerable to invasion, and Tenebrosus gained control over the city. The Rorelent survivors were forced to encamp on land while they decided their next course of action."

"He was a lot of things," Ian said, "but lazy wasn't one of them. During the next few months, he continued his 'recruitment' of human forces."

"That's right," Spencer picked up. "The Rorelent determined that Tenebrosus and his followers were past redemption and that they would have to be destroyed. A leading dewing scientist had just learned how to split the atom. Fortunately, he was on the Rorelent side. The Rorelent staged a battle against Tenebrosus and when the battle had drawn most of the Athenian forces off Atlantis, the Rorelent destroyed it with today's equivalent of a nuclear bomb."

"Tenebrosus and almost twenty thousand of his followers died instantly," Ian explained. "Atlantis didn't exactly sink into the ocean. There just wasn't much left of it when the dust cleared."

"Which spelled the end of the Tenebrosus but not the end of his political ideas," Spencer said. "We had a long period of peace and prosperity, but that all changed when Sebastian Truss came to power. He's dusted off and embraced Tenebrosus's ideas again."

The atmosphere, which had been solemn during the history lesson, turned positively grave at the mention of Sebastian Truss.

"Sebastian Truss is like Tenebrosus reborn," Bruce said. "He has no problem killing humans or other dewing."

"In order to understand the gravity of the current situation," Katherine said, "you have to understand something about our biology. As a species, the dewing's brain functions are faster and more efficient, which makes it possible for us to do things that no human can. We can recall memories, we heal faster, and we live longer than humans. But in one way, humankind is superior to us. You see, we can reproduce only twice in a lifetime."

Evidently this statement was worthy of profound silence, because that's what came next.

"This might not seem like a big deal," Katherine continued, "but it is. A typical dewing will live almost three hundred years. In spite of the extended lifespan, we never have more than two children. Which means that while we struggle to maintain a steady population of less than five thousand, humans outnumber us many million times over."

I knew she meant the two kids thing was important. It was that live-three-hundred-years thing that staggered me. "We live how long?" I asked.

"You heard her right," Ian said. "Three hundred years."

"Holy crap…"

"Pace yourself," he said. "There are more *holy crap* moments coming."

"Do any humans know we exist?" I asked.

"Some of them suspect we exist. The human mainstream, with a little help from us, has turned its back on these people. They're regarded as crackpots. Their ideas aren't taken seriously, but they'd love to get their hands on a dewing. It isn't just the crazies we worry about. Militaries would love to get a hold of us. Humankind thrives on war, and under the right circumstances, we could be used as weapons. If the military couldn't turn us to their purpose, we would become prime targets for genocide. We still have technologies that humans don't, so we could put up a fight, but there are more than seven billion of them, compared to a few thousand of us. The numbers aren't in our favor."

"We don't reveal ourselves to humans under any circumstances," Amelia chimed in. "If we do we're subject to the highest punishment."

Ian made a slicing motion across his throat to illustrate her point.

"The man who told me I was a dewing also said I was unprotected," I said. "What does that mean?"

After an awkward moment of silence, Spencer took the

reins. "The Laurel clan, which is your clan by blood, was the smallest, but known for the strong thoughtmaking that ran through it. And also for taking a determined stand against those dewing who used their joining without regard for human freedoms."

"No one expected the massacre that resulted," Katherine stated quietly.

"Massacre?" I asked.

"The group that follows Sebastian Truss hunted your clan members down and killed them," Spencer explained. "The Laurel clan numbered two hundred and eighty-seven one day. The next day, they totaled thirty-nine. Over the following year, he hunted and killed everyone left...but you."

"That's only because he couldn't find you," Amelia added helpfully.

Katherine shook her head. "None of us foresaw such a terrible thing happening," she said. "The other clans didn't have time to come together to prevent it."

I swallowed a lump in my throat. Whether I knew them personally or not, it was tragic.

"Your mother was special," Spencer said. "The odds were against her from the beginning, but she defied Sebastian over and over again. He wanted her loyalty and control over her joining. He had her captured and tortured, but she refused to give in to him. He was out-of-his-mind angry at her refusal, and thinking he'd weakened her by days of isolation and pain, he went to see her by himself. He was so confident in his own abilities that he dismissed the guard. That turned out to be a mistake. Your mother had been weakened, but she was still one of the most powerful thoughtmakers in our history. She engaged him, and from the damage she inflicted, we believe she almost won the battle."

"He killed her?" I asked weakly.

Katherine's eyes were glassy with unshed tears. "Yes," she confirmed.

Deborah McKye was the woman I'd always think of as Mom, but I longed to know about the courageous woman who was my biological mother. "How old was she when she died?" I asked quietly.

"Twenty-six in human years," Katherine replied. "There was a rumor that she had a child. Most of us dismissed the idea because she was so young, but no one could say for sure. She must have become pregnant when she and your father were on the run from Sebastian. They weren't in regular contact with us during that time."

Across the space between us, Bruce said quietly, "She died bravely. Inspired by the White Laurel, many others defied Sebastian Truss."

"Her name was White Laurel?"

"Her name was Grace, but she's a legend among us," Katherine explained. "We call her the White Laurel because she was heir to the Laurel clan chiefdom and because she had white hair."

"Can you see how things sit for us now?" Ian asked. "The dewing are verging on another war, and considering that the last one ended with bombing an island, it doesn't look good."

I nodded agreement. My head was spinning from so much information.

Katherine gave me a smile of understanding. "It's a lot to take in," she said. "Any more would be overwhelming. We should probably get going, anyway, or we'll miss our reservation."

Everyone stood up. With Amelia at his side, Bruce came to shake my hand. He was an unremarkable-looking man except for the color of his hair. It wasn't really blond but not really red, either. "Your mother was a great woman," he said. "You can call on us if you need anything."

"Thank you," I replied.

Spencer gave me a big smile and a hearty pat on the shoulder, which nearly sent me flying. Then he turned to face his son, and I saw tenderness in his expression. "Can I help you in any way, son?" he asked.

"Just give me some time, Dad."

Spencer wrapped his arms around him in a bear hug. Reluctantly, Ian patted the big man on the back. "Love you, too, Dad," he said.

Katherine put her hands on my upper arms and stared into my eyes. "You look so like your mother," she said before kissing me on the cheek.

I froze, unblinking, until she let me go.

Surprisingly, Luke lingered last. He didn't say anything. He just coughed and gave me a grimacing smile before making an awkward exit from the room.

I turned to the window and looked at the dark sky, wondering if I was more grateful or sad that I finally had some answers. At least I knew the name of the man I'd been hiding from all these years, the man who'd killed my parents...Sebastian Truss.

Chapter Nine

Ian let silence settle between us while a million different thoughts crashed and whirled through my mind. Feeling him watching me, it occurred to me that he was waiting for an emotional breakdown.

"I'm not going to cry," I assured him.

"Are you sure?" he asked. "I think I'd cry if I were you."

I put my head back against the cushions and sighed. "I passed the emotional-breakdown stage when you tackled me on the rocks. I'm solid at the moment. I'm really hungry, though."

Ian laughed. "You're jumping from a life-altering conversation to *I'm hungry*. You can be so weird."

"And you can be so rude. I wish I could hate you for it."

He laughed again. "Don't worry, no one can. Let's see

what there is to eat in this place. Probably not much. I was supposed to go to the grocery store today. Instead, I was parked out back of the Shadow Box with my brains boiling in the heat."

He opened the door of a virtually empty refrigerator. "You should have come in," I said. "Lillian wouldn't have minded. She would have ignored your existence. She does that with most people."

He shook his head. "Lillian is an odd one, but it was because of your shattered nerves that I stayed outside. The last thing you needed today was me hovering over you at work." He looked back into the refrigerator. "I've got bread and some processed cheese slices, so I can offer you grilled cheese or…grilled cheese."

"I'll take the grilled cheese, please."

"Excellent." He removed the bread and cheese from the fridge, opened a tall cupboard and took down the one pan in it. Turning back to see me peering into the unfilled space, he explained, "My parents have owned this place for a couple of months, but Brandy and I didn't move in until last week."

When he bent to look in a drawer for cooking utensils, a lock of his hair fell across his forehead. All my determination to ignore how hot he was evaporated. Tall and lean, he was built more for speed and efficiency than for brute strength. Though, judging by the way his T-shirt stretched across the muscles in his shoulders and arms, he'd have no difficulty defending himself in a fight.

I was just looking, not really interested, I told myself, but the idea of Brandy and Ian living together didn't sit quite right with me anymore. I wondered if there was more going on between them than a cousinly relationship.

"Is Brandy your cousin or your girlfriend?" I asked.

He snorted. "She'd get a laugh out of that one. Brandy is sort of like my sister-in-law. She was my older brother's likeness. A likeness is a dewing's life partner, or mate, for lack of a better term."

"Brandy was your brother's...likeness," I repeated, trying out the new word. "Does that mean they got divorced?"

"Dewing don't get divorced. Once likeness is determined, two dewing can't be separated for very long or they die. Most dewing choose to live with an irritating likeness over dying from the separation. Brandy is what you would consider a widow." All the amusement left his eyes and was replaced by pain. "My brother, Jack, was killed five months ago," he said quietly. "Brandy's parents and sister have been gone for a long time, so she came to live with us after it happened. She's lasted longer than any of us expected, but every day she's less vibrant than the day before. She'll be gone soon, too."

It took me a second to understand what he meant. "Are you kidding me?" I asked. "She's just a teenager and probably one of the healthiest girls I've ever met."

"You didn't know her before, so you can't see how she's changed. It's sheer determination that has kept her going this long. And she's not a teenager. When you asked earlier if any adults live here, I think she qualifies. She's almost sixty years old."

I started to cough, literally choking on my own spit. That would make Brandy older than my human parents. Ian got me a glass of water. "You okay?" he asked, patting me on the back.

I drank water as he put cheese slices between bread, wondering about his age. If Brandy was almost sixty and appeared to be eighteen, how old was the boy next to me? Noticing the expression on my face, he asked, "Why are you looking at me like that?"

"I'm trying to figure out how old you are."

"I was born seventeen years ago, on the twenty-seventh of May."

I breathed a sigh of relief. "At least one thing about you is what I thought in the beginning."

While he lit the gas stove, I thought back to the scarred *V* I'd seen in Brandy's palm. I looked at my own palm to compare it. "Why is the *V* in my palm blue, but the one in Brandy's is more like a scar?" I asked.

He pushed the sandwiches around the hot pan. "The mark starts out subtle and gets more defined over time, and it's not really a *V*." Taking my hand in his, he turned it so my fingers pointed toward the floor. "What does it look like now?"

It took me a second but I got it. "An island?"

"Yep. It's a sign of our original home. The only solid thing we've got left to connect us with it."

When he turned away, I kept looking at my palm, appreciating for the first time the significance of the mark in my flesh. Eventually, my mind returned to more practical matters. "Shouldn't you make a sandwich for Brandy?"

"She won't be back for a while."

"Just out of curiosity, what is her joining?"

"She's a drawer," he replied. "She draws humans like a flower draws bees. She can sense what a human likes and make them think she's just their thing. A drawer can make a human want their company to the point that they'd sign over their life savings or their firstborn child to get it. Most drawers are quite attractive and age slower than other dewing, which is an advantage, because humans appreciate youth and beauty so much."

He put two grilled cheese sandwiches on a plate for me. I was so hungry I almost asked for a third. "I think Brandy has some diet soda somewhere around here if you want one," he said.

I took a bite before responding, "No, thanks."

My stomach growled for more, so I took another bigger bite.

"I told you you'd be hungry," Ian observed.

I chewed and swallowed at record pace. "Very insightful of you," I replied. "You know, you might want to get a table in here. In case your species hasn't heard of them, tables are the four-legged things humans push chairs under."

"Really?" he said with a quirky smile. "Come on, we usually eat in the living room."

The lights of Sin City sparkled out the wall of windows.

"The view here is great," I remarked between bites.

"My parents have a soft spot for Las Vegas. They lived here back in the 1950s, when the town was really starting to grow. My mom loves the view, too. That's what sold her on this ugly house."

I was way ahead of Ian in the process of eating, so I tried to slow it down to a more ladylike pace. "You don't have a television," I commented. "I thought males of any species couldn't live without one."

"It's on the list of things to buy. Actually, Brandy's got a long list going. If we're going to have people over this weekend, we've got to make this place look lived in."

I nodded, and we ate the rest of our food in companionable silence.

I hadn't expected to become comfortable with Ian in so short a time, but he had a way about him. He was at ease in his own skin, and that put me at ease.

Maybe it was the food, maybe it was that I'd finally let my guard down, or maybe it was relief that I wouldn't have to leave in the morning. Whatever it was, I felt more relaxed than I had in years. Even with all the crazy stuff I'd just discovered, I wasn't holding the weight of the world on my shoulders anymore. The room was cool and the sofa was comfy. While Ian texted something, I leaned my head back and let my mind settle into Zen.

I must have fallen asleep, because the next thing I remember, I woke up to the sound of my phone ringing in my pocket. "You'd better get that," Brandy said from across the room.

Looking at my phone, I saw my home number flashing on the screen. I tried to push the sleepy notes out of my voice as I answered, "Hi, Mom."

"Alex said you're at a friend's doing homework tonight. Is everything going well?" she asked with interest.

"We're working through an English project. Things are fine."

"It's late. Did you get something to eat?"

"Yes. Ian made grilled cheese sandwiches for me...and for Brandy." I added Brandy's name because the thrill my mom would get from me spending time alone with a boy would probably send her into cardiac arrest.

"That's good. What time should we expect you home?"

"I should be home by ten."

"Take your time," she said. "Eleven will be fine. Enjoy yourself, and be sure to tell your friends they're welcome to do homework at our house sometime."

"I will," I assured her before hanging up.

Ian had moved to the floor and was sitting with a book in his lap. "Is she worried?" he asked.

"No, she's happy I might finally be getting a social life. Sorry I fell asleep like that."

Brandy sat on the other sofa and pulled her feet up. "Ian has that effect on girls," she joked. "How was the big talk?"

"Long," I replied. "You look great for sixty, by the way."

"Fifty-seven, but thank you."

"Why do Ian and I look like normal teenagers?" I asked. "If we age so slowly, shouldn't we be in diapers or something?"

"We don't age at a constant rate," Brandy explained. "We mature at approximately the same rate as humans until we're around twenty. Then the process slows down."

"Great. I'll add prolonged youth to the benefits of being dewing. Assuming I don't get killed off before I can make much of it."

"Have a little faith," Brandy said. "You've got us to help you now. Speaking of which, I was able to get pretty close to your friend in the black car. He feels like Illuminant clan."

Ian's nose wrinkled in confusion. "I expected Truss or Ormolu clan."

"Me, too," Brandy said, thoughtfully. "Why would someone from the Illuminant clan be looking for her?"

Ian sighed. "Maybe he wasn't. Maybe this guy was going about his own business, the same way Lillian was, and he noticed something that made him wonder about her."

"Maybe," she admitted. "But I don't like it."

"What is Illuminant clan?" I asked.

"There are fourteen clans," Brandy said. "Illuminant clan is one of the more unstable ones. There's talk that they may join with Sebastian and the Truss clan."

"Which would be disastrous," Ian added.

"Since we're being up front about everything now," I said, "there's something I should tell you. Remember how Lillian described a vine tattoo on the arm of the man who left the book at the store?"

"Yes," Ian said.

"There was an embossed design on the cover of the book he left, too. The leather had cracked, so it was hard to make out, but I think it was a vining wreath."

"I was right, then," Ian said. "The tattoo wasn't a coincidence. A vining wreath is the Laurel clan signet. We haven't used signets for more than a thousand years, so not many remember them. I ran across a mention of the Laurel signet when I was doing some research to find out where you were."

I nearly jumped out of my skin. "Could the man with the tattoo have been a Laurel, too?" I asked excitedly.

"That's the weird part," he replied. "Lillian would have felt if he was dewing. She said he wasn't."

"So, why would a tattoo and an embossing on an old book, both in the shape of the Laurel signet, show up at the Shadow Box on the same day?" I asked.

"For any number of reasons," Brandy said. "The design you described isn't that unusual."

Ian and I looked at each other with doubt, but whatever the design meant, we had other worries. "Something else occurred to me," I said. "This guy who's following me—he knows the two of you are dewing? Won't my coming here make him more suspicious of me?"

"Maybe," Brandy replied. "But we have to form relationships with humans in order to exist among them undetected. He's seen the three of us at Fillmore together. It probably won't set off any alarm bells if we're friends."

"You can't be our only human friend though," Ian stated. "That would be odd. Which is why Brandy has invited half the high school over this weekend."

"You're still coming, right?" Brandy asked, hopefully.

I looked at Ian, who was smiling at me. "Yes. I'm going to start acting like a normal teenager."

"Great." She motioned to the empty space around us. "I've got to furnish this place in a hurry. Are you up for a shopping trip tomorrow?"

Doing something as simple as shopping with a girl who wasn't my mother sounded wonderful. "I'll ask Lillian for the afternoon off," I replied.

"Wear comfortable shoes," Ian suggested.

"He's trying to be funny," Brandy interjected, "but he's right. We're going to borrow the Golden One's credit card and make a day out of it."

"The Golden One?"

"That's what I call Ian because he's so shiny and bright." Ian rolled his eyes at her. "Ian's mommy and daddy have mountains of money," she added, giggling.

"Brandy has a small hill of her own money," Ian responded. "I expect to inherit it when she kicks it."

Brandy didn't seem to be offended by his offhanded remark about her death. "You always have been a favorite of mine," she said with laugh and a wink.

"How can you laugh about dying?" I asked.

She tipped her head to the side, considering my question. "I'm not sure why, but the idea of death doesn't bother me anymore."

"It bothers me plenty," Ian said.

"Then it's one of the few things that does," Brandy observed.

Shaking my head at it all, I said, "I should be getting

home."

Ian got to his feet and pulled keys from his pocket. "Just in case the tiger is still out there searching for you, I'll follow you at a distance. Wait while I get my shoes, okay?"

As he left, I smoothed some hair that had come out of my bun. I didn't understand everything that was happening, but it was a relief to be with people who did understand and whom I didn't have to hide around.

"I wonder just how much he told you," Brandy muttered from across the room.

I turned a questioning look at her. "What do you mean by that?" I asked.

Ian came back looking ready to go. "We'll talk tomorrow," Brandy assured me.

My parents were waiting up for me when I got home. They were curled up together on the sofa watching the History Channel on television. They often did that at the end of the day. It was comforting to me. No matter what else in my life was uncertain, their love for each other and for me was never in doubt. Hours ago I'd thought I'd be leaving the next morning, but with Ian and Brandy in my corner, I might get to stay a little bit longer. Maybe a just a few days, maybe a year. Whatever it turned out to be, I'd take every moment I could get.

The next morning I decided Ian was right. Trying so hard to be inconspicuous had made me conspicuous. No other seventeen-year-old girls at Fillmore tried to look like paint on the wall. So I brushed my hair out and let it fall shiny and straight down my back. That alone did a lot to improve my looks. Encouraged, I applied a little pink lip gloss and then debated whether I should keep wearing my glasses or not. Deciding baby steps were best, I put my spare pair on.

Mom was eating breakfast when I came into the kitchen. She took one look at my hair and the pink tint on my lips and her spoon clattered into her bowl. "You look beautiful," she said, reaching out to touch the dark tresses that fell over my shoulder.

I appreciated the compliment but was still unsure about the attention it might attract at school. I fought down the urge to twist it into its usual bun and secure it with chopsticks from the silverware drawer. Mom was wise enough to say nothing more about it, so I ate my cereal in relative quiet.

Someone knocked at the front door as I was finishing up. Mom went to answer it and came back looking euphoric. Behind her trailed Brandy and Ian. "We thought maybe you'd like to ride to school with us this morning," Brandy said.

"Uh…sure," I replied.

I knew Mom was going to get extra mileage out of this impromptu visit. A physical manifestation of people who admitted knowing me was going to push her to the edge. As if on cue, she cooed, "How thoughtful. I always worry that Alison's old car will have mechanical problems and leave her stranded somewhere."

"I take better care of the engine in that car than I do myself, Mom."

"Yes, dear, but it's old," she replied, looking at the attractive young people who were apparently friends of mine. "We've offered to get her a new car," she continued, "but Alison is very independent."

That's when Alex walked into the kitchen, rubbing sleep from his eyes. He scratched enthusiastically under both his armpits before noticing we had company. When his eyes focused in on Brandy, they filled with admiration. "Hi," he said, trying to make his voice sound deeper than it was.

"Hey," Brandy replied.

I struggled not to laugh out loud at my little brother's attempt to impress a fifty-seven-year-old widow. Ian caught my eye. His look said this was the natural reaction to a drawer.

"Would the two of you like a whole-grain bagel and some juice?" Mom asked.

Brandy winked in my direction. "No, thank you. Ian made grilled cheese for breakfast this morning."

Mom tipped her head quizzically. Grilled cheese seemed an odd thing to eat for breakfast, but having seen their empty cupboards, I understood it.

"We should probably get a move on," Ian suggested.

Taking the hint, I hefted my backpack. "Oh, Mom. I might be late. Brandy needs me to go shopping with her."

Mom nodded. From the surprise on her face, I don't think she was able to speak.

It was Brandy's car, a nice white Toyota with tinted windows, waiting for us in the driveway. Ian took the backseat, so I could have shotgun. "How did you guys get through the gate?" I asked as she drove away from my house.

She pointed toward a notoriously grumpy member of

the community. "That man walking the dog. I told him I'm a friend of yours, and he let us in."

"That's completely against our community rules. Did he ask for your phone number, too?"

"He might have, if his wife hadn't been with him at the time," Ian said dryly.

I waited until we were on the main road again, then I said, "I have some questions. A lot of them, actually."

"I'll bet you do," Brandy said. "Why don't you start with the biggest?"

"Okay. I agreed to help you in exchange for what you could teach me, but what do you want me to do?"

"Oh, boy," Ian said. "You should have told her to start with the smallest."

"We want you to use your thoughtmaking to take us to Sebastian Truss," Brandy said, glancing at me.

I snorted. "Are you delusional? I've spent the last three years of my life hiding from him."

"It's a lot more complicated than Brandy just made it sound," Ian said patiently. "My mom and dad's visit last night had nothing to do with a chance layover at the airport. They were in town for a meeting with the other clan chiefs. For the past decade or so, their policy has been to leave Sebastian and his minions alone. In return, they left us in peace. But it was an uncomfortable truce from the beginning, and now there are signs that it's starting to unravel."

"Sebastian is ramping up his manipulation of humans in the United States political realm," Brandy explained. "He's got at least one cabinet member in the current presidential

administration addicted to a sensationmaker of his, and
he's bankrolling the opposing party's main candidate. The
clan chiefs believe he's trying to set himself up as a puppet
master for the president."

"Which would be catastrophic for us," Ian added.
"Humankind has been slow to see how the strings of their
government and economy are being pulled by outside
forces. Sebastian's ego is so big he doesn't see how his greed
will expose us. When humans react to the threat we pose,
we won't be able to defend ourselves for long. There are too
few of us now."

"The meeting didn't get very far last night," Brandy
said. "Someone who knew it was going to happen leaked
information to Sebastian, and he sent a spy. A human spy.
The meeting was stopped when Bruce Dawning got a
glimpse of some thoughts coming from a member of the
catering crew. The human bolted out of the hotel. He was
found dead a few blocks away."

"Which just shows how serious the situation is becoming,"
Ian added. "Sebastian is in motion now. He wants to control
the highest political power in the US, and he's determined
to keep the rest of us out of it. Added to that, he doesn't care
how many humans he has to kill to get what he wants. It's
only a matter of time before he starts killing dewing again,
too. Our kind can't take another massacre like the one that
happened to the Laurels."

"It's a horrible situation," I agreed, "but what can we do
about it?"

"The three of us are going to stop Sebastian Truss," Ian

stated.

"We're going to kill him," Brandy corrected.

Shocked, I just stared at her.

"Technically, you wouldn't be doing the killing," Ian said. "I will. You'll just help out before that."

Brandy read my stunned expression and said, "Think of it as self-defense, not murder. Sebastian would use and then kill you if he could. Killing him first is the smart thing to do."

"The smart thing to do? Nothing about this sounds smart."

"Thousands of lives depend on what we're asking you to do," Ian said. "We can't afford to let Sebastian expose the dewing, but we can't wage an all-out war to prevent it, either. We're going to have to approach this problem differently than our ancestors did. We're going to have to go after the root of the problem. We're asking you to help us do this because it's necessary. It's for the good of us all."

"Even if I wanted to," I said quietly, "how could I help you? I'm practically useless when it comes to thoughtmaking."

"You're little help to us now," Brandy admitted. "But if you're anything like your mother, your powers are extraordinary. If we can teach you how to use them, even partially tap into them, you could be invaluable to us."

"But why does this have to be the three of us?" I asked. "Why not older people who might stand a decent chance?"

"It isn't about age," Brandy said. "Before Jack died, he passed some impressions to me. They aren't the kind of things I can put into words, but when I face Sebastian, I'll know his weakness. And Ian may look like a gangly string bean, but he's got more energy in his little finger than a lot of us have in our entire bodies. He's a trained fighter, too. With the impressions I have and his strength, we can take Sebastian out."

"And me?"

"Sebastian is well guarded," Ian said. "Your thought-making can get us into him."

"There are other thoughtmakers. I assume they know more about what they're doing than me. Why not use one of them?"

"They can't do what we need," Ian insisted. "Besides, my mom saw you with us when we kill Sebastian."

I snorted.

"She saw it in a future vision," Ian said. "She's never been wrong before."

"The more the merrier, right? Couldn't we get more help? Adult help?" Brandy shook her head.

"Spencer and Katherine know what we're going to do. They'll be standing by as close as they can, ready to help out, but a big group of us converging on Sebastian wouldn't work. It would alert him and his people we were coming and we'd never get close enough to him to do any damage. And like Ian said, Katherine saw the three of us there when Sebastian dies. Not the three of us and backup."

"That's a lot of faith to put in fortune-telling."

"It must sound crazy to you, but when someone like Katherine sees something, that's how it will happen."

"She and my dad trust what she saw enough to let

me come find you. It terrifies them, but they support me anyway."

If Brandy and Ian weren't completely delusional, and I could be useful in a fight against Sebastian, agreeing to help them could be deadly. He had killed Jack and my mother, who from what I'd heard had been pretty powerful. Killing me would be like child's play to him. But if by some miracle Ian's plan worked and he did kill Sebastian, the threat to the McKyes would die, too. That was the deciding factor. No matter what happened to me, I had to keep the McKyes safe. They wouldn't be punished for their kindness to me.

"Okay," I said. "I'll help."

Brandy turned to look at me. "Katherine saw us there when Sebastian dies. She wasn't able see if we die, too. This might not end well for any of us."

"I know," I replied.

Ian touched my arm so I would look at him. "I brought you into it," he said. "I'll do everything I can to get you out of it alive."

Chapter Ten

Seeing Michael Larson, Brandy's partner for the poetry presentation, in front of us, she hurried ahead to catch him.

"Doesn't she hate doing high school over?" I asked.

"She wasn't happy about the idea in the beginning," Ian replied, "but it's given her something to think about besides Jack. She's having fun."

Her lovely laugh echoed across the parking lot, making me feel sad. "Does she have to...you know? Isn't there a way to stop it from happening?"

He glanced ahead at her. "It's human for you to want a different outcome, but living without likeness, once you've had it, is worse than death in a lot of ways."

I had trouble believing that, but the whole concept of likeness was new to me and mind-boggling on so many levels. I nodded like I understood, and changed the subject, "Are there any other dewing at Fillmore...other than us?"

"One. Nikki Cole."

That's when I knew why Bruce Dawning had looked so familiar last night. Nikki Cole was his daughter. Her hair was the same reddish-blond shade, and her tiny frame was just like Amelia's.

"I take it from your expression you know her," Ian said.

"We had a little run-in the other day."

He chuckled. "It wasn't pleasant, was it?"

"Nope. I don't understand how someone so mean could be top of the pile here...unless she's a drawer like Brandy."

Ian's face masked over. "She's not a drawer. Nikki uses an age-old technique to get to the top wherever she's at— she identifies those in power and then manipulates them into being loyal to her. I've seen her do it a few times before. Considering how she acts when she's with dewing, her behavior in the human realm doesn't come as a surprise."

"You know her well?"

"I've known her for most of my life. Like you saw last night, our fathers are old friends."

"Do you think Bruce and Amelia told her about me?"

"No, your secret is safe. The Dawnings and Luke Stentorian are the only dewing besides my parents who know what I'm up to. They all think I'm crazy, and that I'll probably end up dead, but each one of them would love to see me succeed. After meeting you last night, the Dawnings know you're the secret weapon I've been looking for. They're just as worried about Sebastian Truss as everyone else is. They won't risk blowing my chance to stop him by telling anyone else about you."

"But Nikki is their daughter. Won't that make her an exception?"

"Nikki is the last person they'd tell. They're extremely protective of her. They don't want her to get involved in any aspect of what I'm doing. Amelia told me point-blank not to talk to Nikki about my plans, and Bruce as much as ordered me to steer clear of her until my business with Sebastian is finished."

As he opened the door for me, I wondered why Bruce had to warn him off so strongly.

The halls were noisy and crowded when we walked to my locker. Ian stood next to me with his shoulder against the wall while I checked my backpack, and I caught the smallest glimpse of the *V* in his palm. Taking his hand in mine, I turned it over. I traced the thin blue lines in his palm with my finger. They were even fainter than the lines in my own palm.

When I glanced up, he was watching me.

"In the beginning, I didn't know what this meant," I said. "Only that it made me different. I tried to ignore it most of the time. Now it means I'm not alone. I kind of like it."

His fingers twined through mine so the marks in our hands laid over each other. My breath caught as a mild electric shock tingled through me. Ian's eyes opened wider, so he must have felt it. "You're right," he said with a small smile. "You're not alone."

I pulled my hand back and felt the current between us break.

"Why are you still wearing those ridiculous glasses?" he asked. "Could you have picked an uglier pair, by the way?"

"The point was to make myself as uninteresting as possible."

"No matter how hard you try, you could never be uninteresting," he said.

I'm sure I had a silly grin on my face for hours after that.

Later, I met Brandy by the cafeteria for lunch.

"We're on for shopping this afternoon," I told her. "Lillian just texted to say it's okay if I take the day off."

"Great," she replied. "I like your hair today. I should warn you that Michael and Scott are going to sit with us during lunch. Connor and a couple of nice girls from my biology class might, too, so there will be a lot of us."

"Thanks for the heads-up," I replied, feeling a bit nervous about plunging headfirst into the social scene at Fillmore. It wasn't that I didn't want to get into it. I did, but I doubted I'd ever be a social diva.

Brandy led the way through the food line and then to a table already crowded with the people she'd mentioned. There wasn't room for me to sit. Ian caught my eye and motioned at the very small space next to him. I shook my head and pointed toward the outdoor eating area, where I intended to go. He got up and followed me outside.

Squinting in the sun, I headed toward a patch of shade at the side of the building and practically dove into the grass there. I leaned my back against the bricks and closed my eyes. Hearing the soft shush of Ian's shoes in the grass, I looked up at him. "You should have stayed inside where the temperature is bearable," I said.

He sat next to me. "I'll take heat over the deafening laughter of Brandy's friends any day," he replied with a hint of his Australian accent coming out.

"Are you sure about that? It over a hundred degrees today and you're not native to Las Vegas."

"It gets hot in Sydney, too."

"You call Sydney home?"

"I do now. I spent my first three years living in LA."

Ian leaned back. As he settled into the shade, his eyes turned from turquoise to deep aqua. It was a fascinating phenomenon. He sighed deeply.

"You okay?" I asked.

"I've just got a lot on my mind."

He carried a lot of responsibility for someone so young. From what he'd said, it had been his idea to find me. For whatever reason, his parents had supported him in his efforts, but it hadn't been their plan.

He reached out and touched a strand of my hair. "Pretty," he said.

"Thanks," I replied, feeling a blush spread over my cheeks. I pushed the strand behind my ear. "Evidently, it's not much like my biological mother's. Who has white hair at the age of twenty-six?"

"No one I've ever met," he replied. "But believe me, it's not a bad thing if you don't look like your parents. I'm sure you noticed I'm definitely my father's son."

"He's bigger, kind of like a huge bear. You're more athletic, like a runner, but the resemblance is uncanny." Ian was surprised. I pushed his shoulder. "Don't take that as a compliment," I said. "It's just an observation."

"You sure?" he asked.

I ignored him.

"Well, looking like my dad comes with a set of problems."

"Like what?"

"Brandy calls me the Golden One, but it's a borrowed nickname. My father is the original Golden One. He became Thane clan chief when he was younger than me. A lot of dewing laid bets he wouldn't rise to the challenge. They thought he'd crack under the pressure. But he didn't. He's proven himself over and over since then. He's kind of famous in a way. Not as famous as your mother, but everybody knows him. If Sebastian Truss worries about anyone, it's probably my dad. Which is why he would never get close enough to Sebastian to do him any harm.

"Anyway, I'm not my father and I don't want to be. My brother was supposed to be the next clan chief. In all the important ways, Jack was more like him."

"You seem to be doing things well so far. You found me. And you're willing to risk your life in a face-off with Sebastian."

"When it comes to facing Sebastian, I'm just finishing what Jack started. When it comes to finding you, I had Brandy's help. I'm worried about the day when I'm on my own." He came off as supremely confident, but he had his own worries. Worries that made going to school at Fillmore seem trivial. It was easy to forget he was just a teenager like me. "How old was Jack when he died?" I asked.

"Ninety-two in human years. To someone who thinks like a human, that must seem very old, but to us it isn't. Jack and I were close in spite of the age difference."

"I'm sorry you lost him," I said.

Ian picked a piece of grass and pulled it into pieces. I could see he wanted to change the subject. He deserved a break. "Why don't we get started on my training?" I suggested.

He tossed the pieces of grass in the air and then watched them float back down. "Sounds good."

Anxious to begin, I scooted around to face him and sat cross-legged.

He laughed. "You look like a little kid on Christmas morning," he said.

I shrugged my shoulders. "Part of me is excited about learning what I can do. And then there's the part that's scared about what you want me to do."

He frowned. "You don't have to do anything that makes you uncomfortable. I mean it. I'm going to do my best to keep you safe. And no one wants to put you in this position less than I do. But right now, you're my best plan and I'm running out of options."

"If it means I can keep my family safe, I'd do just about anything. Don't feel guilty. I want to do this—if I can."

"Okay," he said. "Let's discuss why your abilities are so underdeveloped." His words stung a bit. "All of our joinings start out weak like yours," he continued. "I'm betting your capabilities have developed at a normal rate. It's just a lack of instruction that's holding you back."

"Okay," I replied.

"Before we begin, you need to understand our education is more than following directions. The majority of what we learn comes from feeling how others around us work their minds. That's why our family bonds are so tight. We need each other to learn how to navigate in both the dewing and human realms. You never had the benefit of a dewing family to learn from, so you had to make it up as you went along. It would help if I understood your process."

"There's not much to it," I said. "I think something that I want to put into someone's mind. Then I envision pushing that thought in the direction of whoever I want to take it. Sometimes it works great, sometimes it doesn't work at all. I usually have problems when someone has strong objections or opinions on whatever is going on."

Ian considered this. "It's probably because you're trying to force your thought into a space that's already filled. What if you searched in someone's mind first and found an open place to put the thought into? Then you could kind of slip it in, and the person wouldn't struggle against it, right?"

"I guess so," I agreed. "But I have no idea how to look into a human's mind."

"'Search' is the wrong word. 'Feel' is a better one."

"Sorry, but that doesn't help."

He hesitated. "I want to try something. It's kind of like a shortcut. It might help you learn things faster, but it's… unconventional."

I leaned forward, so my nose was just inches away from his. "Is anything about me conventional?" I asked. "I need to learn this stuff as quickly as possible. Feel free to use whatever you think is necessary."

"Okay," he said with a cryptic smile. "This wouldn't work if you thought the way the rest of us do, but because you think like a human I'm going to access your mind like I did a few nights ago. If you concentrate, you should be able to feel me looking around. Focus on what you feel, so you can imitate my approach. Eventually, you'll develop a method that works best for you, but in the meantime, this should give you a few hints."

"When you access my mind, you're going to make me confide in you, right?"

"Yes, I'll have to breach some of your defenses in order for you to feel how the process works."

"So I'll end up telling you things I wouldn't normally want to?"

He nodded. "If this works, it's going to shorten the learning curve substantially."

"Okay, but don't make me confide anything too personal."

"It's too late for conditions," he said, smiling. "It's a faint feeling, but if they knew what to look for, all humans would know when we joined their minds. I believe you think human enough to experience it like they do, which should give you some unique perspective on how this all works."

That's when I felt the squeezing sensation in my head. It wasn't painful, like it was the time he used it on me in the nurse's office or in his car after the tiger took the book, but it was noticeable. "Did you feel that?" he asked.

"Yes."

"Good. It's important to understand how inefficient it is

to throw thoughts at people. You waste a lot of energy that way, and you won't get the kind of results you want. You have to use control. The beginning step is to try and feel your own energy. It's there, humans just don't think about it much. It's like a bubble that encases your body. Feel for the edges of it, become familiar with it.

"Then take a moment to think about who it is you're going to join. Try to feel the energy around that person, too. Start searching for a connection to the human's energy, and your mind will be drawn to theirs like a magnet. You'll know the link has been established when you feel a tightening, like a rope being drawn taut between you. After a while the process becomes reflexive, and you won't think about it in individual steps anymore."

"Okay."

"The next part of your lesson is where you relax and concentrate on what's happening in your mind."

He started out asking me simple stuff, like my favorite color and where I like to vacation. Then he moved on to more personal things, like what I'd dreamed of the night before, what annoyed me most about my parents, and who my first crush was. A part of me didn't want to talk about some of the things he asked, but I couldn't stop myself. As I concentrated on what was happening, I could tell he was finding the areas of resistance in my mind and then moving his questions around them.

Other than the slight pressure in my head at the beginning, this experience was much different than it had been a few nights ago. That time I'd felt antagonism in connection with Ian's questions. This time it felt…nice.

As I went on answering questions, an energy began to grow between us. It was like an electric current that filled up my mind and then spilled out again into Ian's. In a strange way, the space between us didn't seem to exist anymore. He continued his questions and the mental current transformed into a physical state where every inch of my skin tingled. Ian's face was flushed and his eyes were an even darker blue. He leaned closer to me and his eyes kept flicking to my mouth. We were both breathing faster than normal and I leaned into him, too. Instead of easing off on the mental pressure, he stepped it up and asked what I'd thought of him when we first met.

If my mind had been my own, I might have tempered my response, but under the circumstances, honesty was demanded. "You reminded me of my little brother," I said truthfully.

The current of mental energy between us broke immediately.

"I remind you of your brother," Ian said. "That skinny redhead with pimples I met this morning?"

"It was just my first impression," I said, blinking. "You didn't ask what I think of you now."

He still didn't look pleased.

"Not that this changes anything between us," I said, "but did we just make out dewing-style or something?"

"Yeah," he muttered. "Sorry it was like kissing your brother."

It certainly had not been like kissing my brother.

Brandy must have been suspicious, because she asked

me three times in Art Appreciation what Ian and I had been doing during lunch hour. Fortunately, Mr. Dawson was lecturing on Vincent van Gogh, Brandy's favorite painter, so she let the subject drop when he began a slide show.

Ian was waiting for us in the parking lot after school. Just seeing him caused an electric current to float over my skin. He didn't hold eye contact for long, and I was disappointed. As much as I hated to admit it, I wanted him to see me as something more than useful. Taking a deep breath, I reined my emotions back in. Whatever happened between Ian and me earlier had come about because he was trying to teach me to use my joining. It was important to remember that. The side effects would fade. At least I hoped they would.

Ian kept looking out the back window for my follower. I looked for him in the side-view mirror every few minutes, too. Neither of us was in the mood for small talk, but Brandy was good at making conversation with herself, so the ride passed smoothly. I was surprised when she stopped the car in front of the Shadow Box.

"I haven't seen any sign of your follower today," Ian said. "If we're lucky he's lost interest. I need to talk to Lillian about a few things. Call me if you need anything."

"Will do," Brandy said. Then she extended her hand across me toward him. "Hand it over. This shopping trip is on your mommy and daddy."

Ian rolled his eyes, produced his wallet, and handed her a credit card.

Brandy waved out the window as we drove away.

"The Golden One reminds me of Jack sometimes," she

said. "In personality, not looks."

Her words contradicted what Ian had said at lunch. He seemed to think they were very different personalities. Since she seemed open to the subject, I decided to push for more information. "What was Jack like?"

"You've heard the phrase 'tall, dark, and handsome,'" she said with eyes glowing. "That was Jack. He was really smart and funny, too, with a smile that took my breath away every time. I was nine when I met him. It was my first Thane clan gathering. Ian is something like my second cousin once removed as well as my brother-in-law."

"So you knew Jack growing up?"

"I had a bit of a crush on him through the years, but there was nothing between us until much later when I ran into him at Stanford. I was getting my master's degree in art history there, and he was working at a teaching hospital. As destiny would have it, I broke my sternum in a fall from a horse. My human friends insisted I go to the emergency room to get checked out. Of course I knew it would heal on its own, but I humored them anyway. Jack was my doctor that day."

"So you began dating and got likenessed, or whatever?"

"The dating part followed the getting-likenessed part," she explained. "He walked in, looked up from his clipboard, and there was a complete…mental connection. That's the only way I can explain it. Likeness is a melding of minds and once it happens it can never be undone."

Doing a quick rewind of what happened between Ian and myself during lunch, I cried out. "Oh, no! No!"

Chapter Eleven

"**W**hat?" Brandy asked, mirroring my alarm.

"I think that mental connection, likeness thing, happened to me and Ian this afternoon," I replied in a panic.

She pulled to the side of the road. "Calm down," she said. "I would have sensed it if it had. Hang on—I did sense something."

I couldn't catch my breath. I was starting to see stars.

"It wasn't likeness, though," she stated with certainty. "Explain exactly what happened."

"Ian used his joining on me during lunch. It was supposed to be a shortcut to show me how joinings work. Things started out fine, everything was all business, but then it took a turn."

"So what's the problem?" she asked.

"The problem is…it turned into some kind of weird mind-kissing thing. That sounds crazy, but there is nothing else I can compare it to. Whatever it was that happened, it was most definitely a mental connection, and no offense to Ian, but I don't want to be permanently connected to him for the next three hundred years. I mean, he's great, but I hardly know him, and I'm the last person anyone should be linked to right now. I'm a mess, and there's giant targets on my back. Not to mention I haven't even really kissed a boy. What if there's a dewing out there I'd like better than Ian? If by some miracle I survive this meet and mingle with Sebastian, I should probably check my options before settling on someone for the rest of my life, don't you think?"

Brandy laughed. "Breathe, Alison. Ian became a target the minute he came looking for you, and as far as the rest of it goes, you're thinking human, and look at how things turn out for them. They get divorced 50 percent of the time. We don't pick our likeness, and they don't pick us. It's something the universe determines. The end result is that we are a lot happier with our partners than most humans are with theirs."

"Maybe," I agreed, "but what if he wasn't supposed to use his joining that way? What if we messed things up and destiny can't undo it now?"

"Listen, Alison, you have to believe me. I would know if the two of you had formed a likeness connection today, and you didn't. I felt a pulse of energy at lunch this morning and guessed Ian was up to something, but it's not the kind of energy that comes off a likenessed pair, so relax."

Seeing the sincerity in her eyes, I told myself to calm down. Gradually my heart rate began to slow. "What did happen?" I asked. "Because it was definitely something more than just a confession session."

She shrugged. "Ian connected to your energy on a different level. It's like a separate access point into your mind. It's something we aren't supposed to mess around with. I mean, we all know that access point exists, but since dewing and humans don't form romantic relationships, at least not ones that last, it's pretty pointless. What Ian did today is frowned on, but your comparison is good. It's more like kissing than anything else."

"Why did he do it if he's not supposed to?"

"You aren't human, so technically he wasn't breaking the rules. Maybe he was really trying to help you learn, or maybe he was curious to see if it would affect you at all."

"Please don't tell him I freaked out about this."

"Why shouldn't I tell him?" she asked with a laugh. "He should have warned you what to expect before jumping into your mind that way."

"I told him he could do whatever was necessary," I admitted. "And it was effective. I learned a lot."

She laughed again. "I'll bet you did."

"I'm serious, Brandy. He helped me. I understand joining better now, and I don't want to repay him for that with embarrassment."

"Okay, I won't mention your panicked reaction to the idea of likenessing with him," she agreed. "But it would have made a lovely tease."

Signaling, she pulled back into traffic. She switched lanes and then glanced over at me. "Just a friendly heads-up for you. If he hasn't made it obvious enough, Ian likes you. I think he's almost as confused about all this as you are. Some things you just can't help. I understand your reaction to the idea of likenessing with him. It's a foreign concept. Just know you could search everywhere and not find another man comparable to him. The only one was Jack."

I didn't want to think about likeness. Not with Ian or anyone else.

Brandy pulled into the parking lot of a large home furnishings store. She grabbed her purse from the backseat and then squeezed my hand. "Let's go shopping," she said happily.

A senior sales associate approached us as we walked through the doors. With a professional smile in place, he introduced himself as Todd. He was young, straight, and single. Brandy had him eating out of her hand in a matter of seconds. His squinty eyes never lost their gleaming admiration as he answered Brandy's questions. Her wish was his command and the command of all the workers he managed. She only had to point toward something, and it was whisked away to be wrapped and packaged.

Brandy was decisive in her shopping. She chose curtains, rugs, pictures, and dishes rapidly and convinced Todd to sell us a floor model dining set, two big bookcases, and some accent tables. I was used to Mom changing her mind three times about something before going with her initial choice. This type of rapid-fire shopping was a new experience, and I liked it.

When we finished, Todd's people packed the trunk and backseat of the car with home decor items and then silently drifted away. Todd lingered, telling Brandy the furniture would be delivered the next day. His eyes followed her with a dreamy expression for several seconds before he got up the nerve to ask for her phone number.

She laughed merrily before telling him she was in a serious relationship with someone else. I'm sure his commission softened the blow.

As Brandy maneuvered the heavily laden car out of the parking lot and onto the main road, I heard her sharp intake of breath. "What's wrong?" I asked.

"Dewing at six o'clock."

I quickly checked the side mirror for a black car. I couldn't see one anywhere. "Where?" I asked.

"In the Ford Focus three cars back."

Checking the mirror again, I spotted the correct car. "Is it following us?"

"I'm not sure. It isn't the same person who's been driving the dark car. I'm old enough that once I feel a vibration, it's marked in my memory like a signature. I can tell this is a woman. She feels like Ormolu clan. I'd like to get the license plate number. If we get the plates, I can have Spencer do a little detective work. We might be able to get her name."

Even though we couldn't be sure she was following us, I still felt sick to my stomach when Brandy slowed the Toyota. "Don't freak out," she said. "You feel human. For all she knows, we're just two friends who've been shopping. We're just going to let her pass us and get her license plate number. So look ahead and pretend you've got no interest in her."

I did as I was told. I heard the soft shush as the car passed us and then Brandy said, "She's gone."

She was breathing hard and there were tiny beads of sweat on her forehead. "Something went wrong, didn't it?" I asked.

"No. I just had to be ready to protect you if she was going to try something. Most of the time we don't fight with our fists. It's a mind thing. It takes a lot of energy. If I was healthy, it wouldn't be problem, but I'm not so healthy anymore."

The rest of the way to my house Brandy was unusually quiet. We pulled into my driveway, and she spoke again. "Thanks for coming today. It's always more fun to shop with another girl around."

"I had fun, too," I said sincerely. She was paler than usual. "Are you sure you're okay to drive home?"

"I bounce back quickly," she assured me.

I checked my watch while she drove away. It was seven o'clock, and because I'd traded with Alex, my night to cook. Going straight to the kitchen, I began searching the refrigerator. I did a happy dance when I found a package of ground turkey behind some of Mom's tofu crap. Assuming my dad had secretly bought and stashed it, I got the low-fat cheese, lettuce, and tomatoes out of the fridge. Fifteen minutes later, I had the table set and a dozen turkey tacos ready to eat.

Alex came in saying he was starved. He was fresh from

skateboarding, and his red hair stood up in spikes all over his head. There was a hole in the knees of his jeans. "It's not Tofurky, is it?" he asked.

"Nope. It's the real thing tonight."

He immediately dropped into a chair and started loading tacos onto his plate. "Leave some for the rest of us," I said. His mouth was already full. "What did you make for dinner last night?"

"What do I always make?"

"Macaroni and cheese."

"Yep." The freckles that dusted his nose wiggled up and down as he chewed. He put out a hand. "Twenty bucks, remember?"

I'd been expecting it, so I dug into my pocket for the money.

My dad was next into the kitchen. He kissed the top of my head and glanced at Alex, who was enthusiastic about dinner for a change. "Real meat tonight?" he asked with optimism.

The male members of my family had downed two tacos each by the time Mom came in to eat. "You're all heathens," she said. "I could smell the flesh cooking a block away." She moved two of my carefully crafted tacos to her plate and dissected them. She threw the offending turkey in the trash. "I like your friends," she said. "The girl...Brandy, was it? She seems nice."

My dad and Alex looked up, each of them interested but for entirely different reasons. "She is nice," I replied.

"And the boy, what beautiful eyes he has," she continued.

"Will they come again?" my dad asked. "I'd like to meet some of your friends."

My skinny brother watched me with pathetic hopefulness. "Maybe. Ian and I still have more work to do on our presentation, and I'm helping Brandy with a get-together she's having this weekend."

"Fabulous!" my mother said. "I'll drive you and stop in for a minute to meet her parents."

I swallowed the lump of anxiety rising in my throat. There would be no parents around for her to meet, and I didn't want her knowing where Brandy and Ian lived, in case she decided to make a surprise visit on a different day. I needed to get that thought out of her mind by replacing it with something else.

Calming myself, I felt for my own energy bubble. After a moment of concentration, I thought I knew where the edges of it were. Then I felt for the energy around Mom, and I felt an immediate jolt between us. My mind had joined with hers. I copied Ian's approach and started searching for what I hoped were her thoughts. After a moment, I could tell where they were. I couldn't see the content of them, but I knew they existed as concretely as the table in front of me. I waited patiently for a break between two of them, and when I found it, I slipped *Alison will drive herself* into it.

Mom's expression changed. "Sorry. Of course, you'll drive yourself," she said.

Later that night, I sat on my bed and thought about what I'd done. For the first time ever, I'd been able to override my headstrong mother on something she was dead-set to do. It had been easy once I found the open spots in her thoughts, but I felt guilty about doing it. It was like I'd cheated on a test or something.

I was working on homework when my cell phone rang. The noise startled me. The only people who ever called me lived in my house. Pretty pathetic. "Hey," Ian said when I answered. My heart thumped at the sound of his voice.

"Is this the girl who charged a couple thousand dollars to my dad's credit card today?" he asked.

"I'm innocent. I just pushed the cart."

He laughed. "Guess what I've been doing since Brandy got home?"

"Lugging ten tons of home decor into your house?"

"That is correct. Even with all the stuff she bought, it still looks empty in here."

I rolled back onto my bed. "There's a truckload of stuff scheduled for delivery tomorrow morning, and she's planning to do more shopping in the afternoon. She'll have it ready in time."

"Or she'll kill us both trying," he said. "She's sending me out to get the television, game systems, stereo equipment, and other miscellaneous electronics."

There was a defeated tone in his voice. Knowing Brandy's energy when it came to shopping, I felt bad for him. "Did she tell you we ran into another dewing on the drive home?"

"Yes. A lot of our kind have houses here. They don't always live in them, but Vegas is a fairly popular spot for us. It's probably nothing. Regardless, my dad is trying to find out who's around, and more specifically, who was driving the car."

I felt better knowing Spencer was looking into it. "Is Brandy okay?" I asked. "She was really worn out after… whatever it was she did."

"I think so. She feels well enough to boss me around. She just gave me orders to get some stuff for my room. According to Miss Manners, only heathens live out of a suitcase. Which is ironic because she's living out of one, too."

The mention of suitcases reminded me that he had a life in Sydney to get back to. "How long do you think you guys will stay around?" I asked.

"As long as it takes to teach you what you need to know and deal with Sebastian."

I was quiet for a moment, thinking I would miss him when he left. "Speaking of teaching," I said, "I did something tonight I haven't been able to do before. Mom totally wanted to meet your parents on Saturday, but I mentally suggested I was going to drive myself over, and she changed her mind. She never would have done that before."

"That's really good," he said pleased.

"I've been feeling guilty about it ever since, though."

"I feel that way sometimes, too. Maybe it's because our joinings mess with free will. Most other joinings don't. It's different when I use my mind on another dewing."

"I thought dewing couldn't use their joining on each other."

"We don't use them in exactly the same way," he said, "but we use them."

"Right. Like how you did with me today."

"We can do something similar, but what went on today was a human-dewing thing."

"Brandy told me mind kissing was a no-no. Why did you do it?"

"Mind kissing? Hmm. I told you it would be an unconventional teaching method."

"You did," I agreed with a smile.

"I hoped using that access point would help you understand quickly, because you would be more aware of the process."

"I'd like to argue and be pissed off at you, but as usual I can't. It worked. I would appreciate a warming if you ever decide to do it again."

"That's fair."

I could hear Brandy's voice in the background. She was referring to him as the Golden One. "She just told me to stop wasting time and start putting stuff together," he said. "I'd better go. It's probably going to be a late night for me."

"I can't believe I'm going to say this but…thank you for what you taught me today."

He laughed. "Any time. Good night, Alison."

Putting my phone on the nightstand, I thought about what Brandy had said in the car. *If he hasn't made it obvious enough, Ian likes you.* I had a decision to make. Was I going to let myself fall for him, or was I going to keep some emotional distance between us? I was attracted to him. It was useless to deny that anymore, but my life was a mess. Getting involved with Ian would take my attention off what was really important—getting ready to deal with Sebastian.

And Ian was going to leave when it was all over, anyway. My time in foster care had taught me the heartache of losing someone I loved. With all the other uncertainties in my life, I just couldn't go down that road.

Ian and I could be friends and that was all.

Chapter Twelve

Brandy and Ian didn't drive me to school the next day, but they arrived at the tennis court parking lot just after I did. Brandy got out of her car with a bright smile. Ian looked exhausted. His hair was dark from the shower and his eyes were still glassy from lack of sleep. But he was undeniably hot.

"The house is really coming along," Brandy said happily. "It looks occupied now."

"What time did you guys finish last night?" I asked.

"Around three," she replied.

Ian mouthed *four* behind her back.

"Too bad our kind need the normal eight hours of sleep to function properly," I commented.

Brandy pretended not to hear me. She waved to some

girls and bounded away like a happy puppy. "More party guests for Saturday," Ian said and then yawned. "No sign of your follower this morning. He's been out of range for a while now."

"I hope they've moved on to more interesting things."

"Me, too. Speaking of interesting things, did you get a chance to go over that Byron script yet?"

"Yes. I added a few things, but overall I think it's really good."

"We should get some visuals off the internet to go along with it. Do you want to come over to work on that tonight?"

"I thought you had shopping to do," I commented.

"I should be finished by the time you're done at the Shadow Box."

Brandy had already explained she would be out shopping until late, so I'd be alone with Ian for a while. As much as I enjoyed looking at him this morning, I'd made a decision last night to keep some emotional distance between us.

"I'll come on one condition," I said. "You keep your mind to yourself."

He was amused. "But I thought you liked it. And we still need to train."

"Aren't you under a vow of chastity until you meet your true love, or likeness, or whatever?"

"I told you, I didn't break any rules."

"I know that, but we'd better not go there again. It makes everything…confusing."

"You've probably learned as much as you're going to through that approach, anyway," he said with a grin. "Shame to ban it altogether."

"Once again, you've said something completely inappropriate. Why can't I hate you for it?"

"Because it's true. You can't get in trouble for telling the truth."

"And that my friend, is a lie."

Chuckling, he put a chummy arm around my shoulders. I was going to push it off, but he moved it to answer a text on his phone.

"Luke is here," he said. "He wants me to meet in front of the school. He says he's got something for me."

"I'll meet you in class, then."

"Why don't you come with me? It shouldn't take long."

Luke's appearance was better in the daylight, but he was still far too thin to be healthy. "Thanks for meeting me," he said to Ian. He nodded toward me in greeting. "Business is taking me out of town, and I need to get this to your father as soon as possible. Can you give it to him?"

"He's in California right now. I don't know when he's coming back."

"Keep it until you see him," Luke insisted.

"Okay," Ian replied, taking a small flash drive from him.

Luke waved his thin hand in farewell and then got into a black Maserati.

"That car is nicer than my mom's," I said as he drove away.

"He inherited it when his parents died. They've only been gone a few months. He's been under a lot of pressure adjusting to being a clan chief. He's a nice guy, but not really suited to the role of leader. My dad and Bruce Dawning have been mentoring him."

The first bell rang. "Crap, we're going to be late," I said, hustling up the steps to the front doors.

"You should test your thoughtmaking on Connor this morning," Ian suggested, close behind me. "Let's see if you can stop him from talking for the next hour."

"That's setting the bar pretty high, isn't it?"

"You might surprise yourself."

Five minutes later, Connor sat next to me in room seventeen. He was just about to strike up a conversation when I joined my mind to his. Finding a nice opening between two of his thoughts, I slipped *You don't feel like talking* into it. Connor was confused, probably because the idea was completely foreign to him. After a moment, he opened his textbook and started reading. Ian caught my eye and winked.

Jazzed by my improved joining skills, I practiced every opportunity I got during the rest of the day. I rarely encountered a problem I couldn't go around or through, but each success was accompanied by a twang of guilt and increasing fatigue. By the time the bell rang after Art Appreciation, I was worn-out, and Brandy could see it. "You should take a break for the rest of day," she said as we walked out of class. "You'll get plenty of opportunity to practice your joining later."

"Do you feel drained after doing this kind of stuff?" I asked her.

"I did when I was very young, and I do now that I'm weaker. But when I was in my prime, it didn't bother me at all."

Ian was waiting for us in the north hall. "You don't look so good," he said to me.

Brandy punched him in the shoulder. "You're an idiot."

"Well, it's true," he replied.

"You're still an idiot," she insisted.

I rolled my shoulders, trying to ease out a knot as she walked away.

"It's probably the rebound," Ian said to me.

"What is what?"

"Feeling like you've been hit by a truck. It's probably a result of the rebound."

"It's just been a long day."

"It's more than being tired from a long day," he insisted. "We project energy when we use our joining, and it comes back at us like the flick of a rubber band. You've got to learn to buffer yourself from the rebound."

"You're not making a lot of sense," I said wearily.

"Pay super-close attention then." He put an arm across my shoulders. "You have to buffer yourself after you use your joining. Kind of like tightening your stomach muscles so it won't hurt when you get punched in the gut."

I shook his arm off, shuffled things around in my locker, closed the door, and spun the lock. "I've never been punched in the gut, so that analogy doesn't mean much to me. I promise to think it through tomorrow. Maybe after I've slept eighteen hours I'll understand what you're talking about."

He smiled and put an arm around my waist. "I give good massages," he said with teasing eyes. "I think you could use one."

"You need to work on your smolder," I said. "Maybe lift an eyebrow or something."

He laughed. "I'm only giving it 50 percent right now. When I give it all I've got, it will work so well you won't remember your own name."

"Is there an end to your ego?"

"If there is, I haven't found it yet," he said without shame.

Lillian was at her computer when I walked into the Shadow Box. "How was your shopping trip yesterday?" she asked.

"Good." I replied. I checked out the store to make sure no one else was around. Unsure how to breach the divide between employer-employee and fellow alien species, I tried to think of something significant to say.

All I could come up with was, "So, you're a reader."

She looked up from her computer and rolled her left hand over to reveal the *V* in her palm. The lines were thick and corded like strands of rope. "I'm relieved I don't have to hide this from you anymore," she said.

"You knew about me all this time?"

"It took me a while to figure it out. When I did, I thought it was best to keep quiet. I thought my knowing might make you run away."

She was right. If she'd said one word about me being dewing, I would have run as fast and as far from her as I could get. Lillian had done everything she could to help me, and I had the sneaking suspicion it hadn't been easy for her. "Thank you, Lillian," I said. "Thank you for everything."

"You're welcome." She rubbed the bridge of her nose

in a tired way. "My sister was a thoughtmaker like you," she continued. "I feel a link with her when you're around. It's been a comfort to me."

Lillian was so stoic, I was surprised she'd ever needed comforting. "Was your sister killed by Sebastian like my mother was?"

"She was killed on his orders, so her blood is on his hands."

I nodded, understanding some of her pain. The bells above the door jingled and a harried-looking woman came in. She plopped a piece of paper on the counter. "Can you help me find these?" she asked. "I'm in a hurry."

A long list of titles had been written on the paper. I put on my best customer service face and left Lillian to finish whatever she was working on before I came in. Luckily, perfect recall made finding the books the woman wanted easy. I drifted from one end of the store to the other, pulling volumes as I went. She was so pleased to have finished her book buying in such a short a time that she gave me a whopping two-cent tip.

As I worked on a haphazard stack of books in the self-help section, I wondered how old Lillian *really* was. She looked at least three-quarters of the way through a human lifespan. I figured that meant she was probably three-quarters of the way through the dewing lifespan. Which would have made her approximately 225 years old. If I was right, she would have been born sometime in the late 1700s. My instincts told me she'd been alone a long time. Alone as in not likenessed. I wondered if Lillian's aloneness explained why she chose to live as a rogue. Maybe it was too painful to be around all the other dewing who'd paired off. It would have been rude to ask her about it, so I went about my organizing and let Lillian do her rare book thing.

There had been silence between us for so long that I jumped when she clapped her hands together. "Sorry," she said breathlessly. "I just located something wonderful." She put a hand to her chest. "I've been trying to find this book for more than a year. A dealer in the city thinks he's got a first edition."

She was already on her feet and looking for her keys when she paused. "I don't like leaving you alone."

"It's six thirty," I said. "I'll be fine for the last half hour. Ian says my follower has been off the grid for a while now. Whoever it was must have lost interest, so go get your book."

She looked longingly at her computer. "I don't know," she said.

"Go, I'll be fine."

"Okay, put the CLOSED sign up and lock the door if you feel anything strange," she said, grabbing her purse and walking out the door.

I didn't have much to do for the last half hour. I was so tired and sore from the rebound or whatever that I could have slept on the floor. To fight off drowsiness, I started to clean up the store. No one came in while I dusted the shelves with a feather duster, so I decided to take the trash out a little earlier than normal.

I felt it the moment I walked out the back door—the squeeze as a mind joined mine. Immediately after that, I was

gripped by crushing pain in my head. I dropped the trash
bags and held my head in both hands. Out the corner of my
eye, I saw large man step out from behind the dumpster. He
wasn't wearing a fedora, but I recognized him. He was the
tiger, the man-eater, and he was smiling.

My head felt like it was being compressed from the
inside out. Waves of pain spread from there through the rest
of my body. I swayed on my feet. "I thought so," the man
said with a heavy Eastern European accent. "I couldn't be
sure with the others around, but I thought so."

"What?" I managed to ask.

"You're human enough that I can reach you like this.
The fact that you're not dead yet tells me you're something
else, too. I've spent the last week piecing it all together."

I started to shake. He knew. Three years of hiding in the
shadows was for nothing. The man knew what I was and he'd
come for me. If he didn't already know about the McKyes,
he soon would. The pain coupled with fear for them was too
much. My thigh muscles gave out, and I hit the pavement
like a load of bricks. The asphalt was scorching hot, but the
burning of my skin was secondary to what was going on
inside me. I kept my hands on my head and concentrated on
remaining conscious.

"There have been rumors," the man continued. "Rumors
about the child of the White Laurel. A child thoughtmaker
that would be more powerful than any other because of her
mother's amazing joining and the father's lack of it. It was
clever to place you with humans. Who would think to look
for you among the weak ones?"

The only thing I could do was deny it. "I don't know what you're talking about," I repeated.

His smile grew and the pain amplified another level. "You are going to buy me a place of influence with a powerful man. My clan has been reluctant to join Sebastian Truss, but when they see my payoff, that will change."

The ground under me burned, but I was cold. Cold to the bone with terror. My worst nightmare had come true. The McKyes were going to suffer because of me. My peripheral vision began to shrink. I was going to pass out. The tiger walked toward me. When he moved his foot back to kick me in the head, I caught a glimpse of movement behind him. He must have sensed something, too, because his eyes widened in surprise.

He turned to look over his shoulder as an arm went around his neck, hauling him backward. He hit the ground hard with his head twisted at a horrific angle. Then I heard the popping sounds of bone breaking, and the crushing in my head stopped. Ian got off of him, breathing hard.

"You won't touch her," he said.

I had enough presence of mind to wonder why Ian, who was at least five inches shorter and probably a hundred pounds lighter than the tiger, knew how to kill people with his bare hands. I also wondered why he continued to stand over the broken man while I lay burning on the pavement. A dull ache remained in my head. I had no strength to ask about it or about my family, so I let my eyes close.

"Alison," I heard Ian say, "open your eyes."

I did, briefly, and then felt myself being lifted. He ran

with me in his arms and kept saying things like, "Don't go to sleep," "Stay with me," and "It's going to be okay." He put me in the front seat of his car. Even with my eyelids tightly closed, the sunlight burned into my retinas. I longed for darkness. Not semidarkness, but darkness in its blackest form. I managed to pull my legs up in the seat, wrap my arms around them. My thighs stung as salty tears dropped on them. I probably had second-degree burns on the backs of my legs.

"It's going to be okay," Ian repeated over and over as he drove.

I had a good idea where we were when the car stopped, but I didn't look to find out for sure. I didn't care that much. All I wanted was to lie down in a quiet place and pass out. Ian lifted me out of the car. "My dad will know what to do," he said.

I figured he was trying to reassure himself more than me.

I heard him open the door, and I felt a blast of cool from the air-conditioning. He moved fast but not at a run this time. With every step he took, my head thudded against his chest, making the ache echo and echo and echo again. When the light coming through my eyelids dimmed enough, I opened one of them. We has passed through the mansion's hallway and into the living room filled with new furnishings. He took me down another, darker hallway and into an unfamiliar room.

"Stay awake," he said, laying me down.

There was a shushing sound as an inflatable mattress

took my weight. A moment later, he put a blanket over me. My body had gone from overly hot to overly cold. Rolling myself into a ball, I wrapped the blanket as tight as I could around me.

"I'm calling my dad," Ian said from somewhere in the room.

I kept shivering. Nothing I tried would make the cold go away. The air in the mattress shifted as it took his weight. He sat against the wall and pulled me up so I sat against him. "You're in shock," he said wrapping his arm around me. "It'll just take some time for your body to regulate itself."

His warmth helped a little, but I would have preferred hot coals.

I heard the tones of his cell phone as he dialed and then his rush of words. "Dad, the tiger got to Alison. She didn't go under, but she might if she doesn't get help soon."

Under sounded like a nice place to visit. I started to slip away, but he shook my shoulders to bring me back. "Alison, don't sleep. As long as you stay awake, my dad can fix it. He's catching the next flight back. You've got to hold on until he gets here. You can't sleep. Do you hear me?"

I tried to nod, but my neck ached so badly that I couldn't.

"Alison," he said, "I'm not a healer like my dad, but there is something I can do. Don't fight me when I try."

That was as much warning as I got before he connected to my mind. After what I'd just experienced, I didn't like it one bit. I groaned and fought against him. "You've got to trust me," he said. "I'm not going to hurt you."

What choice did I have? When push came to shove,

he'd win. So I stopped struggling and tried to hold onto consciousness. At first, it felt like he was blindly stumbling around in my mind, bumping into places that already hurt. Then I realized I felt less pain when he moved on to the next spot. This mind touch continued until the vise in my head began to loosen. By the time he broke the connection, living seemed a viable option once again.

Grateful, I turned my head to look at him. He was shaking and ghostly pale now. His eyebrows were drawn together, and his breathing was shallow like mine. It took only a moment to understand why. "You took some of the pain." I whispered.

"I took as much as I could," he replied shakily. "Don't sleep until my dad gets here. Promise me."

"I promise."

"What about the McKyes?" I managed.

"They're fine," he assured me.

I accepted that. Ian was all about the truth and honesty. He wouldn't lie to me.

He touched something on his phone and death metal music started blaring full blast from it. He tossed it on the mattress and held me tight with both arms. We sat that way, listening to the world's worst music as we fought pain and sleep.

I fought as much for him as I did for myself. He'd saved my life and then taken part of my suffering. The very least I could do was stay alive to thank him for it.

Chapter Thirteen

Sometime later, I heard the door open and knew Brandy had come in.

"Look at the two of you," she said sympathetically. She came and knelt by the mattress. "Spencer and Katherine are coming back in their jet," she continued, smoothing my hair. "They should be cleared to fly in a few minutes. I expect them to be here in about an hour."

She got up to leave, but Ian called her back. "The cars and the body," he said. "They're still at the store."

"I'll call Lillian. We'll take care of it," she replied.

"Please call my parents," I muttered. "Tell them I'm spending the night with you. If others are looking for me, I don't want to drag my family into it. They can't fight like you guys can."

"Okay," Brandy said and quietly let the room.

When Spencer Thane burst through the door, Katherine was right on his heels. They came straight to us. Spencer put a hand on his son's head, and Ian pushed it away. "I'm okay," he muttered. "It's fading already. Work on her first."

Spencer put his hand on my forehead. Then he closed his eyes in concentration, and a pleasant warmth spread through my body. The knots in my head untied and my breathing returned to normal. Spencer was sweating when he turned away from me.

"Thank you," I whispered.

I closed my eyes and knew he was working on Ian when the tension in his body relaxed behind me. His arms loosened and slid limply to his sides.

"Help me lay them down," Spencer said.

Katherine pulled me away from Ian and arranged me more comfortably on the mattress. I could feel Spencer do the same with Ian.

"We'll just let them rest," Spencer said as the left.

The room was lighter when I woke up. I stretched out one leg, and that was enough to tell me I was going to be stiff for a long time. My body felt bruised, like I'd been used as someone's punching bag. With a small groan, I straightened out my other leg.

I'd forgotten Ian was next to me. He sighed in his sleep. His breath was soft on my neck. Out of nowhere his body twitched. The movements triggered a flashback of what had happened behind the Shadow Box. A crystal-clear picture of the tiger flashed onto the big screen in my mind. I saw the sadistic joy spread over his face as he mentally tightened his grip on me. I saw myself topple to the burning pavement and heard my own moans of pain. Then Ian came running toward the tiger and leaped onto his back, pulling him backward.

In the seconds that followed, I processed what I hadn't before. In spite of a broken neck, the tiger's mind was still active and alive. He'd withdrawn from my mind so he could engage Ian in an unseen mind warfare. The camera in my mind cut back to Ian. He radiated incredible heat as he stood over the tiger. He was fighting in a way I couldn't see or understand, but I knew the moment it was finished, because he came to me. Uncertainty and disgust were written all over his face. He'd killed the tiger, and he regretted it.

Shutting my mind to the memory, I turned toward the boy who'd saved my life. His body twitched again and his gold eyebrows drew together in his sleep. I noticed a small worry line at the inner corner of one of them. It was definitely something new. On the inside and on the outside, Ian was scarred by what he'd done. And he'd done it for me.

I reached up to smooth the line with my finger. His eyes, still hazy with sleep, opened. "I'm sorry," I whispered, "I didn't mean to wake you up."

I gently touched the line again. "What are you doing?" he asked.

Embarrassed, I tucked my hand between my body and the mattress. "Nothing. Sorry."

"You're so weird sometimes," he said sleepily. "I like that about you."

"That makes you weird, too," I replied.

As he watched me, his expression changed from sleepy to aware. He was going to kiss me. I shouldn't have let him, but I held still and felt the feather-soft touch as his lips met mine. My heart thumped and my stomach tensed as he did it again. I tipped my chin up and met his third kiss.

He fell back asleep, and when I knew he was too far gone to wake up again, I rubbed the worry line once more.

Sometime later, Brandy walked in carrying a tray loaded with breakfast food. "I thought I should wake you," she said. "The Golden One's parents will be back soon."

Ian yawned loudly and then shifted to sit up. I watched him for the signs of the regret I'd sensed during the night but couldn't find any. He reached for a piece of toast off the tray. "I thought they'd stay here," he said around a bite.

"Such a forgetful boy. There aren't any beds here, remember, and your mom didn't want to sleep on the floor or the couch. They went to a hotel for the night."

Talking about Ian's parents brought all sorts of fears to the forefront of my mind. "What about my parents and Alex?" I asked anxiously.

"What about them?" Brandy replied.

"Fedora man said he'd been following me for days. What if he passed information about them to Sebastian Truss? What if his people have them?"

"Fedora man," Brandy repeated with a smile. "That's a nice nickname for that... Never mind. To answer your question, if he'd known for sure who you were, he would have had your parents or Alex stuffed in the trunk of his car when he went to get you last night."

Ian nodded his agreement. "It would have been easier to get you to go with him that way."

"He wasn't certain enough to risk involving your family," Brandy continued. "He needed to get you alone to figure it out, and Ian took care of things before he could pass any information on."

I remembered the tiger's words as I knelt on the pavement having my mind crushed. *I've spent the last week piecing it all together*, he'd said. I breathed a sigh of relief. Brandy was right—the tiger had had most of the pieces, but he hadn't been sure I was dewing until he accessed my mind for the second time.

"I'll have Lillian go to your neighborhood and feel for anything out of the ordinary," Brandy offered. "She called me five times during the night and then again at the crack of dawn to check on you. She hates herself for leaving you alone at the store. This little assignment will make her feel useful. It might also keep her from calling me every half hour."

"And it's a good precaution to take," Ian said. "If she feels anything strange around your neighborhood, she'll let us know."

"What did you tell my mom last night?" I asked.

Brandy smiled down at me. "Only that you were staying here with me," she replied.

"And she was okay with that? She didn't want me to wear a tracking device or something?"

"Nope. As long as you're with me, she figures all is well."

Ian devoured another piece of toast in two bites.

"Brandy is great at inspiring confidence in overprotective parents," he said, wiping his fingers on a napkin. "Speaking of which, when should we be expecting mine?"

"They were starting the drive over here when they called," Brandy replied, "so any minute now."

Ian glanced down at me. "You can't sit up, can you?"

"No," I replied dejectedly.

He patted me gently on the shoulder. "Not to worry, young one," he said sarcastically. "My dad lives for this kind of thing. He'll have you fixed up in no time, and you'll be a favorite with him forever because of it."

"I doubt that," I mumbled.

"Why do you doubt it?" Brandy asked.

"Ian killed another dewing because of me, and one look at Spencer's face last night told me Ian put himself in a really bad position taking my pain. They're going to have a hard time getting over the moral and mortal danger I put him in."

Brandy shrugged. "You're thinking human again. Remember destiny? You were meant to live, and the tiger was meant to die. Ian was just an instrument in the process. As far as what he did by taking your pain, he knew very well what he was in for. Isn't that right, Golden One?"

Ian nodded before downing a glass of orange juice.

I appreciated Brandy's reassurance, but I knew something was wrong where Ian was concerned. I'd seen it on his face last night. I cared too much for him to stand by and let remorse eat him from the inside out. I was going to talk to Spencer about it.

Brandy took the breakfast tray while Ian chewed the last piece of toast. "You didn't leave any for Alison," she said. "For a skinny kid, you sure can eat."

He didn't deny it. "Got to go," he said. "My parents are here."

I watched him walk away and tried to reconcile the boy in wrinkly jeans and a loose button-down with the guy who'd killed another dewing to save my life.

A few minutes later, Spencer came striding through the door like a giant bull. "How are you feeling today?" he asked.

"Like I spent the night getting kicked," I replied. "I know the tiger attacked my mind, but my muscles are all messed up."

"Don't push yourself," Spencer said in a calming tone. "The body always reacts to an attack on the mind. You need a few days to get your strength back." He sat beside me, sending my side of the air mattress upward with a whoosh. "You got a double whammy last night. Your human thought patterns made your mind vulnerable, but the tiger attacked your essence, too."

"He attacked my what?"

"Your essence. That's the energy that runs just beneath your skin."

"So my energy got beat up?" I asked, to clarify.

"Yes. I was able to fix the damage in your mind last night, but there's only so much I can do to heal your essence. I'll help you a little more now, but you'll probably be stiff and sore for a few days."

I tried to figure out how to ask all of the burning questions in my mind. Finally, I decided on a direct approach. "Before you fix me, can I ask you some questions?"

"Sure," he responded kindly.

"I understood enough of what happened last night to know Ian put himself in a bad position when he took my pain. I'd like to know *exactly* what the danger was."

"He took your pain just as he might have done for any human," Spencer explained. "The process isn't difficult. It's a simple redirection of a human's thoughts toward ourselves." He chuckled. "We don't do it often, because when we redirect the pain, it comes back at us with twice as much force."

"So there was no risk of him dying or anything?"

Spencer laughed again. "No, just a lot of pain."

Glad to have that cleared up, I launched into the next topic on my list. "Ian killed the tiger to save me. Obviously, I'm more grateful than I can say, but he's suffering because of it. It haunts him that he killed another dewing. I think he's going to need therapy or something."

Spencer paused. "This is going to sound cruel to you, but it was crucial for Ian to stop the tiger last night. He knew if he didn't, you'd end up dead or the tiger would tell Sebastian about you. If you haven't guessed it already, Ian has remarkable energy. After the Laurel clan was massacred, Katherine and I had him trained to fight as humans do. He's been honing those skills most of his life. The tiger would have known the instant Ian engaged him that my son was capable of killing him. If he had backed off, Ian would have backed off, too, but he didn't. In a way, the tiger chose to end his life last night.

"As far as Ian's mental health goes," Spencer continued, "I don't consider what happened last night a bad experience for him. I wouldn't wish it on anyone, but he's headed toward a violent confrontation. Feeling some of the emotions he did last night might serve him well when that time comes."

I still thought it was crazy that Spencer and Katherine were okay with their son risking his life in a fight with Sebastian. "I don't understand how you can you let him go ahead with what he plans," I said.

"It isn't a question of what I want anymore. It's about the greater good."

"Even if it means you lose both of your sons?" I pushed.

Spencer looked at his hands. "I received confirmation yesterday that Sebastian has control over another cabinet member in the administration. At the rate he's manipulating the political powers of this country, we'll have to go to war against him within a year. The best option is to have him replaced as clan chief, but that doesn't seem likely. It would take an internal uprising, and most of the Truss are completely dedicated to him. We're working that angle, but it will take time. More than we've got, I fear."

"Couldn't you just send him a box of poisoned chocolates or something?" I asked.

"We've considered all our options," he replied with a small smile. Then he passed a hand over his eyes. "Unfortunately, they're limited. Not only is the Illuminant clan showing signs of joining with the Truss, the Ormolu clan is too. To top it off, we've got a mole to deal with. The time and location of our last clan chief meeting was leaked."

"I heard about that," I said. "Maybe your mole is a blessing in disguise. Maybe he or she could be coerced into giving the clan chiefs some information to use against Sebastian."

Spencer shook his head. "It may be months before we catch the mole. I want to stop this thing before the next presidential election. But the clans can't agree on how to do it. Every day that we let Sebastian go, he grows stronger. I've already lost one son, Alison. Believe me, the last thing I want is to lose Ian, but I've had to accept that for the good of our kind, Ian, Brandy, and you will fight Sebastian Truss in the very near future."

"And it has to be us because Katherine saw it in a vision? It sounds so crazy to me."

"I'm sure it does, but Katherine's visions are flawless. She saw it a few weeks after Jack died. In her vision, Sebastian was killed by someone in the line of succession for a chiefdom, a fading likeness, and the daughter of the White Laurel."

In my opinion, only one of the three he mentioned was a certainty…me. "Ian said she couldn't say if any of us would make it out alive?"

"She couldn't. But she saw Sebastian dead. As horrible as the outcome might be, it's enough to justify the risk. This isn't about me and what I want. This is about what is right. I know it's small comfort, but Katherine and I will give the three of you whatever assistance we can when the time comes."

I'd already accepted the only hope for my family's safety

lay in killing Sebastian Truss. I wanted to argue for Ian and Brandy's sakes, but I didn't, because I knew their devotion to the cause.

"Trust destiny," Spencer said with a small smile.

"I don't like destiny very much."

"Everything happens for a reason. In time, you'll find destiny is your friend."

I doubted it. "How long am I stuck lying here?" I asked. "I need to, um, go to the bathroom pretty bad."

Spencer's good humor came back, and he laughed. "It will only take a few minutes to get you fixed up enough for that."

Chapter Fourteen

When Spencer left, I went to the adjoining bathroom and found a clean towel in the linen closet. Turning the water on, I stepped under the rain shower faucet and let hot water work on my stiff muscles and joints.

Ian's hygiene products didn't include hair conditioner, so I was left with a tangled mess to comb out afterward. I found a flimsy-looking black comb in his shaving kit and did the best I could with it. The poor thing bent and lost a few teeth as I ran it through my snarls. By the time I was finished, the comb was ruined. I said a few words of respect and then buried it in the trash can.

After getting dressed again, I opened the bathroom door and found Ian lying on the air mattress with his arm over his eyes.

"Nice shower?" he asked in a weary voice.

"Yes. I'll have to buy you a new comb, though. I killed the one from your shaving bag."

He moved his arm to look at me. "You'd better."

"Where is everyone?" I asked, going to sit next to him.

"It's Saturday. We have people coming over, so Brandy is out getting more stuff for the house. My parents have gone to the grocery store, and I just finished hanging the flat screen. I have a list a page long of other stuff I'm supposed to get done before zero hour." He checked his watch and sighed. "But I had a pretty rough night, so I'm taking a break right now."

"Does Brandy allow breaks?"

"No. Please don't tell her."

I looked for the worry line near his eye. It was still there. "I'm sorry you had to kill the tiger last night," I said. "I mean…I'm grateful, but I know it was a terrible thing for you to have to do."

He didn't respond immediately, but when he did, he was firm. "I'm not sorry for what I did, and I would do it again if I had to."

"You look *very* sorry about it in my memory."

"I was confused, but I didn't regret it. It was easy for me to kill the tiger. In the moment, it was as easy as breathing. I'd expected to struggle with the concept at least, but I didn't. How messed up does that make me?"

"So you think there's something wrong with you because it *didn't* bother you to kill someone who was going to murder me? That makes you the weird one. You came thousands of miles from your home looking for me, and when you found I was a poor excuse for a dewing, you didn't abandon me. I know you wouldn't have, even if I hadn't agreed to help you. You could easily ditch this plan to fight Sebastian and fly back to Australia to live your life, but I'm pretty sure you won't do that, either. Maybe you're full-on crazy, but you're not a heartless killer."

"I hope you're right," he said with another sigh. He took a lock of my wet hair in his fingers. "It was pretty nice of me to save your life, wasn't it? Is that why you kissed me?"

There were a lot of reason why I had kissed him, but I wasn't going to tell him all of them. "I am grateful," I said. "But in general, I don't kiss guys for that reason."

"So you kiss a lot of guys?"

"No, you're the first one, but we can't do it again."

"Ouch," he replied.

I smiled down at him. Our kiss had been a mistake. His plan to leave Vegas when we finished with Sebastian hadn't changed. And we had other more important things to be concerned with. "I think it was probably pretty good for a first kiss," I said, "but I don't want to be kissing anyone right now. I don't need or want to be distracted while I learn what you and Brandy can teach me. You should limit your distractions, too. We need to concentrate on confronting Sebastian right now."

Ian smiled wickedly. "You're right, but when this is over, I'm going to kiss you again."

"You keep telling yourself that," I said.

I left him lying there to rest while I went to explore

Brandy's newly decorated living room. The room had undergone a complete transformation. An enormous oriental rug in shades of red covered the tile. On top of it, the sofas had been rearranged to face each other. Four sophisticated-looking club chairs joined the seating group. A large leather ottoman sat in the middle, and lamps were artfully arranged around the perimeter.

A flat-screen television had been mounted to the wall above the fireplace. Floor-to-ceiling bookcases flanked it, with chic decor items adorning the shelves. An enormous table complete with leather-upholstered chairs sat under the dining room chandelier. Pottery had been arranged in the center to look carelessly artistic.

"Holy cow," I muttered.

"I agree," said Katherine from nearby. "I'm glad you're feeling a little better. Spencer wants to start on your training first thing tomorrow morning."

"You're staying to help?"

She took my hand and led me to one of the sofas. "If the five of us work as a team, we should be able to get you up to speed in no time at all."

"I need all the help I can get," I said sincerely. "Couldn't you use your futuretelling to see if we're still alive after Sebastian buys it? That would really motive me."

"My joining doesn't work that way," she replied. "As much as I want to know certain things, I can't decide what the future will tell me."

"Oh," I said dejectedly.

Katherine studied me for a moment and then said,

"Your eyes are so much like hers. Her hair was the opposite color, of course, but her eyes were the same unusual shade of gray. Would you like to hear more about her?"

"I would."

She patted the back of the sofa encouragingly, so I settled in to listen.

"About seventeen years ago," she began, "Sebastian kidnapped several dewing children. One from each of the fourteen clans opposed to his actions. He offered a choice to the clans—disband and pledge our loyalty to him, or he would kill our children and continue kidnapping and executing others.

"He took your mother as the Laurel hostage. It was a strange choice because she was a lot older than the rest, and being a thoughtmaker, she was dangerous, too. You see, thoughtmakers are unique. If their energy is strong enough, they can use their joining on other dewing. Sebastian probably took her because your grandfather was the Laurel clan chief and he wanted that leverage in particular. He had to have regretted the choice immediately, because he put her under heavy guard with special precautions to make sure she couldn't use her joining to escape."

Katherine paused in her story when Ian came in rubbing his eyes. "Hello, sweet boy."

He waved at her and plopped down in front of a bunch of cords hanging from the television on the wall. "This is going to take forever," he muttered.

"Need help?" I asked.

"No. Go ahead and listen to my mom," he replied.

Katherine smiled at him as he bent his head over his work. "Your mother did get free," she continued, "and if she had run, she would have stood an excellent chance of getting far away before anyone figured out she was missing. She didn't run, though. Now that I know she was a new mother herself, I can better understand her choice. She stayed long enough to free the rest of the kidnapped children. They varied in age from just a couple of months to fourteen years old. What she did next, no thoughtmaker had ever done before or has ever has since. She mind-cloaked the Truss. None of them sensed her or the children as they left the compound they'd been held captive in.

"Spencer and I, along with the rest of the clan chiefs, were meeting not far away. We were all emotionally wrecked by the kidnappings, but we had to consider our options at that point. Given our population, you understand how we feel about bloodshed. Some saw giving in to Sebastian as the best way to stop the killing. Others thought that would only make it worse. A loud argument was in swing between the Ormolu and Dawning clan chiefs when someone knocked at the door.

"She must have followed our vibrations, because she walked in followed by twelve bedraggled children. She was holding Ian, only six months old at the time, in her arms. I still get chills when I remember her gray eyes, wild from the rebound, as she handed him to me."

Across the room, Ian cursed, waving a pinched finger in the air.

We turned to him. "Sorry," he said. "Go on."

Katherine chuckled softly. "Your mother gave us a gift that day," she continued. "Obviously, we were overjoyed to have our children back, but it was more than that. She gave us a taste of victory, too. She renewed our determination to stand against Sebastian and all the evil he stands for.

"When Sebastian found the children gone, he was out of his mind with rage. He wanted to punish Grace, to see her suffer for what she'd done. Overriding his longing for vengeance, though, was his desire to control her power. He put his energy into setting a trap for her. A year or so later, he captured your father to lure her in. Even then, she wouldn't give him what he wanted. She wouldn't use her thoughtmaking for him.

"In a fit of anger, Sebastian made the mistake of seeing her alone. She was very young, but she was extremely powerful. With no one around to intervene, she engaged him in an essence fight. She wounded him in some physical way. The strange thing is that whatever she did didn't heal right."

"I thought we can heal from anything," I said.

"Typically we can. That's what makes Sebastian's injury so difficult for us to understand. No one but his closest advisor knows what exactly is wrong with him. He hasn't been seen in public for years." Katherine's eyes filled with tears. "My son Jack was a gifted healer and physician. That's why Sebastian had him captured. He wanted to be healed."

It was completely out of character for me, but I reached out and patted her hand awkwardly. She smiled through her tears. "Since your mother's death, no other thoughtmaker has been able to duplicate the thought cloak she pulled off," Katherine continued. "Sebastian has spent the last decade hunting them down and making them try."

In awe of the mother I'd never know, I asked, "What joining does Sebastian have that makes him so powerful?"

Ian swore again and raised another pinched finger in the air. "He's a freaking shapeshifter," he said.

"That's right," Katherine said. "He put his joining to good use two hundred years ago by providing séances for royalty in Europe. During the course of an evening, he would appear as dead relatives to those that tipped him highly enough. It isn't his joining that makes him powerful. It's the power of his essence. Sebastian's mind energy is very strong." She watched her son with profound love and sadness. "We hope Ian's is stronger."

"What will happen to the Truss when Sebastian is gone?" I asked.

"No one knows for sure, but we hope his followers will disband."

"So risking our lives to kill him might be for nothing," I said quietly.

"No," she said, "Sebastian has to be removed from power. If his followers continued to give us trouble, we'll deal with them. That part won't be as difficult."

I wasn't convinced, but I heard Spencer's voice over my shoulder ask, "How's the patient?"

"I can move now," I said. "Thank you for your help."

"It was the least I could do. If it weren't for your mother, we wouldn't have Ian around to connect the television to the sound system."

I looked at the boy my mother had carried in her arms seventeen years ago. His hair was curled up at his collar and his oddly colored eyes were alight with aggravation as he struggled with a bunch of knotted cords. "Did you know about all of this?" I asked.

With his gaze still locked on the cords, he replied, "I grew up hearing about it."

I wondered then if my mother had gone back for the other kidnapped children that day because she thought I might need Ian and the Thanes in the future.

In the back of my mind I heard the word "yes."

Chapter Fifteen

"You're a decorating genius," I said when Brandy walked in later. "The transformation this place has gone through is amazing."

"Brandy has a PhD in art history," Katherine said proudly, "but she's been working as an interior decorator for the last couple of years."

"No wonder shopping with you was so easy," I commented. "You actually know what you're doing."

Brandy shrugged. "I had grand aspirations for this place. I wanted to leave one last mark on the world, even if it was only an interior decorating mark. Time has handicapped my efforts, though. It will be a miracle if I get the basics how I want them before people start arriving."

"What can I do to help?" Spencer asked.

Brandy nodded toward the mess of cords hanging from the television. "Can you help Ian finish the electronics?"

He looked doubtful but said, "I'll try."

Katherine and I followed Brandy into the kitchen. "I bought some more plates," Brandy said. "They need to be washed."

"I can do that," I volunteered.

Brandy handed me a stack of plates wrapped in tissue paper. "I stopped by your house and picked up some clean clothes for you. No offense, but you look like you slept in those."

"No offense taken," I replied. "I did sleep in them."

She pointed to a bulging suitcase by the door. "Voilà."

"It looks like you packed enough clothes for a week."

"Enough for a few days. You are officially our houseguest through Labor Day."

"My mom is okay with me being away from home for three whole days?" I'd never even been away for more than a night.

Brandy winked at me. "I think she trusts me."

"She didn't make a fuss about me calling home at regular intervals or anything?"

"No. Why would she? I explained you were busy working on your presentation for English class and helping me with things here."

"You are *very* good," I said with admiration.

She smiled like what else did I expect, and then removed a set of rust-colored pillows from a shopping bag.

A furniture delivery team called to be let through the

gates as I was rinsing plates.

Brandy didn't seem pleased. "That's cutting it close," she grumbled.

"Choosing furniture for four bedrooms takes time," Katherine replied patiently. "We promised to pay the delivery people twice their usual fee to get it here quickly."

The first items carried in were for Brandy's room, two nightstands, a dresser, and a bed, all in a light wood that looked cheery even wrapped in plastic. "No more funky inflatable mattress," she said bounding down the hall after the deliverymen.

"It was my idea to furnish the bedrooms," Katherine explained. "I think she planned to close all the bedroom doors so people wouldn't know they were empty. But we're going to keep the house, so it seemed right to get the furniture now. She wasn't happy about my interference. I told the delivery team to bring her stuff in first, hoping she'd like what I got for her enough to forgive me."

"I think it worked," I said.

Still untangling knotted cords, Spencer said, "One of Katherine's greatest talents is diplomacy."

She winked at me. Ian's mother was a gentle manipulator. "I think we'll have to put you in one of the smaller rooms," she said. "Your things should be brought up next."

An hour later, I sat on the new bed in my temporary room and looked around. Like the rest of the house, the walls were painted a neutral putty color. A thick white carpet covered the floor. Windows and a set of French doors let in the plentiful Las Vegas sunlight. The furniture Katherine had chosen for the room was dark and contemporary looking. I liked the clean, hard edges of the pieces and the stark contrast between the wood and lighter tones in the room much more than the fluffy Pepto-Bismol pink of my room at home.

Katherine knocked on my door and came in carrying a comforter set. "I wasn't sure what colors you like," she said, unzipping a bag and dumping a bundle of linens out. "Going on nothing but a guess, I chose this blue gray for you. The shade matches your eyes."

I was touched by her thoughtfulness. "They're beautiful, but I could have made do with one of the air mattresses and a sleeping bag."

"Believe me, you're going to need a nice place to sleep tomorrow night."

I was already nervous about my training, so the foreboding tone in her voice didn't help matters. Picking up on my feelings, she reassured me, "You're going to be tired more than anything else."

I hoped she was right. "Thank you for helping me feel so at home here."

I'd set to work making my bed when there was a brief knock on my door. It opened and one bright turquoise eye peeked in. "Come in," I said.

Ian pushed the door open and hauled my luggage into the room. "I brought your suitcase," he said. "This thing weighs a ton." He hefted the bulging bag to the top of my dresser. Then he looked around the room. "It's nice in here," he commented. "Suits you in a way. You'll appreciate having a real bed to sleep in tomorrow."

"I wish you people would stop saying that."

He looked apologetic. "It wasn't in my plan to throw everything at you at once, but my dad thinks it will work better this way. Don't misinterpret that as him calling all the shots. He thinks he's the boss, but I'm the one running this show. I've been doing it from the start. I gave in to him on this because the more you know, the safer you'll be."

I laughed softly. In some ways the two of them were so much alike. They were both confident, determined leaders and because of that they would always butt heads.

"What's so funny?" he asked.

"I was just thinking about you and your dad."

"Anyway, he thinks the tiger might have talked about you before I killed him. Not to Sebastian. To someone else in the Illuminant clan. If they come looking for you to finish what the tiger started, you'll need to be able to protect yourself. You're going to get a crash course in thoughtmaking, mind defense, and essence fighting over the next two days."

"And it's going to hurt," I deduced.

"I told you the learning curve would be steep. Pain will help you climb it faster. Which gives you all the more reason to enjoy yourself at the party tonight."

Brandy passed by the open door of my room. "Better get a move on, you two," she said. "People will be here soon."

"Promise me you'll *try* to have fun tonight," Ian insisted. "No thoughtmaking yourself into invisibility."

"I promise. Now, go away."

He complied, whistling some random tune as he left.

I closed the door and went to inspect the contents of my suitcase. I found the only two dresses I owned laid out on top of everything else, a subtle hint from Brandy to dress up, not down. The first was the bright sundress my mother bought during our school shopping trip last week. It was formfitting until the waist, then it flared like a parachute and ended at midthigh. The length was all wrong for someone as tall as me. It made my torso look too short compared to the rest of my body.

Tossing it onto the bed, I inspected my second option, a shirt and skirt combo. The shirt was a pale pink chiffon over a darker pink shell. The skirt was dark gray and fitted. I'd worn the combination to a Christmas party for my dad's business the year before. I'd looked like a librarian. No way was it right for a high school get-together. Catching a glimpse of the embellished pocket on my favorite pair of jeans poking out from under another of my shirts, I pulled them out and held them up. They were worn in and did great things for my butt. I'd never worn them to school for exactly that reason. I set them next to the chiffon shirt and liked the dressy against the casual. I settled on that option and checked in my suitcase again.

Brandy had packed my set of hot rollers. I'd owned them for two years and never so much as plugged them in. *What the heck*, I thought. It was time to find out if my hair had the ability to curl. After sorting through the other clothes, I noticed my neglected cosmetics case stuffed into a corner. Curling my hair with hot rollers was one thing—I couldn't really mess that up, or so I hoped. Applying makeup was another matter entirely. I'd probably come out looking like a clown. Hoping not to overdo things, I retrieved the pink lip gloss I'd used the day before and some mascara.

Thirty minutes later I stood on the edge of the tub to get a full-length look at my efforts toward self-beautification. To be honest, I didn't recognize the girl staring back at me from the mirror. She was tall and slender, with loads of shiny hair that lay across her shoulders and down her back in soft waves. She had wide gray eyes framed by thick lashes. Her bottom lip was full and there was a nice blush in her cheeks.

For the first time since enrolling at Fillmore, I felt really good about how I looked. Jumping down from the tub, I went to find my sandals.

No one in the crowded living room noticed me at first, so I had a few seconds to study the battlefield before throwing myself into the mix. The girls were in the kitchen and the boys were sitting in various places around the television. "Sudden Death" by Megadeth blasted through the sound system Ian had hooked up. I saw Connor's head bobbing among the other male heads in the room. He was playing Guitar Hero.

There was no route around the boys, so I put my game face on and stepped into the middle of them. If I hadn't been so nervous, I might have found their reaction funny. Face after face turned toward me with interest but without a speck of recognition. Contagious silence spread among the group until all conversation stopped.

I said, "Hi," accompanied by a little wave.

Silent stares resulted.

"Hey, Alison," Ian said, looking at me as though I was a stranger.

"Hey," I replied before continuing toward the kitchen.

I got a soda and leaned against the counter, listening to the gossip around me. As usual, Brandy was in the middle of things, laughing, talking, and putting even the most self-conscious girls at ease. When she got a break, she came over to get a soda. "Wow. You clean up nice," she said, giving me a wink. "Half the guys in here can't stop looking at you, and Ian looks like a kid in a candy shop. In case you're confused, he's the kid and you're the candy."

I laughed. "It's been so long since I dressed up for anything, I wasn't sure it was me when I looked in the mirror. And it's all thanks to you."

"I do what I can," she replied, smiling.

Probably sensing my nerves, she stayed near me as I settled into the rhythm of things, then she wandered away to talk to a girl standing on the fringes of the group. Inspired by her social grace, I turned to my nearest neighbor, intending to strike up a conversation. Before I could say anything, I felt something on my skin. It was warm and it hummed a little. That's when Nikki Cole walked into the room.

Her strawberry-blond hair was pulled up to showcase her delicate features. Her shirt and skirt had been carefully chosen to emphasize her small, curvy figure. She radiated confidence like Ian did, but it came off cool and detached rather than inviting. She drew human attention, both male and female. It was the steady vibration coming from her that held mine. Her cornflower-blue eyes turned toward me and a sneer crossed her pretty face. She remembered me, but her eyes didn't linger. They moved to Ian, and her sneer was replaced by a smile that transformed her face into radiant beauty.

Crossing the room to him, she touched his forearm in a familiar way. Ian looked down at her, and the strangest thing happened to me. The energy in my body, more specifically just under my skin, began to heat and bubble. I'd never experienced anything like it. Brandy's arm brushed mine, and she flinched back. "You're burning up," she whispered in alarm. "Take some deep breaths." I did what she said. "Whatever you were thinking when your energy heated up, don't think of it again for the rest of the night," she ordered. "Do you understand me?"

"Not really."

"I'll explain later," she said. "Just control what you think about, okay?"

"Okay," I replied, determined not to think of the pretty dewing girl who'd gone straight toward Ian and was now chatting him up. Brandy grabbed Felicity Nathanson and pushed her up next to me. "You two know each other, don't you?" she said.

Felicity was meant to distract me from thinking about Nikki, and I silently thanked her for it. "Felicity, right," I said cheerily. "We had biology together last year. We were lab partners once."

She smiled. "Starfish dissection."

Felicity wasn't really popular, sporty, musical, dramatic, or brainy. She was one of the kids filling the cracks at

Fillmore. Like I'd tried to be. Feeling a connection with her, I said, "This is a great party, isn't it?"

"Yeah. I was surprised Brandy invited me. But she's so nice, and her cousin is in my trig class." She had stars in her eyes when she mentioned Brandy's cousin. I did my best to ignore that. I asked her what other classes she had, and as she finished reciting her schedule, I looked up to find Ian walking toward us.

"Hi, Felicity," he said with a smile for my companion. "Mind if I steal Alison for a minute?"

"Uh, no," she replied.

He took my hand and towed me toward the group of boys and Nikki.

"Why do you want to steal me?" I asked suspiciously.

"I want you to come and play."

"Guitar Hero? I don't know…"

He didn't let go of me until I was standing in front to the television holding a fake guitar. If anyone had bothered to ask, I would have told them not to start me out on the beginner level. I was fiercely competitive with Alex on the game and could play most songs with my eyes closed. I goofed up a little at first, but halfway through I was pursuing guitar greatness. As I finished the last chord on my third song, I banged my fake guitar in pantomime. Turning around I saw a sea of faces frozen in astonishment.

Everyone's surprise seemed pleasant, except for Nikki's. Her eyes were filled with intense dislike.

"Sorry about that," I said. "I guess I got carried away."

My statement was greeted by a round of applause, and

then Michael Larson said, "Well, no one is going to beat that. Time for a new game."

A little overstimulated by that much attention, I headed for the patio and some fresh air. I let myself out and then stood looking down on Sin City. The door opened and closed behind me. I didn't need to look around to know it was Ian.

"That was interesting," he said, coming to stand next to me.

"I play that game a lot with my little brother," I explained. "There hasn't been much else for me to do on weekends. Alex loves video games, and he appreciates a worthy opponent. According to him, I have mad skills."

Ian laughed softly and then turned to a different topic. "You felt her come in, didn't you?"

I knew he was referring to Nikki. "Yes. I've been feeling vibrations all day, but I didn't know what they meant until I felt one at the exact moment Nikki came in. Do you think Nikki felt me, too?"

"I'm sure she didn't," he said. "Brandy told me your essence rose in reaction to her, but Nikki didn't respond."

"Why did it do that, the boiling-under-my-skin thing?"

"You just got a taste of what it feels like to warm up for a fight."

"But I don't want to fight with Nikki."

"Maybe not consciously, but you don't like her. You told me that yourself. Maybe subconsciously you think she's a threat to you."

I considered that. "It's probably that I'm worried she'll figure out what I am."

"Even if she did, it wouldn't matter," he assured me. "Your mother saved one of her cousins from Sebastian Truss. Her clan owes you as much protection as mine does."

I remembered Bruce and Amelia's reaction to me three nights ago and I believed him. Neither of them would do anything to jeopardize my safety. I still felt uncomfortable about Nikki, though. I didn't trust her.

"She seems to like you," I said, glancing at Ian's handsome face and beautiful smile.

He laughed again and turned to lean his back against the railing. "It's social power Nikki likes," he said. "She's more into Luke Stentorian than me. He already heads a clan. I'm still waiting in line."

The idea of ugly Luke likenessing with beautiful Nikki was very gratifying. "They'd make an interesting couple," I said.

"Nikki thinks so. She's been stalking him ever since his parents died. Poor Luke is no more in control of who he can likeness with than any of the rest of us. Nikki thinks it will increase her odds if she spends a lot of time with him, though. He likes her well enough, but he's struggling to adjust to his new life and responsibilities. He doesn't need the kind of pressure she puts on him. He probably left town more to get some space from her than to do business."

"And with her main prey out of range, you've been elevated to top target?"

"It appears that way, but Nikki is too predictable for my taste," he said, leaning in close to me. "Once you understand her character, there are no real surprises anymore. I prefer a little weirdness to liven things up."

"Which explains why we get along so well," I said, putting my hand on his chest to push him back.

He didn't budge. Against my will, my breathing slowed, and my eyes lingered on his mouth. Thankfully, Connor poked his head out the door. "Alison, you up for Dance Revolution?" he asked.

I took a deep breath. "I've already made a fool of myself once tonight," I replied. "Why not do it again?"

"This I've got to see," Ian said, following me in.

Chapter Sixteen

Within an hour's time, everyone's anxiety had disappeared, so boys and girls were mingling with enthusiasm. Twice I'd demonstrated how Dance Revolution should be done. As I laughed and talked with the kids around me, I wondered how I'd managed to go so long without this.

I was bummed when the power went out around eleven. It was no use stumbling around in the dark even though everyone wanted to keep the party going. They talked about meeting up at other places in town. It didn't take long for everyone to leave. Everyone but Nikki.

She'd cornered Ian by the TV.

I was on trash duty, so I headed their way with a flashlight and a garbage bag. I picked up a couple soda cans and heard Nikki say, "You should come over to my house. My parents will be out late. We can watch a movie…or something."

"I have to help clean up," he replied.

She looked my way and spoke in a voice that was meant to be overheard. "Brandy's little friend…oh…I mean big friend seems to have things under control."

"I can't," Ian said patiently. "I've got some stuff to do tomorrow. I can't be out late."

Realizing she wasn't going to prevail, she smiled up at him. "Maybe next time."

"Maybe next time," he agreed, taking her by the elbow. "Let me walk you to your car."

I shoved another can in the bag.

"I can't stand that girl," Brandy said from across the room.

"I'd like to let my big self drag Nikki up the stairs by the hair and hang her from the roof by it," I said. "I wonder what she'd think of me then."

Brandy chuckled. "I'd pay to see that."

When Ian came back, he went straight to the utility room and flipped the breaker back on. "You turned the power off," I said in disappointment.

"That's the deal I made with my mom. We've got a busy day tomorrow."

Spencer and Katherine walked in. We all stood silent, looking at the mess around us.

"Apparently the party was a success," Katherine observed.

I put another soda can in the garbage bag and yawned. Spencer came my way and took the bag from me. "You have the night off, young lady," he said.

I stifled another yawn. "I can help."

"No. You need to get some rest," he insisted. "I'm sure you're still sore from the tiger's attack. Better take advantage of some sleep."

Without adrenaline coursing through me, the aches in my body were back. "Okay," I said reluctantly, "but I'll do the dishes tomorrow. You can leave them in the sink."

Spencer pushed me gently out of the kitchen. "I'm an expert dishwasher," he said. "I've been doing it for almost two hundred years now."

Ian caught me by the arm when I stumbled on the rug. "Come on, sleeping beauty."

On Katherine's orders, all the bedrooms had been locked during the party. I leaned against the wall while Ian ran a hand along the top of the door frame, feeling for the key to my room. The only boy at the party who came close to being as attractive as him was Michael, and he'd take a distant second.

Ian's gaze lingered on me after he unlocked the door. Maybe mine lingered a little long, too. I was too tired to stop myself. "Thanks," I said, pushing away from the wall.

He blocked my way into the room. "You made quite an impression tonight," he said. "At least ten guys asked me your name. I told them it was Kate."

I laughed. "Kate?"

"It's all I could come up with on short notice."

He smiled down at me, and the soft light around us caught the green flecks in his eyes. Like a moth to a flame, my gaze was drawn to his mouth. I remembered feeling safe when he slept behind me, and the warmth of his lips on mine when he kissed me. A piece of me wanted that again. Ian's gaze flicked to my mouth, too. If I tipped my chin up, he'd kiss me. Warmth spread over me, tempting me to do it, but I took a deep breath and swallowed. Then I pushed him gently out of my way. "I flew my freak flag high tonight," I said.

His smile deepened. "You'll never be invisible at Fillmore High again. It was good to see."

"Thanks."

"Good night, Alison," he said with a twinkle in his eyes.

"Good night," I replied, closing the door between us.

I went to the bathroom and brushed my teeth. The girl in the mirror looked a lot like she had before the party. Her hair was wavy and shone in the light. Her light gray eyes were still wide and framed by lots of dark lashes. The difference was the dreamy expression in them. She was changing from the inside out. It was coming on fast, too. I wasn't sure if I was ready for it.

Morning came too soon for me, and it was accompanied by a profound longing for home. The first thing I did was call Mom's cell phone.

"Hi, sweetie," she answered.

I knew she was trying to hide it, but I could hear anxiety in her voice. "What's wrong?" I asked.

She sighed. "My car got broken into at the gym this morning. I'm with the police and insurance man right now."

An uneasiness made the hairs on the back of my neck rise. "How bad is it?"

"It could be worse. They smashed the back window and riffled through the glove box, but they only took the navigation system. I should have known better than to park along the street. There's been a lot of this kind of thing around the gym recently."

"Do the police have any ideas?" I asked.

"No, not yet. But I'd sure like to be there when they catch the guy. No one messes with my baby this way."

I smiled, knowing her baby was the car.

"How is everything going with you?" she asked. "How was your little get-together last night?"

Remembering the mess I had to clean up, I choked back a laugh. It hadn't been a little get-together. Brandy had turned it into a full-on party. "It was fun," I managed. "I got to show off some of my gaming skills. Alex would have been proud."

"I'll tell him," she said. "I'm sorry to cut this short, sweetie, but the police need me to answer more questions."

"Okay. Be careful, Mom. This isn't the safest town in the world."

"I know. I will."

I hung up feeling troubled. Mom had talked about a string of break-ins near her gym, so it wasn't like it came out of nowhere. But it worried me. If Spencer was right, the tiger had told someone that he was suspicious of me. "Suspicious" was the operative word. He hadn't known for sure who I was, so why pass specifics along, right? Thankfully, Lillian was planning to drive by my neighborhood throughout the day. She'd let us know if anything changed.

Whatever my concerns, the best thing was to get trained as soon as possible. I dressed for pain in shorts and a T-shirt. My hair was still wavy from the hot rollers. I pulled it back in a ponytail so it wouldn't get in my way. Then I was ready.

Well, maybe not ready, but I wouldn't stand on the sidelines anymore. People I loved were in danger, and I had to learn how to protect them.

Chapter Seventeen

The house was quiet when I made my way to the kitchen. All the vibrations around me hummed at a low frequency. I thought I was the only one awake until I found Katherine wrapped in a silk bathrobe, sitting at the dining room table. Her chestnut-brown hair lay smoothly over her shoulder as she sipped a cup of tea. She looked up when I walked in. "Ready for today?" she asked.

"I've waited a long time to learn what I can do with my mind. I suppose a bit of pain is a small price to pay for the education."

"That's a brave girl," she replied.

I got the milk and cereal out while Katherine stared silently into her cup. When I sat next to her, she reached to get something from off the floor. "Brandy found this in the tiger's car," she said, handing me a long, flat item wrapped in tissue paper.

I knew without opening it what was inside. Removing the tissue paper, I found the same book I'd seen lying on the floor at the Shadow Box.

"It's a genealogy of your clan," Katherine explained. "We hesitated to give it to you at first, but ultimately…it seemed more wrong to keep it from you."

A musty odor wafted toward me when I opened the cover. The first pages were yellowed with age and covered in a flourishing calligraphy I couldn't read. "Names and birth dates," Katherine said, pointing at the writing. "Under each bold line is a death date."

I skimmed more pages, feeling the life and death that ran through them. Tears clouded my vision when I realized I'd never know the stories behind the names. There was no one left to tell them to me. Farther in, the names shifted to English spellings written in an atrocious calligraphy. I could only make out a few of the letters. Seeing a scrap of paper marking a place near the end of the book, I turned there.

The writing was still difficult to read, but I interpreted one of the names as Grace Laurel, followed by a set of dates that meant nothing in the Western European calendar. "Saul Laurel" had been penned next to it with another set of dates. Below them both was written, "Jillian Laurel."

Katherine pointed at the third name. "That's you," she said. "Jillian Laurel."

I'd never thought about my original name. I could only remember being called Alison, the name the state of Nevada had given me. Jillian seemed an odd name to me. I didn't really like it. Shaking my head at the strangeness of it all, I pointed to the name above mine. "And this is my father?"

"Yes. There's not much I can tell you about Saul. I only met him once, but from what I read in the book, he was a dewing without joining."

Remembering that the tiger had referred to my father that same way, I asked, "What's a dewing without joining?"

"In rare instances, a dewing will be born without the ability to join a human's mind. They have all of our other abilities. In fact, their essence energy is often exceptionally strong. But when it comes to a human's mind...they can't connect. Dewing without joining pass a special energy to their children. It's as if the child's joining is stronger because the parent wasn't able to use theirs."

I thought about what she said and what it meant to me. "So, if I was a normal dewing, one who had been raised in a dewing family instead of a human one, my joining would be super strong?" I asked.

"Given the talent you probably inherited from your mother, and the latent energy you got from your father, yes."

"Too bad I got messed up being raised in a human family, right?"

"It remains to be seen how messed up you are," she replied with a kind smile. "All the raw talent and ability is in you. We just need to show you how to use it."

I looked at the names of my parents again, and then turned a few more pages in the book. The writing stopped halfway down one of them. The pages behind it were blank, because the Laurels had been murdered. There were no other names to put in the book. My hands trembled as I thought about it. Katherine took them in hers. "It tells only a part of your story," she whispered.

"It's so awful. Even the children and babies were killed. I can feel all of the hope that died here."

"It's not a hopeless story," she insisted. "There is much to mourn, but the story isn't finished. There's still one name in the book...yours."

"Who filled in these dates?" I asked, pointing to what I assumed were the most recent deaths.

"Probably the last person alive from your clan," Katherine replied.

Ian came in. "Are you sure the man who left the book with Lillian wasn't a Laurel like me?"

"Lillian has issues," he said, "but she can feel vibrations just fine. That guy didn't have one. She's sure he was human."

"Why would a human have this book?"

Ian made a bowl of cereal for himself and took the seat opposite me. "One of your clan must have given it to him before they died."

"Then there's a human out there who knows about us," I said. "He had a tattoo that looks like the embossing on the cover of this book."

"Maybe he just liked the design," Katherine suggested. "A Laurel could have used their joining to convince him to get the book to you at a particular point in the future. The human could have had this book for years, waiting to pass it off. If the design appealed to him, he might have had a tattoo artist copy it."

It was a plausible explanation for the tattoo, but the implications behind it made me angry. "For this book to reach me now, there had to be a Laurel out there who knew about me when I was younger. That means they knew I was in the foster-care system. They could have gotten me out. Why didn't they get me out?"

Ian leaned in to look me in the eyes. "I can't imagine what growing up was like for you, Alison, but Sebastian was hunting your clan down. If you'd been with a Laurel, no matter who it was, you would have been killed, too. Your clan was trying to protect you."

Logically, he was right, but seeing the book in front of me brought up all of my old abandonment issues. I closed it.

Spencer came in bright eyed and ready to work. He stopped short when he felt the glum atmosphere in the room. "Am I interrupting something?" he asked.

I didn't want to explain, so I put on a happy-to-see-you smile and said, "What's the plan today?"

Like a drill sergeant, Spencer handed out orders, and we went to work moving all the furniture off the big rug in the living room. Spencer said it would be less painful for me to land on the rug than the tile floor beneath it, and no one wanted me to knock myself out if I fell on the furniture. From this, I inferred I would be falling a lot.

My first lesson was self-defense, aka controlling the boiling energy under my skin.

When Spencer and I took up positions standing across from each other on the rug, he said, "Brandy told me you heated up when you sensed Nikki last night. The heat you felt is typical of what happens during a fight between two dewing. We don't do it a lot these days, but there was a time when we did. When we fight, our energy or essence comes to the surface. We concentrate this energy and then project it out at our opponent. The strength of the projection doesn't correlate to the strength of the body, so you may face someone much larger than yourself and have no trouble fighting them off. Similarly, you could fight someone a lot smaller and find yourself in big trouble."

"The heat was under my skin," I said. "How do I concentrate it, let alone...project it?"

"You have control over the energy during a fight, just like you have control over it when you use your joining. Feel the energy under your skin; let it build in you until there's no more room. When you do that, it's concentrated and your mind can control it. From that point, you can use the energy as a weapon or a shield."

"Uh...that sound complicated."

"How do babies learn to walk?" Spencer asked me. "They learn by trying and failing until they understand how to do it. Eventually their muscles take over, and they don't think about how they're doing it anymore. This lesson will be unpleasant. You will fail before you succeed, and it will hurt. But pain is a great teacher. It will help you master the skills you need faster than anything else."

Though I wasn't thrilled, I didn't have much of a choice.

"When you feel the attack, gather your energy," Spencer said, moving behind me. "Let it build through you, and then push it out at your attacker."

"Kind of like punching someone?" I asked.

"Yes, kind of like punching someone. The important thing to remember is that you can be killed if your mind energy is crushed. Most of the time our physical bodies will regenerate, but our minds won't. In a fight to the death, your opponent will make you feel pain all over your body, hoping you will turn enough protective energy away from your mind so he can reach in and crush it."

"Okay," I said, trying not to shrink from the idea. "Regardless of the pain I feel, I have to keep energy around my mind."

"Exactly," Spencer said. "If you were ever to get into a fight to the death, your opponent would have to mortally wound you as well as crush your mind. We call the two together a finishing."

I remembered seeing Ian break the tiger's neck before their mind war. "I understand," I said.

He motioned for Katherine to join us. She walked toward me, and I tried to see her as a threat instead of a really nice supermodel.

"I'm going to access your human thought patterns and help you as much as I can," Spencer explained from behind me. "Katherine is going to attack."

"I hate this," Katherine muttered.

Brandy shot me a thumbs-up from across the room. Ian didn't look as optimistic.

The minute Katherine attacked, I felt like I'd been kicked in the stomach. This feeling was quickly followed by a gentle pushing in my mind, which I assumed came from Spencer. The pushing made me firm up the energy around the middle part of my body. At the same time, I struggled to keep constant energy around my mind. Just as I was able to push back enough to equalize the pressure around my stomach, Katherine kicked me in the back. As I fought to equalize the pressure around my back, she kicked me in the shins.

I collapsed to the floor with a moan.

Katherine fell to the rug next to me and started smoothing the hair away from my face. "Alison, are you all right?" she asked.

"Fine," I replied, rolling onto my back.

"You can't coddle her," Spencer said. "You have to keep up the attack."

She looked up at him with her eyes burning. "I can't do this, Spencer. It's like fighting a child. I'll help you with what you plan tomorrow, but I simply can't do this part."

"Okay," Spencer agreed. "Brandy needs to save what energy she's got, so I guess it's up to you, Ian."

Ian put his hands up in protest.

"I can't help her and attack her at the same time," Spencer said. "You know as well as I do, this has to be done. She won't be able to protect herself if she doesn't learn."

"It's not a kindness to leave me the way I am, Ian," I said from the floor. "You know it isn't."

He walked forward and helped me up. Then he took Katherine's place in front of me, and the process began again. Each time I successfully pushed the antagonistic energy away, it moved to a new place. Every now and then, I felt Ian take a jab at my mind to make sure I hadn't let my energy drop there.

The energy beneath my skin generated heat as it worked and in reaction, my skin beaded with sweat. I could feel heat coming off Ian, too. The light hair at his neck slowly darkened with sweat and his face flushed. I had to work ten times harder than he did, so my face was probably tomato red the entire time. I burned like a furnace as he mentally kicked the crap out of me.

Just when I thought I couldn't take anymore, Spencer called for a break. Ian's essence drew back from me, and I stood swaying in the middle of the rug. He gathered me in a hug, letting me lean against him. "I need to sit down," I said against his chest. Then I slipped through his arms like I was covered in butter and landed on my butt. "This is fine," I muttered.

Katherine brought us both a bottle of water. I gulped mine down and asked for more.

She kindly refilled it for me and then answered the intercom ringing in the kitchen. "Lillian's here," she said to everyone.

I was on my second refill when Lillian walked into the room. She looked awful. Her normal helmet hairstyle was flattened in places and sticking up in others. Under the light jacket she was wearing, her purple shirt was buttoned wrong. She'd spilled something on it, too. She came toward me and, getting to her knees, pulled me to her bony chest. It was very uncomfortable. "I should never have left you alone," she said into my hair.

I appreciated her concern and would have said so, but the room had started to spin around me. Fighting nausea, I closed my eyes tight. I don't know when she let me go, because the next thing I knew, I was waking up on one of the sofas. The house was cool and mostly empty except for Ian. He was sitting on the rug a few feet from me, playing a game on the Xbox. I reached out to touch his shoulder and he turned to me. "You're awake," he said.

"Yes, how long was I out?"

"About an hour."

"Man, I felt terribly motion sick. I thought I was going to throw up."

"You will throw up eventually," he said. "Everyone does."

"You went through this, too, then?"

He paused the game. "It wasn't exactly like what you're experiencing. I knew what I was getting into, and I had more time to get used to it. It's a biological process as much as anything else. We burn incredible amounts of energy when we fight, and we burn more when the rebound hits us. There's a lot to it and the body can only take so much. I threw up a couple times before I figured out how to handle it."

I smiled at him. "I can't imagine your mother puking. She's too elegant for it."

He smiled, too. "She may be the one exception."

"Who taught you to do it?" I asked.

He looked back to the game. "Because of the Laurel massacre, my dad wanted me to learn early. He had Jack start teaching me when I was five."

"That's really young, isn't it?"

"Yes," Ian replied with a haunted look in his eyes. "I understand my dad's reasoning now, but at the time, it seemed…cruel. Fortunately, Jack was a patient teacher. He tried to make certain parts of it into a game. But the true nature of essence fighting is ugly, and you can't hide that." He shrugged. "You do what you have to."

I could see he didn't want to talk about it anymore, so I changed the subject. "Where is everyone?"

"Out to dinner. There's not much food left in the fridge."

I stretched and then thought about school for the first time. "We've got to finish our poetry presentation," I said. "I added a few things when I looked it over at the Shadow Box, but there's still more to do. We haven't had a lot of time to work on it."

"I'll put the graphics together tomorrow while you're getting the other half of your training."

"The part where everyone jumps into my mind?"

"Yep."

"I'm a little worried about mind kissing your dad."

Ian's bright eyes met mine. "It won't be the same," he warned. "And my parents don't know I did it like that. I'd rather not have to explain it to them, okay?"

"Are you asking me to lie, Mr. Honesty? I thought you didn't do that."

"I'm not asking you to lie. Just don't bring it up."

"You'll owe me," I said.

"You'd think saving your life and doing the majority of our project would make us a little closer to even."

The others came in carrying Chinese takeout, and when Katherine set things on the table, Ian and I hurried toward it like starved animals. After we ate, Lillian volunteered to do the mental kicking, which came as a relief to Ian. Any remorse she might have felt about leaving me alone at the store had faded. She didn't hold back or cut me any breaks. She believed in tough love and beat me a lot harder than Ian had done.

Like Spencer said, pain was a great teacher. The harder Lillian kicked me, the better my reaction time got. In a relatively short period, I was relying less on Spencer's direction and more on my own instincts of self-defense. By the end of the tutorial, I was able to counteract her pummeling and keep the energy level around my mind intact without any outside assistance.

It was a big accomplishment, and everyone was pleased. Especially me. When Spencer announced that my training was over for the day, I fell to the rug again. The rebound was making the room go into hyperdrive rotation. My stomach lurched. I tried to get up and run for the bathroom but didn't make it. I puked Chinese food all over Brandy's new rug.

Even emptying my stomach didn't help the sickness. I curled into a ball of misery. Spencer picked me up and carried me to my room. "You'll feel better tomorrow," he insisted before leaving me on the bed.

I didn't want to go to bed sweaty and stinking of vomit, so I got up and made my unsteady way to the bathroom. I started the water and let the tub fill around me. After scrubbing myself thoroughly, I put my pajamas on and went back to bed.

With the covers pulled up to my chin, I started going through some kind of reverse heating. Before my bath, it felt like I had fire under my skin. Now I couldn't stop shivering. My teeth were chattering when Ian let himself into my room.

"Are you cold?" he asked.

I nodded and he said, "It happens that way."

Then he lay down on the bed and curled up behind me. He put his arm around my waist and pulled me tight against him. He yawned. "It only lasts a couple hours," he said.

I fell asleep almost immediately.

Chapter Eighteen

I was alone the next morning. I could feel the reassuring hum of Ian's energy somewhere nearby, but at heart, I felt lost. I yearned for the comforts of home. I wanted to eat seven-grain organic cereal and runny tofu lasagna. I wanted to spend a few hours playing video games with Alex and then scratch my lazy old dog behind the ears.

With a lonely feeling, I stumbled toward the Laurel book on top of the dresser. I clutched it to my chest and I climbed back in bed. I breathed in the musty smell of the pages before running my index finger over the names and dates on them. In a pathetic attempt to bond with my biological parents, I let my fingers rest on the names of Grace and Saul Laurel. Closing my eyes, I concentrated, hoping for some feeling of connection with them. When I opened my eyes again, they automatically focused in on the other name on the page.

Somewhere in the space around me I heard a voice say, "Jillian Laurel."

Startled, I looked up from the book. Of course, there was no one else in the room with me. I slammed the book closed.

"Are you awake, Alison?" Katherine asked just outside my door.

"Yes," I replied.

She opened the door. "I wanted to see how you're doing this morning."

"I've been better," I replied honestly.

She came gracefully into the room and sat on edge of the bed. "You were a real trouper yesterday. I'm sorry we can't go easier on you."

"I don't want you to go easy on me. I've accepted that pain and the rebound will be part of the learning process." Then, remembering my bout of motion sickness, I said, "I'm sorry about your rug, though."

"Don't worry about it," she replied, taking my hand. "You look sad this morning."

"I've only been gone a couple of days, but I miss home."

"I'm sure you do."

"I shouldn't even call it home."

"Why is that?" she asked gently.

"My first memory is of walking through a big door into a room where a new foster family was waiting for me. The curtains were red, and the carpet was brown. I remember exactly what everyone was wearing. I remember it smelled like cigarette smoke. I remember thinking, *these people aren't going to love me*, but I went to them anyway. Just like I did when it came to all of the others. I liked Mr. and Mrs. Greenspan the best," I said reminiscently. "They had two older children of their own, and they seemed to really like me, too. I wanted to stay with them, but they didn't keep me. After that, something inside me died.

"When the McKyes came along a year later, I was just a shell of a child. It took two years of their patience and love for me to come to trust them. And when the walls I'd built came down, I was finally happy. But it didn't last. After meeting the dewing in the park, I crawled back into the half life I'd lived before. For their safety, I can't be Alison McKye forever. I'll be all alone again without a steady place to call home."

She took my hand. "I saw something in your future yesterday. I wasn't looking for it, so the vision came as a shock, but I saw you happy. Very happy." Her eyes shone a little in the dim light. "And you weren't alone."

I snorted. "Are you sure you weren't hallucinating?"

"Everything happens for a reason. Even the hard stuff."

I wanted to believe that was true, but I didn't.

By the time I made my way into the kitchen, everyone had already eaten breakfast. Ian was sitting at the table behind his laptop. He gave me a bright smile before returning to whatever he was working on. Not wanting to interrupt him, I ate my cereal and looked at the others in the room. Katherine and Brandy were sitting together on one of the big sofas. Brandy's vibration was weaker than it had been the night before. Her laugh was vibrant, her eyes were bright, but her internal energy was fading fast.

With a hollow place in my stomach, I looked for Spencer. His huge frame cast a shadow as he stood staring out the wall of windows. He was talking on his cell phone and seemed agitated. Hanging up, he strode to the center of the room. "We've got another situation," he said. "The Sterling clan chief's went early to our meeting location, and they found a spy among the cleaning staff there. Just like before, the human bolted and was in the middle of a seizure when they caught up to him. He said one word before dying. Any guess what it was?"

We looked at him questioningly.

"'Stentorian,'" Spencer said in disgust.

All of my alarm systems started firing at once. "That's Luke's clan," I muttered.

"Yes," Katherine said. "What's going on, Spencer?"

"That sniveling, sneaking, conniving Luke Stentorian must be our mole," he replied heatedly.

"Couldn't it be someone else in the Stentorian clan?" Katherine asked.

"Who besides Luke would have known the location of our next meeting?" he asked in return. "Luke has been on the inside of our circle since his parents died, the perfect place to gather all sorts of damaging information. He doesn't have much of a backbone, we all know that, but I tried to help him."

"At least you know who the mole is," Brandy said. "All

you have to do is catch him."

Spencer was still furious. "Oh, I'll catch the little coward, and when I do…"

"What about the flash drive I gave you?" Ian asked. "Is there any information on it?"

"It was just stupid poetry stuff," Spencer said in disgust. "Luke's random musings about life. I can't figure out why he wanted me to have the garbage, unless it was to throw me off track."

I got to my feet. "My mom's car was broken into yesterday," I said.

Every face in the room turned to me. Their expressions suggested I was really missing the point. "Luke knows who I am," I explained. "He knows my name, and my mom's car was broken into yesterday. What does that suggest?"

"There's no reason to suspect the two are related," Spencer said, coming toward me. "However, I understand why you're concerned. Luke could pass a lot of information about you on to Sebastian, but he's known who you are for days. If he'd said anything to Sebastian, I'm sure your family would have been taken by now. I have the feeling that our traitor will hold onto most of the really valuable intel for a while. At least until he's sure of getting an enormous payoff. If we catch him soon, we can keep him from telling Sebastian anything more."

I paced the kitchen. "What are we going to do in the meantime?"

"I'll make some calls," Spencer said. "By this afternoon, I should have a couple of dewing here to guard your family.

I'll have to invent a plausible reason for what I'm asking my friends to do, but I've always had a creative streak."

It wasn't enough. "Shouldn't we be guarding them right now? At least until the other dewing arrive?"

"We don't want to rush in and surround your family," Ian said. "That would be a red flag to anyone watching. As much as possible, we have to pretend everything is normal."

"I'll call Lillian," Brandy said, retrieving a phone from her pocket. "She won't mind running surveillance again today."

I nodded my thanks, and Spencer started dialing on his phone, too. He stepped out onto the deck to talk.

"What about the clan chiefs' meeting tonight?" Ian asked Katherine. "If Luke is the mole, he would have given Sebastian all the details."

"We'll change the location and time," she said, searching her purse for her phone.

While the people around me made calls, I looked at my bowl of soggy cereal.

"You'd better eat it," Ian stated. "This is going to be another long day."

I didn't doubt his words, so I started shoveling cereal into my mouth. I chewed and swallowed without tasting. All I could think of was Luke telling Sebastian my mother worked out at Forever Fitness off of Forty-Fifth.

Five minutes later Spencer came striding back inside. "Time to get to work," he announced. "The best way to mitigate any damage Luke might do is to teach you everything we can."

"I'm ready," I said.

"We are going to work on defending your thoughts today," he explained. "Being raised in a human family has put you at a disadvantage that none of the rest of us face. You're vulnerable to all the joinings of other dewing. So you're going to have to be aware of your own mind at all times in order to keep others out of it."

"There is a second part to the lesson," Ian added. "As a thoughtmaker, you might be able to access the mind of another dewing. My mom told you that, remember?"

"Yes, but I tried it on you and Brandy several times the day we met. It didn't work."

"That was the day you hit your head and nearly passed out in class," Brandy said. "I don't think you were at your best."

"True," I agreed, remembering that my thought transference hadn't worked very well on anyone else, either.

"We know other thoughtmakers can use their joining on dewing, so we'll just have to assume you have the same ability," Spencer continued. "We don't share your joining, so we can't explain how it works, but we hope that showing you our minds will give you enough information so you can figure the process out."

I nodded my understanding and immediately felt the familiar squeezing of Spencer's mind linking with mine. Absent the discomfort of our previous encounters, I was able to feel his approach clearly. It was like a butterfly landing here and there in a garden of flowers. Everywhere he touched felt better when he left. The process went on until I had a decent understanding of what a healer's mind would feel like.

When he finished, he motioned for Brandy to take his place. "Haven't you already done this on me...like a million times?" I asked her.

"I haven't, actually. It's nice to be friends with someone without my joining occasionally. It reassures me I'm not a complete fraud. I chose to get to know you without cheating."

That was a relief. It was good that I'd liked her because of who she was, instead of having some voodoo-like joining make me think I did.

Brandy's mind aligned with mine in a quick and direct way. I felt her search for information and knew it was a violation of my privacy, but I didn't mind so much, because she was feeding me my own version of pleasant thoughts at the same time. It was like having someone ask my favorite ice cream flavor and then being fed dish after dish of it. Somewhere in the back of my mind, I knew I was going to regret eating so much, but in the moment it was delicious.

"Got it?" she asked after a few minutes.

"Yep," I said, with a full mental stomach.

Katherine was unsure when she sat in front of me. "I don't know if this will work," she said. "It depends on whether or not destiny wants to tell me anything today."

Her approach was subtle. I had to really focus to catch the details of it. After a few moments, it felt the way music sounds. The beats of her thoughts matched my own and then jumped ahead a bit. Her eyes had a faraway look as she worked. The process continued until I understood what a futureteller's mind felt like. When her eyes came sharply to focus, I asked, "What did you see?"

Her eye wandered to Ian. "Nothing," she said, getting up to leave the room.

She'd seen something that involved Ian, and it wasn't good. I didn't have much time to dwell on it, though, because Spencer motioned for Ian to begin. He gave me a look of warning. "It will be more like the first time than the second," he said.

"I'm ready," I said, and the process began again.

I tried to follow the path he took, but it was more complicated than the others. It felt antagonistic again, too. It wasn't butterflies, it wasn't music, and it wasn't eating ice cream. It was real manipulation, direct pressure applied to my free will. He didn't waste time with warm-up questions this time, either. "What is your greatest fear?" he asked.

Most people would probably have answered, "Spiders," "Monsters under the bed," "Terminal illness," or "An eternity in hell." But I hesitated. The pressure he applied went straight to the core of my mind, and it made me furious. *How dare he rob me of my secrets*, I thought. I pushed back at the pressure of Ian's mind until I felt his energy shift backward. Then I pushed harder, and with a giant flex of mental muscle, I hefted his energy out of my mind.

He was surprised. "What happened?" Spencer asked.

"She just skipped ahead a lesson," Ian said. "She kicked me out."

"Try it with me," he said delighted.

I felt his approach and though there was no hostility in it, I pushed back against his energy and refused to let him in.

"Very good, Alison," he said. "I didn't expect you to get so far so fast."

I was pretty proud of myself, but I'd forgotten about the rebound. The room tipped to the side, and the cereal I'd eaten felt like it was crawling up my throat. I squeezed my eyes tightly closed to steady myself.

"She needs a break," Ian said.

"She's earned one," Spencer responded.

Opening my eyes, I looked toward the wall of windows. I hadn't been outside in three days. "I'd like to go for a drive," I said.

Ten minutes later I was drinking in the hot, polluted air of Las Vegas and loving it.

"Air-conditioning, or windows down?" Ian asked.

"Windows down, please."

I laid my head back. Warm wind brushed against my face like soft kisses. I let my arm dangle out the window. Imagine Dragons's "Demons" came through the speakers. "This is one of my favorites," I said.

"I know," he said, turning the volume up. "I checked your playlist yesterday."

I smiled. "Stalker school again?"

He drove the back streets while I slumped in the passenger seat and practiced breathing. All the pressure and stress of the past three days seemed to evaporate. When he pulled into the shade of a tree at a well-watered park, I felt a lot better about life.

Ian leaned back in his seat, too. "Why did you throw me out of your mind when I asked your greatest fear?" he asked, looking over at me. "Are you afraid of dying? That's the answer most people give."

"I don't fear dying so much," I replied honestly. "After the party the other night I realized I've been half alive for most of my life. There's really not much difference between half alive and fully dead, is there?"

"Are you afraid of fighting Sebastian Truss?" he pressed.

"No. I've gotten pretty comfortable with the idea of pain recently."

"What is it, then?"

I watched a dog run up to a magpie in the park. The bird rose in flight and hovered above a dog as if taunting him. I wondered what it would feel like to fly away from danger. Maybe it had a nest and a mate to go back to. He was lucky if he did.

The fear I wasn't going to tell Ian about was my reality. I was going to be alone for the rest of my life.

When we got back to the house, Spencer put me to work trying to thoughtmake Brandy. I started off feeling optimistic, but after trying to push thoughts into her mind for half an hour, I slumped into the corner of the sofa, utterly discouraged. As far as I could tell, it was impossible to thoughtmake another dewing.

Thanks to sharing my mind with four of them earlier, I'd learned dewing thoughts were different than human thoughts in some important ways. Human thoughts were jumbled and erratic, tumbling over each other in a sort of fight for supremacy. They were constantly jumping from one thought to another, which put the human mind on a kind of thought overload.

The dewing mind ran a straighter course. Their thoughts flowed from one to the next smoothly. There was no fighting, jumping around, or switching back and forth between tracks. The result was that dewing thoughts had a power and efficiency human thoughts didn't.

Half an hour of searching also showed me there were no open places between a dewing's thoughts. They ran continuously like a long stretch of rope. There were no spaces to slip a thought into. I was on the verge of giving up entirely when it occurred to me I might be going about the process all wrong. I couldn't push my thoughts through an open place, but maybe I could wrap a thought around the strand that was already there.

Brandy had lost interest in my attempts to thoughtmake her and was watching television. I searched in her mind for a specific thought, and then formed *Your ear itches* in my mind. I used my energy to wrap that thought around hers like a tight hug. It was intensely difficult, and the rebound hit me hard, but it was worth it when I saw Brandy reach up and scratch her ear.

Quickly, I formed *Your other ear itches* and wrapped it around her thoughts. The room seemed to shift and dip to the other side as my energy came back at me, but Brandy scratched her ear again. Pushing the motion sickness away, I wrapped *You're thirsty* around her thoughts.

Brandy got up from the sofa and headed toward the

kitchen. "Where are you going?" I asked.

"To get a drink," she said. "I'm thirsty."

I jumped to my feet, shouting, "Yes! Yes!"

Everyone looked at me like I'd finally snapped under the pressure. I tried to calm myself. "Are you really thirsty?" I asked. "Or do you just *think* you're thirsty?"

Brandy considered, and then an excited expression crossed her face.

"It was a thought," she squealed. "It was one of *your* thoughts!"

I started jumping up and down.

Brandy and Katherine joined me half a second later. Through a haze of happiness, I saw identical expressions of relief on Spencer and Ian's faces.

Chapter Nineteen

Later that night, I choked down some kind of vegan casserole with a smile on my face. Of course, Mom wanted a full debriefing of my weekend and everyone involved in it. I answered her questions between bites of gooey mush with more than usual eagerness, and then joined Alex in the living room. He had a new video game warmed up and waiting. After giving me a royal beating at it, he asked if I could get Brandy to invite him to her next party. I wouldn't answer.

When he left to do his homework, I curled up in my dad's recliner. Coming into the room, my dad kissed me gently on the forehead and told me he loved me before going to bed.

They were all asleep when I went upstairs. Out my window, I searched for the dark SUVs I knew would be tailing my mom, dad, and brother for the next few days. I couldn't see them, and the drivers were too far away for me to feel, but Spencer's friends were out there somewhere. It was a huge relief.

I was still sore from beatings I'd taken the day before, so I filled the tub and added lots of watermelon-scented bubble bath to it. As the water soothed me, I went over the dewing skills I'd learned that weekend. I could defend myself when another dewing attacked my essence, and I could protect myself from others' joinings. I could even do thought transference with other dewing, which was a big accomplishment. But there was still a gaping hole in my abilities. I couldn't act offensively. I couldn't fight back with my essence, and that really worried me.

When I'd talked to Ian about it, he wasn't bothered. He told me my abilities would be needed before and after but not during the attack on Sebastian.

I didn't like the idea of Ian and Brandy going at Sebastian while I stood on the sidelines. So I planned to make Ian teach me how to fight. But not tonight. Tonight I was going to sleep in my bed, in my house, and tomorrow morning I was going to eat seven-grain organic cereal like the daughter of a hippie should.

Brandy picked me up for school the next day. "Where's Ian?" I asked, missing the sight of him.

"He's taking Spencer and Katherine to the airport. He'll meet us at school."

"Spencer and Katherine are leaving?"

"Katherine changed the location for the clan chief

meeting. Apparently, it's not going to happen anywhere around here. Only clan chiefs know where and when it will take place. As an added precaution, they've agreed to suspend communication with the outside world until it's over. They won't be gone long."

"I hope it works."

"Me, too," Brandy agreed. "They have got to come to a consensus about what to do. If they don't, it might be all-out war between the Truss and us. I don't fancy blowing up another island or maybe a continent this time."

"Could we do that?"

"It wouldn't surprise me."

As we exited the gates of my community, I felt two dewing vibrations coming from a car parked down the street. Brandy tossed a short wave in that direction, and the driver flashed the car's lights

Ian met me at my locker. He wore his usual T-shirt, worn jeans, and Vans. My heart did unwanted flip-flops at the sight of him. I told myself to get a grip. "You ready for our presentation?" he asked brightly.

I pointed toward my temple. "Perfect recall, remember?"

"How could I forget?"

I quickly clicked through my locker combination, checked my reflection in the mirror, and straightened the picture of my dog on the door. After moving my notebooks around, I glanced up and saw Ian watching me with a troubled expression.

"What's wrong?" I asked.

"Watching you do your weird locker stuff reminded me

we still don't know who took the pages from your notebook. They weren't in the tiger's things. Dad and I searched his car and the hotel room he'd been staying in, too."

"So someone else was messing around in my locker," I said apprehensively.

He nodded. "It appears so, but I haven't felt anyone around that shouldn't be."

My suspicion immediately ran to Nikki Cole. Her vibrations wouldn't seem out of place at Fillmore. Just thinking about her made the energy under my skin start to heat up.

Ian smiled at me. "Cool it," he said.

"Sorry, but it could have been Nikki. I'm telling you, something is up with her. She could have broken into my locker, taken my stuff, and then disappeared into everyone else around here."

"Just because Nikki has had the opportunity to take your things doesn't mean she did. What would her motivation be? She can be mean, but why would she break into your locker?"

"You said she hangs around Luke Stentorian a lot," I said. "He's the mole, so maybe she's helping him spy on me."

"I really doubt Luke told her over burgers and fries that he's helping Sebastian Truss. Their relationship isn't that close."

"How do you know?"

"I know because I have eyes in my head. Luke was never comfortable around her. He wouldn't have confided in her that he was spying for Sebastian, let alone asked her to help him."

"Maybe. I just feel like she's part of something bigger."

"Are you sure you aren't just jealous?" he replied, looking amused.

"Of what?"

"Nikki wants to spend time with me...you do, too."

"When we're done with Sebastian, Nikki can have you all to herself," I assured him.

He laughed. "Your mouth says one thing, your eyes say the other."

"You are so full of yourself."

English class was already full when we got there. I stopped dead in my tracks a few feet inside the room. My mouth immediately went dry, and the blood drained from my hands and feet as I looked at my classmates."

Ian bumped into my back. "What is it?" he asked, putting a hand on my elbow.

I shook my head. "I've never given a presentation," I said. "I always figured a way out of it before. I think I'm scared to talk in front of all these people."

"All these people? There are only nine of them. The first time is always a little scary. You'll be fine."

"I won't. I can't talk in front of them," I insisted.

"If you screw up, you can thoughtmake them into forgetting about it later."

Although true, it didn't make me feel any better. When I didn't move, Ian gave me a gentle push. Connor patted the chair next to him. Thankful for his friendly face, I made a beeline for it. "You look...not good," he commented.

"Do I?"

"Take some deep breaths," he suggested.

Nervous or not, I follow directions well. Unfortunately, I overdid the breathing and a pins-and-needles sensation started in my fingers before moving on to the rest of my body. I grabbed Connor's arm. He read the situation well and pulled my chair, with me sitting in it, away from the desk. "Put your head between your knees," he ordered, "and stop breathing so fast."

I did as I was told. Ian's Vans approached. "What's wrong with her?" he asked Connor.

"She started to hyperventilate."

A moment later, Ian's face was near mine.

"Jeez, Alison," he whispered. "It's just a little in-class presentation. All you have to do is read the photo in your mind."

"I can't do it," I whimpered.

He sighed once. "Don't push me out of your mind, okay?"

He used the kissing approach this time, and all sorts of pleasant sensations quickly replaced the tingling in my fingers and toes. I took in a long cleansing breath as Ian's sunshine floated over my skin. "Better?" he asked in a whisper.

"Better," I replied.

"Good. Let's get this over with."

Sitting up, I pulled my chair toward my desk. Connor gave me a reassuring smile, and then I felt her. Nikki was standing in the door looking in disbelief from Ian to me and back again. Ian nodded in her direction. She put a hand up in response but glanced at me again before leaving.

"She knows," I said.

"She can't understand why I'm mingling energy with a human," Ian replied, "but she doesn't know."

When class started, Mrs. Waters announced the order of our presentations. Ian and I were first.

"Gordon Lord Byron was born on the twenty-second of January, 1788, in London, England," I heard myself say. "He is considered the seminal poet of his time."

I managed to get through the rest of my part, and though my delivery sucked, I didn't leave anything out. Ian did great. He was a talented speaker and Byron's life provided ample material for him to joke about. The audience laughed at the appropriate times and gave us a round of applause when we finished.

I stumbled back to my seat, relieved. Ian had taken the desk near mine. He grabbed my hand and squeezed it. Physical contact on top of an overload of energy made my head spin. To top it off, when our eyes met, I couldn't look away. From across the room, Brandy threw a pen at us. It landed loudly on the desk in front of me, breaking the spell. She shook her head and Ian pulled his hand away.

Brandy fell in step with me after class. "You're humming," she remarked disapprovingly. "I don't think Ian's parents would approve of the type of energy floating around here."

"I had to do it," Ian said, coming up behind us. "She was paralyzed with fear."

"Too bad the side effects will make both of you useless for the rest of the day. You didn't think about that, did you?"

"Useless for what?" I asked.

"Ian won't will be able to defend himself if someone should attack. His energy is too wrapped up in yours," Brandy explained.

Remembering Ian's worried look at my locker that morning, I asked, "Why are you bringing up the possibility of an attack now? What is it the two of you aren't telling me?"

"She's just worried about the missing pages of your notebook," Ian said. "The same as me."

I looked at Brandy's face and knew there was something else going on. They were keeping something from me. When we stopped at my locker, I forced the issue. "What's *really* going on?" I asked. "You're both checking your backs, and mine, too."

"We'll tell you after school," Ian said.

"If it's something that involves my safety, I think I have the right to know now."

Brandy looked from me to him. "She's right."

Ian gave in. "Two dewing from the Ormolu clan were killed last night," he said. "Sebastian ordered it."

"Apparently, they had information to sell to him," Brandy added.

"Why have them killed if they had information?" I asked.

"We think Sebastian expected information about you," Ian explained. "He flew into Seattle to hear it himself. When he got something else, he had the Ormolu killed."

"So, now we can assume he knows I really exist. I'm not a myth anymore."

"We think so," Brandy admitted. "We aren't sure how much information Luke passed along, but Sebastian is still asking questions, so he doesn't know who you are or where you're living...yet."

My worst fears were being realized. Everything I'd tried to prevent was on the verge of happening. "What am I going to do?" I asked.

"Nothing," Brandy answered. "Spencer's friends are already guarding your family. Until Spencer and Katherine get back, I think the best thing is to continue on like you're a normal teen going to high school in Vegas."

I didn't have a better suggestion, so I shrugged in agreement.

"Brandy was right when she said I didn't think things through," Ian commented. "I shouldn't have accessed your mind that way in class. It puts us both at risk. Brandy will have to protect you if something happens, so stick to her like glue."

"Who's going to protect you?" I asked.

He didn't answer. Probably because the answer was "no one."

"I'll probably last five minutes defending you," Brandy said, "but I'm a better bet than he is. Consider me your shadow."

"Okay," I said, trying to convince myself that a very dangerous situation wasn't rapidly spinning out of control.

Brandy was waiting for me outside of my fourth-period class. "Hello, shadow," I said.

"Hello, glue," she replied. "Ready to eat?"

"Good. I'm hungry."

Again, I felt Nikki's vibration before I saw her. She ducked into a classroom just ahead of us. There was something familiar in the feeling of her vibration this time. Brandy noticed me tense up and correctly guessed the reason. "Nikki is harmless," she said.

"Why has she been spying on me, then?"

"After feeling the energy outside of English today, she probably thinks Ian has a massive crush on you. It happens sometimes, but at a certain point in the relationship, both the human and the dewing are repelled by each other. Nikki assumes Ian will come up against a brick wall before anything serious can happen. She's probably just curious what he sees in you."

"I don't trust her. She wants to be more than friends with Luke. She might have sold me out to get close to him."

"Relax, Alison. Whatever she wants with Luke, she wouldn't betray her family. They stand as firmly against Sebastian Truss as the Thanes do."

They kept saying that, but I'd never really believed it. Just because her family was against Sebastian didn't mean she was. When we passed the door Nikki had gone through, I looked inside. She was sitting demurely at the front of the class. Her eyes met mine for a fraction of a second. There was no hatred in them, just a veil of inquisitiveness. I knew then that she was really up to something.

By the time we got our food in the cafeteria, Brandy's groupies had assembled at their usual table. Ian must have needed space from their loud laughing, because he was sitting at the next table. Without looking up, he moved his backpack from the chair next to him and waved me toward him. His blond head was bent over a book.

"Are you planning to ignore me all lunch hour because you're mad about what happened in class?" I asked.

"No," he said. "I just want to finish this book."

"How can you be absorbed in a book when Luke Stentorian is on the loose and Sebastian is on the verge of finding me? And when I say *me*, I mean *us*."

"Like Brandy said, the best course of action right now is to act normal. Besides, this is a great book."

I checked the cover. He was reading *The Man in the Iron Mask*. Not a light read, and he was nowhere near the end. I didn't want to sit around twiddling my thumbs for the rest of lunch period, so I decided to practice my skills. I formed the thought *I'd like to see the Eiffel Tower* and wrapped it around the thoughts in Ian's mind. The rebound made me draw a painful breath, but he looked up and into the distance.

"What's up?" I asked innocently.

"It's weird," he said. "I was just thinking about the Eiffel Tower. I've seen it before—twice, actually. I wasn't very impressed either time."

"I'm getting better and better at this."

"It was you," he said with a grin. "Try it again."

When I accessed his mind next, I could tell he was watching for me, but I quickly wrapped *I think I'll have tofu lasagna for dinner* around his thought strand. Expecting the rebound, I steadied myself before it hit.

"No way!" he said.

I'd lied when I told Brandy I was hungry. I wasn't. I pushed my tray away. "I think we should talk business," I suggested. "It's time for you to tell me exactly what it is you want me to do when we confront Sebastian. I'll be able to prepare better if I know what my role in this whole thing is supposed to be."

He thought about it and then nodded. "Let's talk outside."

I followed him out of the cafeteria, and we sat in the shade with our backs against the school just like we'd done before. "So what impossible thing do you want me to do when we meet Sebastian Truss?"

"It's what we need you to do before we meet him that's important. We need your thoughtmaking to get us close to Sebastian. Apparently, he's moving around a bit, which isn't a good sign. But he lives in Washington, DC, in a compound that looks like a mansion from the outside. He passes himself off in human circles as a rich eccentric, contributing to lots of philanthropic causes and political campaigns. The favors he collects for his donations allow him to place his followers in highly sensitive economic and government positions all over the world."

"Why do you need thoughtmaking to get close to him?"

"DC is Sebastian's playground," Ian replied. "His followers are all over the city. They're especially concentrated around his compound. If we run into one of them, Brandy and I will register as Thane clan, and we won't be able to get anywhere near Sebastian."

"So you need me to thoughtmake you into a different clan?" I asked.

"No. We need you to make them think we're humans and then get us inside Sebastian's house for a personal audience with him."

"If I manage to get you inside his house, how can I possibly arrange for you to see him alone? Won't there be other Truss there?"

"Fortunately, most of Sebastian's supporters get their nights off," Ian explained. "Whatever damage your mother did when she fought him has made him self-conscious. Most shapeshifters are vain anyway, but his injury has turned him into a recluse. Only his assistant, a cousin of his named Maxwell, stays at the mansion full time."

"How do you know all this?" I asked.

"We have our own moles."

"What about Sebastian's likeness? Won't she be there?"

"He's never had a likeness."

Like Lillian, I thought. "What will you and Brandy do if I'm able to get you in to see him?"

"We'll fight him in the way we showed you this weekend."

"Two against one."

"Believe me, it isn't the numbers that will put Sebastian at a disadvantage."

"Wouldn't it be better if it were three against one?"

Ian gave me a warning look. "All we want you to do is get us in to see him. Then you sit tight while Brandy and I go to work. We can't teach you enough in the time we've got to make you a threat to his essence."

"If he's got such a strong mind, and he's defeated so many others, what makes you think you and Brandy stand a chance against him?"

"Jack was able to relay some impressions to Brandy before he died. It's nothing that can be put into words, but there's a weak point in Sebastian's mind. It's imperative we get to him while Brandy is still alive, so she can use what she felt to find that weakness herself. She's our real weapon. She can't kill him herself, but we hope she can tell me where to hit him so I can do the job."

The look on my face must have shown my doubt.

"I know it seems crazy dangerous, but we'll do it. We have to," Ian said, helping me to my feet.

I sat in fifth period thinking Ian's plan depended on me. If I didn't get us inside Sebastian's house undetected, that would be the end of it.

My thoughts had to be wrapped around the thought strands of each dewing. Identifying and then thoughtmaking the numbers of them I expected in DC would sap me of energy. The rebound alone would likely kill me. In order to get them in, I'd need to cloak my thoughtmaking the same way my mother had done when she walked away from Sebastian with twelve children in tow. I had to figure out how she'd worked her shortcut in order to help my friends — and the clock was ticking.

I was so consumed by my new responsibility that I forgot to check my locker at the end of the day.

Chapter Twenty

The minute I walked through the door at the Shadow Box, Lillian accessed my mind. Thankful for the opportunity to practice my defensive skills, I gathered my mental energy and tried to push her out. I couldn't.

"What have you been up to?" Lillian asked suspiciously.

I checked around to make sure there was no one else in the store before answering. "I had stage fright before my presentation in school today, and Ian…helped me."

Lillian rolled her eyes. "That was a stupid thing to do."

She never disappointed when it came to speaking boldly. I put my apron on and started straightening books behind the counter.

Her eyes practically bored a hole in my back. "There's something else going on, isn't there?" she asked. "Something more than an excess of energy has got your mind in a whirl."

I met her gaze. Of course she would pick up on my emotional turmoil. She'd accessed my mind as a reader. I put an armload of books on the counter. "I need to figure out how to cloak my thoughtmaking, so I can get Ian and Brandy into Sebastian's mansion. The giant problem is that I have no idea how to it. It seems destiny doesn't care, because it's pushing the timeline up."

"You heard about the killings," Lillian stated.

My shoulders slumped. "Yes," I admitted.

"Have a seat by the window," she ordered.

Lillian disappeared somewhere in the back of the store while I sat in an overstuffed chair. I heard her moving things around and doubted she'd find whatever it was she was looking for. I hadn't made a dent in the mess back there, but she came back carrying a thick notebook.

She sat in the chair opposite me. "This was my sister Angela's," she said, laying the book open on her lap and running her veined hand over it. "She sent it to me the week before Sebastian's people found her. It's the only thing I have left of her." Glittery tears filled her eyes as she continued. "It's not really a journal. It's more like a day planner with her thoughts written in it, but toward the end, when Angela was being hunted, she was trying to develop the kind of mind-cloaking your mother used. She wrote about some of her attempts in here. Maybe there is something in this that can help you."

She handed the book to me.

"I'll return it to you," I promised.

"No," she said firmly. "It's yours now. I don't think Angela meant for me to have it forever. Perhaps she knew another thoughtmaker would need it someday."

She told me to stay put and look through her sister's writings for the rest of my shift.

A quick glance through the pages showed me her sister had written everything from grocery lists to a few lines of poetry in it. Not knowing what might turn out to be valuable information, I decided to start at the beginning and work my way through. I'd made it about a quarter of the way when my cell phone rang.

"Hello," my mom said happily. "We're having dinner out tonight. Alex wants pizza, and since it's his birthday, I'm giving in. Can you meet us?"

With everything else going on, I'd forgotten about Alex's birthday. "Probably. Where are you going?" I asked.

"California Pizza at the Mirage. We're bowling at Batcat's afterward."

"Okay, I'll drive over after work."

"Sounds good, sweetheart. I have to go. I can't steer this shopping cart and talk on the phone at the same time."

"Sure, Mom," I said, envisioning a cart loaded down with gifts for Alex.

At seven o'clock, I was sitting in my car outside the Shadow Box still reading Angela's journal. On Ian's orders, I was waiting for Brandy to come before leaving Lillian's protection. Brandy was going to tail me to the Mirage and then stake me out from a nearby spot.

Seeing Brandy's white Toyota coming, I closed the

notebook and turned the key in my ignition. I got nothing but a clicking sound as a result. Brandy pulled up and rolled her window down. My eyes went immediately to Ian in the passenger seat and stayed there.

"I knew your car was due for a breakdown," Brandy said.

"What's wrong with it?" Ian asked.

"It won't start. The engine won't turn over at all."

I got out, locked my doors, and then slid into Brandy's backseat.

"Hmm," Ian muttered. "Nothing about the car look tampered with, did it?"

"I didn't notice anything unusual."

Ian and Brandy exchanged anxious looks. "What's wrong now?" I asked.

"Sebastian's men killed another dewing in Seattle this afternoon," Brandy said. "She was Stentorian. We think Sebastian is trying to find Luke, too."

"We've got to do more to protect the McKyes," I said.

Brandy shook her head. "We can't send for more protection. A bunch of dewing surrounding your house would be like yelling, 'Hey, Sebastian, look over here.'"

"We've got day and night coverage on each member of your family," Ian said. "We'll keep things as they are until my mom and dad get back."

"When will that be?"

Neither Brandy nor Ian could answer that question.

Alex and my parents were waiting for me under a palm tree outside the casino. My dad motioned for Brandy to roll her window down. "Where's your car, Alison?" he asked me.

"Everyone's negative energy finally killed it," I replied grumpily. "It wouldn't start after work."

"I think there might be a problem with the alternator," Ian volunteered.

My dad shook his head. "I'll have it towed to my garage tomorrow."

"Why don't you kids come in and eat with us?" my mom suggested. "We're celebrating Alex's birthday, and then we're going to bowl. We could use some extra players."

Brandy and Ian hesitated, probably because they had bigger issues on their minds. "Come on," my dad insisted. "It's the least we can do after your family fed Alison all weekend."

"Okay," Brandy said, accepting the invitation. "We'll meet you inside."

So, in spite of the danger closing in all around us, I found myself celebrating my adopted brother's fourteenth birthday in the company of my two new friends. My dad ordered four pizzas, and we were all painfully stuffed by the time our waitress brought out dessert with a candle burning on top. Alex was not too old for birthday wishes, so he closed his eyes and concentrated before blowing out the little flame.

We all clapped, and then he began opening gifts. I felt an edgy excitement as I handed mine over. I'd done my shopping at the Shadow Box. I'd picked three books in the Star Wars series and wrapped them in the cartoon section from one of Lillian's newspapers. Alex wasn't a big reader, but I hoped an action-packed series might change that.

"Those are great," Ian said when Alex put them on the table.

Alex looked doubtful. "Really?"

Ian smiled. I loved that he was a nerd like me.

When we got to the bowling alley, I put on a pair of questionably smelly shoes and prepared myself for humiliation. I was good at most sports, but not bowling. The heavy ball always seemed to stick to my fingers longer than it should, and perfect recall did nothing to improve my aim. Helpful hints only made me mad, so basically I provided comic relief by bowling gutter balls all night.

After completing two pathetically low-scoring games, I sat back to watch the others. Dad and Brandy were having lots of fun. They were content with their mediocre performances. Mom was giving Ian a real run for his money. But Alex, who was doing his best to show off for Brandy, was the star of the show.

He was smart, funny, and most importantly he had a good heart. Someday he'd have a girlfriend. Weird. There weren't a lot of teen boys who would consider a night out with their family and sister's friends a good time. Whoever the girl ended up being, she would be lucky. I hoped I'd be around to meet her.

Alex came to sit next to me. "Thanks for the books," he said.

I laughed. "That's so genuine. It's like I gave you a plate of vegetables to eat. Just promise me you'll give reading them a chance."

He put a hand over his heart. "I promise."

I rustled his hair like I used to do when we were younger. On his way back to the lane, Ian punched him in the upper arm. It was a typically male gesture that brought an enormous smile to my little brother's face. Ian caught my eye and winked.

During the next break, Ian sat with me. "Why, when you're so good at everything else, do you suck at bowling?" he asked with laughter lighting his eyes.

"I've wondered that myself."

We watched Alex roll a strike and then glance at Brandy to see if she'd been watching him. Ian leaned back and smiled, "I'm glad I got to spend some time with your family tonight," he said. "They're great. And it was nice to do something human. It took my mind off of Sebastian for a full thirty minutes."

He left to go bowl. I was getting perilously close to crossing the line. I'd been fighting it from the beginning, but my feelings for him were getting stronger. I wouldn't let that happen. It was okay to be his friend and enjoy his company, and I could appreciate that he was hot, but that was as far as it could go. After what had happened in the classroom, well, it would be too dangerous if we took whatever this was any further. We didn't need the distraction, and I didn't need to hurt any more than I already would when he went home.

Mom called the party quits, and Ian and Brandy drove away, promising to come pick me up for school the next day. I rode home in the backseat of my dad's Mercedes, feeling the comforting vibrations of Spencer's friends the entire way home.

For once, I pushed all the bad stuff aside and just enjoyed time with my family. I wasn't sure how many more of these moments I would have.

Chapter Twenty-One

I opened my locker the next morning and knew something was wrong. A quick look around and I figured out the picture of Tsar, my dog, was missing. Thinking maybe the adhesive had come loose, I searched the bottom of my locker and the floor but didn't find anything. The Low Tack on the inside of the door was still wet. I knew then that the picture hadn't fallen off. It had been taken.

It was a picture of Tsar, sitting on his haunches with his slobbery tongue hanging out. Near him was our mailbox. "Red Canyon Estates" was spelled out across it. Our house showed in the background. Visible at the top left-hand corner of the picture were the five metal numbers above our garage.

My heart thumped. Someone had taken my picture

because it was proof of my address.

I closed the locker door with a bang. I didn't bother spinning the lock. Someone from Sebastian's camp already knew the combination, anyway. Pulling my cell phone from my backpack, I dialed Mom's number. She answered on the second ring, but before she could even say hello, I asked, "Are you okay, Mom?"

There was a moment of confused silence, and then she said, "I'm fine, Alison, but judging from your voice, you aren't."

I improvised. "My stomach is bothering me, probably from all the pizza we ate last night. I was wondering if you're feeling it, too."

"No, I feel wonderful," she replied. "But then, I only ate the cheese pizza. You carnivores deserve indigestion."

I made myself laugh at her joke. "Maybe you're right. Are you teaching at the gym this morning?"

"Yes, but you left your calculus homework on the kitchen table. I'm on my way to drop it off at the school office for you."

"Thanks," I said, heading toward the main doors of Fillmore. "I'll meet you out front. The bell hasn't rung yet. How soon do you think you'll be here?"

"Two or three minutes."

I hung up and considered whether or not I should get Ian and Brandy from class. Telling them about my missing picture and the danger it suggested was high on my list of priorities, but I wanted to see my mom and know she was safe first.

Using all seventy-two inches of my height and muscle, I pushed my way through a throng of kids. Standing on the top step, I had a good view of the parking spaces in front of the school, as well as traffic on the main road. When I saw the bright blue paint of Mom's rental car coming, I walked down the steps to meet her. The late bell rang behind me.

I caught a glimpse of something moving across the street and felt the tickling of an unfamiliar vibration. It was coming from a woman dressed in a too-tight skirt, a silk tank, and four-inch espadrilles. She stood leaning against her idling car. When Mom pulled to the curb, she got a cell phone out of her bag.

I reacted by running at her full speed. I didn't know what I planned to do, but I couldn't let her take my mom. She was staring at the rental car and didn't see me coming until it was too late. I tackled her to the ground. She recovered quickly, and the look of surprise on her face was quickly replaced by a look of comprehension. I was ready for her when her essence reached out and struck me in the stomach. I pushed back against it, equalizing the pressure. Then I slammed my fist into the side of her face. She clawed at my neck and her energy hit me in the back. I fought through the pain and punched her in the jaw. Then her energy left me. She was concentrating on something or someone else.

Pushing her wrists against the cement, I glanced up and saw Brandy leaning over my mom, who had fallen to the ground. Before I could hit the dewing woman a third time, someone grabbed the collar of my shirt and hauled me up. In midair, I realized it was Ian. He steadied me on my feet, looking furious. The heat coming off him told me he was engaged in an essence fight with the dewing woman.

"Go check on your mom," he said through clenched teeth.

Over his shoulder, I could see Brandy had maneuvered my mom so her face was turned away from us. She hadn't seen what happened.

A black SUV pulled up behind the dewing woman's still idling car, and a very tall man got out. He was one of the dewing who was supposed to be protecting my family. "Where were you?" I yelled, striding toward him.

Ian grabbed my hand, practically spinning me back to him. "Get your mom out of here," he said to me. The dewing woman was bleeding and unconscious on the pavement.

I accepted the wisdom of his suggestion and turned back.

When I got to her, my mom was trying to explain to Brandy what had happened. "I think I passed out," she was saying.

"Don't worry, Mrs. McKye, the ambulance is on the way." Mom tried to sit up, but Brandy eased her down again.

"Stay still," I urged. "The paramedics should check you out before you try and move."

When I looked up, Ian was hefting the dewing woman into the back of the SUV. The tall dewing got in the driver's seat and drove away. I smoothed the hair away from Mom's face. "What happened?" I asked her.

"I don't know. I was fine one minute, and the next I had the worst headache of my life. It came and went so fast."

The ambulance arrived and the paramedics started to check her out. "Her vitals look good," one of them said to me. "We'll take her in to the ER so she can get a thorough checkup there."

"That's not necessary," Mom insisted.

"Just go to the hospital, Mom. That's what Dad would want. I'll drive your car over after I check out at the school office."

I held her hand until they loaded her into the back of the ambulance.

The minute the ambulance door closed, Brandy grabbed my arm and marched me out of hearing distance of the onlookers. "What were you thinking when you ran at that woman?" she hissed.

"Isn't it obvious? She was waiting here to snatch my mom."

"No, she wasn't. She was sent here as an observer. She was probably looking for information, anything out of the ordinary. You certainly gave it to her when you attacked her."

Brandy's words fanned the flame of my own anger. "I am sick of all this," I said, with hot rage burning in the pit of my stomach. "I'm sick of worrying every second of every day that someone is going to get to my family. She attacked my mom."

"She attacked her after you charged her. Sebastian will certainly figure everything out when one of his spies turns up missing from the front of Fillmore," she retorted. "If you'd just done as I asked, if you'd just let us take care of things, we would have stood a real chance. But no, you had to rush headfirst into the situation and ruin everything."

"This isn't a situation anymore," I said. "This is a catastrophe. That woman started texting at the very moment my mom drove up to the school. She was waiting for her to arrive. Someone out there knows about my family."

"What's going on?" Ian asked, coming to stand next to us.

"It's all been for nothing," I said. "Three years of hiding, and it all means nothing. They have the picture of Tsar, by the way."

Ian and Brandy were confused. "Who's Tsar?" Ian asked.

"My dog. My house number and the name of our development showed in the picture, too. It's a sick way of saying 'gotcha.'"

Ian sighed in frustration.

"I just want it over," I said, putting a hand over my eyes. "Sebastian needs to die or I do. The McKyes are good people. They loved me when no one else did. I won't let them become pawns in his sick game."

"I think you know what this means," I heard him say to Brandy. "You should probably go back to class. I'll talk things over with Alison."

I felt Brandy's hand on my shoulder. "I'm sorry I yelled at you," she said. "I didn't know they had your picture. I would probably have attacked the woman, too. I'll call tonight to see how your mom is doing."

I nodded as she left, but I was still furious. Ian pulled me in for a hug.

"We have to do something," I insisted, "and soon."

"I knew the time was getting close," he said. "The clan chiefs can't make a decision, Brandy is getting weaker each day, and the killings have started again. The dewing you just punched got a text off before you clobbered her. I think it's safe to assume Sebastian knows you're here."

"It's just a matter of time before he comes for me, right?"

"Yes, but this might work to our advantage. We know he went to Seattle because he thought he was going to get information about you. I'd be willing to bet he'll come to Vegas if he knows you're here. I assume he'll have to make some arrangement on his end, but he'll likely give the order to have you picked up within the next day or so. We need a change of plan."

"Okay, what do you want me to do?"

"Maybe nothing. We could let Sebastian's people come for you. Brandy and I will stick close. Then when they try to pick you up…I'll get one of them to tell us where Sebastian is, and we move on as we planned."

Maybe it wasn't the best plan, but it would get me to Sebastian fast, and that's what I wanted. It was going to be him or me. "I just want one thing," I said, pulling back to look at him. "I want an army of your dad's friends around to protect my family."

"They'll be here by this afternoon," Ian agreed. "I hate putting you in this position when you're still so vulnerable."

"I'm ready," I stated.

He picked up my hand to look at my reddened knuckles. "You've got a great left hook, by the way."

I examined my hand more closely. My knuckles were swollen and smeared with dried blood. "I thought I was a pacifist," I said.

He chuckled. "We need to tell Brandy what we're going to do."

"I'm cutting for the rest of day," I said. "I need to check on my mom at the hospital and drive over to the Shadow Box. I need to talk to Lillian."

"I'll go with you. At least until you get to Lillian's. Then I'm going to talk to your mom's surveillance team. They screwed up today." With his arm over my shoulder, we went back inside.

"Think you can thoughtmake the secretary into checking us both out for the day?" he asked.

"I could do it in my sleep," I replied.

Lillian was waiting for me when I got to the Shadow Box that afternoon. The minute she saw my face, she asked, "Sebastian found you, didn't he?"

The answer must have been written in my expression, because she said, "We are sometimes at our strongest when we don't have the luxury of overthinking things."

She led me to a chair by the window and we sat down. "What are you going to do now?" she asked.

"Let Sebastian come for me. When he does, we fight him."

"Sounds like suicide," she said.

"You're always so optimistic."

She thought a moment. "I've lived a long life. I'll come, too."

I laughed. Lillian would never change. "I can't have you come. I need you to look out for the McKyes. Ian said he'll have extra people on it, but I don't know them. I'll be able to concentrate better on what I need to do if you're protecting them, too."

"Fine," she agreed. "But I'd give almost anything to see Sebastian Truss die."

"I promise to give you all the gory details if I survive. In case I don't, I want to say thank you for watching over me all this time and for giving me the perfect job. I love you for that."

Lillian was a little shocked that I'd said I loved her, but I did. She was sour and grumpy most of the time, but she'd looked out for me. I'd come to depend on her without knowing it. I'd really miss her antisocial attitude when I left. She gazed out the window for a moment.

When she looked back at me, her eyes were watery. "I wasn't always like I am today," she said with a sad smile. "I know what people think of me. They think I'm distant and unpleasant. But I wasn't always like this. I was young like you once. I had family and friends. I was full of hope, happiness, and dreams." She shook her head. "But over time, my hopes were disappointed. Those I loved died or moved in different directions, and my happiness dimmed.

"In order to cope, I withdrew from everyone. I thought I could limit the pain that way, but another kind of pain took its place." A tear rolled down her softly wrinkled cheek. "There are two kinds of emotional pain. The pain of loving and letting go, and the pain of never loving at all. I've come to believe that never loving at all hurts worse. My advice is to love with an open heart. If you have to leave the love behind, at least you have memories to take with you."

I knew how much it cost Lillian to open herself up like that. She sniffed and wiped away the tear. Then she was back to her stoic self. "Did you find anything useful in Angela's notes?" she asked.

"No, but I haven't gone through all of them yet."

"Why don't you sit here and read through the rest of the notebook? I'll take care of the store today."

"Thanks, Lillian. I've got to make a call and check up on my mom first. Then I'll get right to it," I said.

She gave me a half smile and then walked away.

I made myself push through Angela's entries until I reached the last one. *They came to the house,* she'd written. *John and I held them off, but we're on the run now. My sister has been forced to run as well. We can't seek shelter in the clan. We pose too great a danger to them. If I could figure it out, if I could break through the barrier, I would have something to bargain with. I would have something to trade my life and John's for. Tomorrow will be the end one way or another. He's sent an army after us this time. I can sense the Truss all around us. In all my years, I've never sensed such greed in a clan before. It shrouds them like a cloud…I told John to run, but he won't. He says he'll die anyway. He'd rather be close to me when it happens.*

I closed my eyes. As sad as the last entry was, there was something in it, a clue. I made myself feel the differences between human thoughts and dewing thoughts as I reread it.

I felt again the open places in the human mind that allowed my thoughts in and the steady ropelike thought strand in the dewing mind where no open places existed.

Then it happened. Like seeing a four-by-five photo switch into a panoramic view, my outlook was widened and deepened.

Human thoughts were choppy and messy. So much so that they diverged from the thoughts of other humans. Human thoughts were messy but unique to the individual, shooting off of a main thought like the branches of a tree. Dewing thoughts were like a rope that connected all of their minds together. That's why Angela had been able to feel the greed of the Truss around her. That's why dewing could sense one another and feel clan affiliation. It even explained likeness to a certain degree.

Somewhere deep in the dewing mind, beneath the thought strand I already knew was there, there had to be another strand. One that ran between all dewing at once, a sort of shared consciousness.

Angela had been looking for a way to break through the dewing thought pattern. There wasn't one, but what if a thoughtmaker could wrap around the strand of shared consciousness? Was that cloaking?

The voice in my mind whispered, *Yes.*

I couldn't be sure if the process worked until I tried it out.

At ten to seven, Lillian came to sit at the window with me again. She thrust an envelope into my hands. "For unexpected expenses if you decide to leave," she said. I checked inside and found a couple thousand dollars in cash. I started to object and hand it back to her, but she refused to take it. "There's one condition. When you finish Sebastian Truss, you have to contact me."

We both knew that would depend on whether I was still alive. "I will," I promised.

We sensed Ian coming before the bells above the door jingled. "I can't decide if you're really brave or truly insane," Lillian muttered, looking up at him.

"What's bravery or sanity when you've got destiny on your side?" Ian replied.

Without a good-bye for either of us, she got up and headed for the back of the store.

Ian sat next to me. He wasn't in a hurry to start a conversation. He just hummed while looking out onto the street. A feeling of peaceful connectedness washed over me. Ian was my friend. Maybe in a different life, we could have been more than friends. Whatever it was between us at that moment, I liked how it felt to be around him. I gave myself permission to enjoy it.

We watched the shadows grow a little longer on the street. "I'd better get you home," Ian said eventually. He got up and pulled me to my feet. "You ready to go?"

I took a last look around the Shadow Box. "Yes," I replied.

I walked in the door of my house, knowing my life would never be the same. I wanted to make something special for the last meal I would share with the McKyes, but it was late, so I made spaghetti. The dinner was quiet. No great bruises up the side of my head to talk about, no sleepovers to discuss, and no birthdays to celebrate. Mom was okay, and my car was back in our garage. My dad said it had been an easy fix—it just needed new spark plugs.

I took mental snapshots of my family doing the normal things I'd taken for granted for years. Mom was recovering from the dewing's attack at my school and lying on the couch to rest. There was no doubt in my mind she'd try to go to the gym the next day. My easygoing dad, who saw the bright side of any problem, was watching the news. And Alex, the gangly boy who'd been my closest friend during the last three years, was playing Xbox in the den.

The next morning, I packed my backpack the same way I'd done for years. Then I sneaked into my parents' room and took Mom's turquoise bracelet, the one the same color as Ian's eyes, from her jewelry box. She rarely wore it, and I felt sure she wouldn't realize it was missing for a while. I took one of my dad's fancy handkerchiefs out of his drawer. It smelled like his cologne. Holding it to my nose, I breathed in and let my mind show me all of the wonderful memories I had of him.

Once Alex had gone down to breakfast, I searched through the drawers of his desk. I found a picture of him playing with Tsar and another of us warring at some video game. I figured he'd know if those went missing, so I settled for taking a couple of pretty rocks from his collection. Hiding these treasures in my backpack, I went downstairs to breakfast.

Brandy called while I was clearing my place. "Can you

pick me up today?" she asked. "I left the headlights on last night and ran the battery out."

"Sure, but can't Ian jump it with his car?"

"He left early. He's already at school."

"I'll be there in ten minutes," I said.

It wasn't part of my usual routine to kiss my parents before leaving for school, but I did it that day. Mom and Dad were surprised but also pleased. The happiness and pride I saw in their eyes as they looked at me nearly broke my heart.

Alex moved fast when he saw me coming. So I smacked him on the top of the head as a farewell gesture…and then I left.

Chapter Twenty-Two

"I haven't felt any of Sebastian's people around," Brandy said as I drove out of the Thanes' gates. "They're bound to show up soon, though."

Brandy seemed fine to me, but as we drove I could tell her energy had dropped again during the night. It was best that Sebastian was coming for me. She was fading too fast to wait. That thought made me choke up a little. "Thank you, Brandy," I said. "Thank you for being my friend. Thank you for helping me with all of this."

"Of course," she replied with a smile. "I wish I could see the future like Katherine. I'd like to know how things turn out for you and Ian."

"You mean if we live or die? I'd like to know that, too."

"You'll live," she said with a certainty I didn't share.

"But that's not what I mean. I think you two are good for each other. Maybe destiny intends for you to be together."

"I don't think I'm meant to be with anyone," I said quietly. "At least not for very long. I know you care for Ian. Believe me, you don't want him to get tangled up in the mess of my life."

She laughed. "Messes don't scare Ian. He likes to sort them out."

"Some of them can't be sorted out."

She tipped her head to the side. "But there's a lot of fun to be had while you try."

I smiled at her and then said, "I'm going to miss you."

"Don't be sad. I'm going to be with Jack again. My death shouldn't be a sad thing to anyone."

"You think you're actually going to be with him again?"

"We have no religion or teachings about what happens after we die, but I've always felt that we continue on. Even though I can't see him, I feel Jack around. I know he'll be waiting for me when I'm done here."

I thought back to the times I'd heard that voice speak to me. In my heart, I'd always known it was my mother's voice, the voice of the White Laurel. As crazy as it once would have seemed to me, maybe Brandy was right and we did exist in some form after death.

"I'm going to ask you to do something for me, Alison," she said, sounding very serious. "I know you're unsure about the future, but I need you to help Ian. He and I dealt with Jack's death together, but I'm the one that came out of it in better shape. Ian not only misses Jack, he feels guilty about taking his place as heir to the clan chiefdom. He can't see himself in that role, and it hangs over him. If you don't want to stay with him, at least check in on him from time to time. Help him remember this time in his life and what he's accomplished."

I pulled my car into a parking space and cut the engine. "I will."

Brandy reached over to hug me. She pulled my head to her shoulder and patted my hair the way a mother would a child. It was the first indication she'd ever given that she was three times my age. Then she pushed me back to arm's length. "You deserve to be happy," she said. "Remember that."

"I'll remember."

Reaching into the front of her backpack, she pulled a folded paper out. "This is for you. Don't read it until our business with Sebastian is finished."

I nodded and put the paper in my pocket. Brandy was smiling when I looked up.

"I think the Golden One wants to talk to you," she said, pointing toward Ian, who was coming our way. She pretended to get a phone call when he opened my car door. Motioning for us to go ahead, she winked at me.

"Are you ready for this?" Ian asked.

"Ready as I'll ever be."

Aware that hostile eyes were probably watching, I kept my expression neutral when I glanced over at him. The sun glinted off his light hair and brightened the color of his eyes. *He's the most beautiful man I've ever seen.*

In a strange parallel, he whispered, "You're beautiful."

I laughed. "I didn't know you had vision problems."

"I don't. I thought you were beautiful the first time I saw you standing in line at registration. In spite of those ugly glasses and your reluctance to return a smile."

"You're beautiful to me, too, Ian."

"Of course I am," he said, cocking his head to the side.

I pushed him hard in the arm. He just laughed. When we reached the side doors of the school, he put his arm around my waist and pulled me between the brick wall and a tree that sheltered us from onlookers. He put his hand on the back of my neck, and my eyes closed in response. I leaned into him when he kissed me gently on the lips. "We're going to get through this," he whispered.

I opened my eyes. "I hope so."

"We will," he insisted, making me look at him. "You have to believe it as much as I do. You never backed down from anything we threw at you this week. Your abilities run as deep as any of us hoped they would, and you learn on the fly. You will be strong today, and Brandy and I will be right behind you."

"Are you scared?" I asked.

"A little, but fear isn't a bad thing for me. It quickens my reaction time."

I thought about my conversation with Spencer the day after Ian killed the tiger. He said his son was a trained fighter with extraordinary energy. I knew that was true. I'd seen what Ian could do with my own eyes. I hoped desperately that his abilities would be enough when he fought Sebastian.

"Don't get killed," I ordered.

He hugged me tight. "That's second on my to-do list. First on my list is to make sure you don't get killed."

Chapter Twenty-Three

The snatch took place in a crowded hallway between third and fourth periods. I couldn't feel any dewing vibration around, so it was a complete surprise when a needle punctured the skin on my upper arm. I had enough time to turn around and look for the human that had given me the shot, but there were too many people around to tell which it had been. Fear tightened my chest as the world around me shrank to a tiny pinpoint of light.

I woke up facedown on a mattress with no idea where I was. It took me a few seconds to remember what had happened. Rolling onto my back, I felt a heaviness in my body from whatever drug they'd given me. I rubbed my eyes, trying to clear the haze from my mind.

Sitting up, I realized I was wearing a white dress with

lace at the hem. It didn't fit well. The arms were too short, and the middle was baggy on me.

Concentrating, I felt for dewing vibrations. I could pinpoint three. One came from the next room. I knew exactly whom it was coming from. The other two were farther away and unfamiliar to me. I was in no hurry to see the dewing in the next room, so I walked to the window and parted the curtains.

In the soft dusk, the Las Vegas Strip was already lit up like Christmas on steroids. I'd assumed Sebastian would fly me out of Vegas as soon as he could. For the first time ever, I thanked destiny for proving me wrong. Being in Vegas, at least for a little while longer, would make it easier for Ian and Brandy to find me.

I checked around for my backpack and found it resting against the dresser. My jeans and T-shirt were nowhere to be found. I would have changed back into them if I could.

A tray had been left on the dresser. An assortment of small sandwiches and cakes as well as a crystal pitcher of ice water had been artistically arranged on it. There was also a soft-looking shawl folded over the end of the bed and a pair of white slippers with shiny beads in the shape of flowers over the toes. The ugly slippers upped the creep factor significantly.

I'd read accounts of ancient human sacrifices in which the sacrifice was fed and dressed in the finest before being strapped to an altar to have his or her heart ripped out. Icy pins prickled down my spine. To keep myself from losing it, I repeated *Katherine saw Sebastian Truss dead* over and over in my mind.

I couldn't bring myself to sit on the bed again, so I went to the double doors at the far end of the room and flung them open. The outer room was just as lush as the bedroom, but one thing in it didn't fit the setting. Luke Stentorian was sitting hunched in chair in the middle of the room. His mousy brown hair was standing on end, and he had his face in his hands. When he looked up, he was his usual sickly self, only with two days' beard and wrinkled clothes.

"Hello, Luke," I said with contempt.

His eyes were watery when he replied, "Hello, Alison."

"That's all you've got to say?" I mocked. Sitting in a chair opposite him with my back ramrod straight and my fists clenched, I continued, "I thought you'd try for something more dramatic, like, 'Prepare to be crushed by my pal Sebastian.'"

Luke looked down at the floor again.

"I'd ask why you're here," I said, "but it's fairly obvious. Sebastian left you to guard me, didn't he? By the way, how does it feel to work for a monster like him? Is it everything you imagined it would be?"

"I don't work for Sebastian," he muttered.

"Spare me the act. I'm not that stupid. You've been sending him information about the clan chiefs. You're the freaking coward who ran to tell Sebastian who I was. You're the reason I'm here, you sickly creep."

"I'm not," Luke said quietly. "I would never work for Sebastian. My parents hated him and what he did to your clan. I would never betray their memory…or you. Sebastian's people drugged me and dumped me here without telling me why. I was only half conscious when they brought you in."

"Play it that way, Luke," I said with a sneer.

"I'm not working for Sebastian," he repeated.

I glared at the skinny, sweating man in front of me and wanted to believe he was lying.

But somehow I knew he wasn't.

I wanted to be mad at someone, I wanted to hate someone, and I wanted to hit someone. But it wouldn't be Luke.

"Why are we here, Alison?" he asked in a pathetic voice.

"I'm here because Sebastian wants to control my joining."

"No one has come since they dropped you in the bedroom. There are two guards at the door. They switch off with other Truss every hour."

"How many dewing do you think Sebastian has here?"

He concentrated and then said, "Around thirty. I can't understand how Sebastian got so many of his clan into the city without Spencer knowing."

"Spencer has been gone for two days," I informed him. "If there are thirty Truss in the casino, they outnumber Spencer's friends at least three to one."

"What are we going to do?" Luke muttered.

"Are you any good at essence fighting?"

"Not really."

"That's one thing we have in common. I'm not, either. But we have to be ready to fight. This thing is going to come down to a good old-fashioned knuckle-busting essence crushing. That's all I can tell you."

I felt an energy shift outside the door. I heard grunts of

pain and thumps as bodies hit the floor and walls. There was fighting going on in the hallway. I ran to the door, feeling for confirmation. When door pushed inward, so did a rush of heat. Brandy smiled up at me. Behind her I saw Ian's blond head drive into the stomach of one of the door guards. The guard grunted and tried to sideswipe Ian's feet. Ian dodged and twisted the man's arm behind his back before driving him to the floor. I heard the air gush out of the guard's lungs and knew Ian had finished him. The other guard was already dead a few feet down the hallway.

Ian got up, breathing hard. Brandy tried to stop me, but I rushed out to him. Ian didn't even look at me. He pushed me out of the way and stomped toward Luke. The poor man tried to back away, but Ian punched him in neck before he got two steps. Luke fell on his back.

"Stop," I yelled.

When Luke turned blue and collapsed onto the floor, Ian grabbed his feet, pulling him out flat. Then he rammed his foot into Luke's abdomen.

"Stop," I yelled again, grabbing Ian's arm. "He's not working for Sebastian."

The look Ian turned on me was full of hostility. I took a step back. It was like he didn't recognize me. Steadying myself, I grabbed him by the upper arms and felt them tense under the pressure of my grip.

"It's me," I said, trying to shake him. "It's me."

His eyes cleared, and I knew he was finally listening. Luke shifted a fraction. Ian watched like he wanted to deliver another kick.

"Listen to me, Ian. He had nothing to do with any of this," I said as calmly as I could. "Sebastian's people brought him here the same way they brought me...against his will and drugged."

Ian took a deep breath and nodded.

"Luke says there are at least thirty of Sebastian's people here," I said. "How did you get past all of them?"

"We used a couple humans to sneak us in," Brandy replied. "I think Sebastian expected a full-frontal attack, not just the two of us. Stealth was on our side for a few minutes, but he knows we're here now."

"We're like fish in a barrel," Luke muttered. "We've got nowhere to run."

"Running isn't part of the plan," I said.

With her head tipped to the side like she was listening, Brandy said, "Two Truss are coming this way."

I ran to get my backpack from the other room. "I guess we're on the right track, then," I responded.

"I couldn't feel Sebastian's vibration when we snuck in," Brandy continued, "but he's definitely here now. There's no mistaking the malevolent vibe I'm getting. The four of us are finally in the same place at the same time."

I looked down at my dress and slippers. "I think I've been dressed up for a special meeting with him."

Brandy pulled a face. "You look awful in that."

"I agree," I said.

"We've got about thirty seconds," Brandy said, tipping her head to the side again.

Ian had gotten it back together. "Whatever happens,"

he whispered, "don't let them separate the three of us. Use your thoughtmaking to keep us together."

I nodded and stepped away from him. Then something occurred to me.

I knelt next to Luke on the floor. He was slightly blue tinged and bleeding from his nose. "Luke, pretend you're passed out when Sebastian's people get here. If they leave you alone, even for a second, get out of the casino. Find Lillian and tell her where we are. Do you understand?"

His eyes were glazed, and he didn't respond.

"Say you'll do it, Luke. Get out and find Lillian."

His eyes focused but he didn't say anything.

"If you don't say something, Luke, I swear I'll hit you again," Ian hissed.

"I'll do it," he muttered. "I'll do it."

"They'll be here in five seconds," Brandy said.

Ian glanced over at me. "Put up enough of a fight to make it seem real, but we'll go with them."

"Okay," I said and then four Truss rushed into the room.

The temperature went up as we fought, but it was over fast. A heavyset woman with her hand squeezing the back of my neck said, "You'll be seeing Sebastian now."

I found her thought strand and wrapped *Take the other two* around it. The room spun from the rebound. "We might as well bring them all," the big woman said.

Brandy caught my eye and winked.

They took us to the elevator and up another floor. When the door opened it revealed a grand apartment. Everything around us glistened and gleamed like it had been polished with money. Even the air smelled like cash.

Two of the Truss guards stayed by the elevator while the remaining two herded us down a wide hallway to a set of gilded doors. When they opened, a great tsunami of vibrating evil washed over me.

He sat behind a desk placed in front of a large window that looked over Sin City. Heavy red curtains at the sides of the window created a stagelike effect with Sebastian as the star.

He was a remarkably normal-looking man, medium build with graying hair. He was probably about Lillian's age. "You can leave now," he said to the Truss flanking us. "If I need you, I'll call for you."

They bent their heads like they would to a king, backed out of the room, and closed the door. Sebastian's face broke into a smile. It was the smile of a wolf about to devour its prey.

Thinking defensively, I formed the thought *You don't want to hurt them* and tried to access Sebastian's mind. He seemed to be waiting for me, and with one shove, he pushed me out. *Why can he feel me in his mind when no other dewing can?* I wondered.

"I've been waiting for you," he said. "Well, waiting for the Laurel, anyway. This is a momentous occasion, something I've waited almost three hundred years for. It's a thrill to have the Thane clan represented while I make my proposal."

I wasn't in the mood for games or stalling. I wanted whatever he was planning to come out in the open. "What do you want from me, Sebastian?" I asked.

His eyes bored into mine with something akin to hunger. That look did more to damage my resolve than anything else. I glanced to Brandy for reassurance and saw she was already fighting his essence. She stood too far away for her heat to reach me, but her face was a mixture of concentration...and pain.

In contrast, Sebastian appeared perfectly composed, and he was carrying on a separate conversation with me. I formed the thought *Leave her alone* and was going to slip it into his mind, but Brandy stopped me. "Stay out, Alison," she insisted. "You're getting in my way."

"You look like your mother," Sebastian said, staring at me. "She was a good friend of mine."

"I doubt that," I replied. "I've been told she hated you."

He shrugged. "Love...hate...two of the strongest emotions any species can feel. "They're so alike in their intensity, so exciting in their own ways."

"The difference is she wanted to kill you."

"She did give it her best," he acknowledged. "Such a strong energy. Much stronger than Jack's likeness here," he added with a quick look at Brandy. "Though I did expect her to be dead by now."

"Not yet," Brandy said through clenched teeth.

Ian looked from Brandy to Sebastian and then back to Brandy again. I could tell he wanted to join the fight but didn't want to mess up whatever Brandy was doing.

I couldn't stand by watching her suffer, so I started to form another thought.

"Stay out of this, Alison," Ian whispered.

"He's right, thoughtmaker," Sebastian said. "There will be plenty of time for us to get to know each other better when I'm done with the Thanes."

Out the corner of my eye, I saw Brandy start to shake. She had broken out in a sweat, too. "It's not right," she said loudly. "He's not like us."

Ian had been waiting to hear something from her, something that would give him an idea where to hit Sebastian. "What does *that* mean?" he asked.

Brandy abruptly dropped to the floor. Ian ran toward Sebastian. He made it halfway across the room and then fell to his knees. Sebastian seemed surprised. "You're strong for someone so young," he said. "But not strong enough."

I didn't know exactly what was happening, but Ian was in trouble. I wasn't above hitting old men when I had to. I started toward Sebastian, too.

His energy hit me like a hammer to the knees. I heard my own breath wheeze out. Stunned by his strength, I stumbled backward. I tried to access his mind again. He was waiting for me but too preoccupied with Ian and Brandy to shove me out immediately. I had enough time to feel something familiar about it before he shoved me out.

Brandy moaned and rolled onto her back. Her bright eyes met Ian's and then mine. She smiled her lovely smile and then her vibrations ground to a halt.

"Brandy," I cried.

"That was child's play," Sebastian growled. "She was as good as dead the minute she walked through the door. I won't even have to finish her." He leered at me. "I've waited a long time for you, young Laurel. Your mother's final gift to me was acknowledgment that you existed."

I barely heard him. I was choking back tears. My dear, beautiful friend was gone forever.

"Aren't you curious why a dewing of my age has not likenessed?" he asked me.

I pulled myself together. Brandy would want me to fight even if the only weapon I had was a sharp tongue. I wiped my eyes. "I assume it's because you give off disgusting energy," I said.

He barked a laugh at my insult, but he was perspiring now, too. "You and I are unlike other dewing," he said in a superior voice. "One of our greatest advantages is that we can choose our own likeness. I've been waiting for a thoughtmaker. One strong enough to deserve likeness with me. Together the two of us will unite the dewing, deal with humankind, and provide leadership that will ensure survival of our species."

"Any luck finding that unfortunate woman?"

"She just walked through my door," he responded with a sickening smile.

"No," I heard Ian growl.

Sebastian turned to him. "This has nothing to do with you, boy."

As I understood what the ugly dress I was wearing meant, bile rose in my throat. "There's not a snowball's chance in hell of me likenessing with you!" I yelled at the evil old man.

"Come now," Sebastian said. "This is the city of chapels and weddings. And there's so much I can offer you in return."

In front of my eyes, he morphed into the shape of my human mother. "I won't make you choose between the humans you love and the dewing," my mother's voice said. She changed into someone who looked freakishly like my dad. "Come home, Alison," my father's voice said. And then my dad became Alex, with his face contorted in pain. "Help me," he wailed.

"It's not real," Ian said from somewhere that seemed far away.

I came back to myself and forced Sebastian out of my mind.

"That's right, thoughtmaker. I know about your humans. In fact, I know where each one of them is at this very moment. My Truss are poised, ready to bring them to me the second I give word. Make this easy on your humans and on yourself. Likeness with me and insure their safety."

Desperate, I reached into his mind one more time. I felt that something familiar again before he could push me out. He was weakening. He could barely close the door this time. Unfortunately, Ian was weakening faster. The line near his eye was deeply furrowed, and his breathing was shallow. I wondered how much longer he could fight.

I started toward Sebastian once more. His energy hit me in the stomach. I crumpled to the ground and saw a cruel joy on his face, so similar to that on the tiger's face behind the Shadow Box that night. For some reason, that gave it all away. I finally understood why his thoughts felt familiar to me.

He hid it well, but underneath the ordered dewing-like

thought pattern was a jumbled human one, which cleared up what Brandy had meant when she said, "He's not like us." It also explained why the wound my mother had given him hadn't healed right, and why he could feel my presence in his mind when no other dewing could.

"You are a sickness, Sebastian," I said. "You've brought human greed into a species that has a natural aversion to it. You're like a virus, spreading your perverted half-human thoughts through their shared consciousness."

Sebastian's eyes burned. "You guess correctly, thought-maker. My mother was human and my father was dewing. You and I have much in common, though, growing up as children of two worlds." His eyes focused in on me. "You don't see it, do you?" he asked. "You don't have to be human or dewing. Being both makes you a race unto yourself. A superior race, with human ambition and dewing power."

I heard Ian fall to ground. I went to him and grabbed his hand.

"All that is missing in my life," Sebastian continued, "is a partner. Together we can build Atlantis again and rule the world."

"Isn't world domination kind of tired?" I asked with disgust.

"It's world leadership," Sebastian corrected. "Imagine how idyllic this planet would be if Tenebrosus had succeeded eleven thousand years ago. Think of the human wars that would never have occurred, of the human suffering that could have been avoided if we'd shared our technology with them. The dewing would never have been reduced to such paltry numbers. Both species would have lived long and productive lives with such vision in place."

And humankind wouldn't have been able to think or act independent of their dewing captors, I thought.

Pretending to consider what Sebastian was saying, I asked, "What about the Thane?"

"What of him? He'll be dead soon."

My mind worked fast. Ian was going to die if I didn't do something fast. I needed to get Sebastian to direct his energy at something else, so Ian could recover a bit. I had one option. Sebastian had said, "You and I can choose our likeness." That's what I'd do.

The time was right to use what Angela's notes had shown me. I searched the mind of a Truss guard outside the door, looking for the thread of shared consciousness. It was thin and buried deep, but I found it. I formed the thoughts *The Laurel escaped. She's out of the building.* Wrapping it around the small rope was ten times as hard as regular thoughtmaking. The rebound made breathing difficult. I swallowed deeply. If the cloak worked, it might not make a difference anyway.

Then I let the memories replay in my mind. I saw the sweet joy on Brandy's face as she talked about Jack. I saw Spencer kissing Katherine in the kitchen when he thought no one was looking. Then I saw Ian sitting next to me after the pages in my notebook were taken. Ian jumping on the back of the tiger to stop him from crushing my mind. Ian holding me after he'd taken my pain. Ian laughing as I played video games, and Ian promising that he'd keep me safe.

Leaning down, I brushed the soft gold hair back from his face and touched the worry line by his eye. Then I kissed him. *The Laurel and the Thane have likenessed,* I put into Sebastian's mind. The recoil was violent, rocking me backward.

"No!" Sebastian yelled.

I took a deep breath and steadied myself for what was to come. Like a diesel truck, his essence slammed into mine. Now that he thought I belonged with someone else, I was worthless to him, and he hated me.

The full weight and power of his mind was something I'd never imagined. A few days of practice was nowhere near enough to prepare me for this type of attack. I shook as his energy closed around me, and I heard myself moan. Then there was a tingle in my mind as Ian joined my fight. With his guidance, I began to push back against Sebastian instead of withdrawing to the pain in my body. Sebastian advanced anyway, and my agony intensified. I fell to the floor. That's when I felt the energy around my mind crack.

"No, Alison!" Ian yelled, and his mind joined mine more fully.

Sebastian smiled in a vile way. "That was a mistake, infant Thane," he said. "You can't save her if you're dead."

The energy in the room shifted. Sebastian had found an opening into Ian's mind. An opening created when he'd overspent his energy to save me. Ian's face reflected his suffering, and worst of all, his acceptance.

Sebastian's cruel eyes glazed over. "You chose wrong, young thoughtmaker, just as your mother did. She chose a dewing without joining, and you chose a Thane. Neither of you is good enough to serve my purpose."

I hardly cared anymore. I couldn't change Sebastian's mind about me. He wanted me dead, and I was losing Ian. If I was going to die, I was ready.

Then I heard the voice in my mind. *"Don't stop the fight, Jillian! You're stronger than you think!"*

My only coherent thought was to wonder why my dead mother kept talking to me all the time. But then the burning started. It began like a slow flame in my stomach that grew white hot and branched out into my arms and legs. *This is it,* I thought, *this is death.* But instead of feeling my energy die out, it expanded like natural gas igniting.

I felt so full of heat I wondered if my body had become engulfed in flames. As my vision cleared, I saw Sebastian's eyes shifting all over the room. We weren't alone. Neither of us could see them, but we were surrounded by a number of unseen dewing energies. They felt familiar to me. I recognized one of them as Brandy. I thought I recognized anther as Angela, Lillian's sister. One of them was my mother, the White Laurel.

I got to my feet. All the pain of the last few minutes was replaced by white-hot energy. Gathering this power in my mind, I pushed it out at Sebastian. The drapes at the window ignited from the heat, and I saw fear in Sebastian's eyes for the first time.

"You're not a thoughtmaker," he said in a strangled voice. "You're a...conduit."

"Just think of it as karma coming back around to kick

you in the ass," I said, pushing the energy out again and wrapping it around Sebastian's neck. I imagined myself squeezing as tight as I could.

Sebastian transformed into a gasping invalid. He moaned and leaned forward in his chair, his aged body contorting in pain. I waited for the shield around his mind to break. It didn't take as long as I thought it would. He was already spent from fighting Ian and Brandy. When the crack appeared, I reached forward with my essence and let the energy inside me crush him.

His body slipped off the chair and onto the floor. Then I saw the wound my mother had left him with all those years ago. His left leg was missing...entirely.

The rebound hit me all at once, and I dropped like a stage puppet. "*You must finish it,*" the voice in my head said.

I made myself crawl to Sebastian's limp body. I picked up his head and started to turn it the way I'd seen Ian do to the tiger's. Someone burst into the room yelling, "Fire!"

Startled, I dropped Sebastian's body. Through smoke I could see the man looking into the room. He was dressed like one of the cleaning crew and was likely the human Katherine had seen the future through.

"Call 911!" I yelled at him.

The fire from the drapes cast a reddish glow in the room. "*Finish it,*" my mother's voice repeated.

I turned to Sebastian, but a hissing sound caught my attention. The ceiling was on fire, too. The sprinkler system above us came on, but it didn't slow the flames at all. I crawled to Ian. I wouldn't let him die alone. When I found him, there was no sign of life in his body, but I put my cheek on his chest and waited. Gradually, I felt a low hum and then a faint vibration. Then I heard a heartbeat, and his chest rose. He coughed loud.

"You're not dead!" I cried. "You're not dead!"

He opened his eyes slowly, and I started to laugh. An absurd reaction, really, but I laughed and laughed.

"Did you finish Sebastian?" Ian asked weakly.

I felt for his vibration. There was nothing there. "I crushed his mind," I replied, looking toward the body. "I think he's dead enough."

"You have to make sure," Ian insisted.

So I crawled back into the middle of the steamy room and found Sebastian's body just as a piece of the ceiling came falling down. Rolling aside in the nick of time, I watched what remained of him burn under the rubble.

"We have to get out of here now," I yelled to Ian. "The entire ceiling is coming down!"

I went back to him and helped him sit up. His movements were feeble, but the light of life was returning to his eyes. "More dewing are here," he said anxiously.

"I know. I tried something new. I think it's time to see if it worked."

Ian leaned heavily on me as I helped him to his feet. Suffering from the rebound myself, I'd never been so thankful for my six feet of lean muscle and size-ten feet. I managed to support him into the hallway but stopped when someone came running toward us.

"Lillian?" I asked. "What are you doing here?"

"Rescuing you," she shouted. "The casino was crawling with Truss, but they all left in a hurry. It's like they were chasing something invisible. We've got to get out before they come back."

She rushed me and Ian toward the emergency exit. Looking down the long flights of stairs, I could have cried. "There's no way we can get him down these," I said.

Spencer burst through a door a couple of flights below and came running up to us.

"Thank goodness," Lillian said, letting Ian's weight fall on his father.

Like it was nothing, Spencer hefted his son over one shoulder and started down the stairs.

"What about Brandy?" I asked remembering her lying dead on the floor in the burning room.

"There's nothing we can do for her now," Lillian said, wrapping a skinny arm around my waist to help me. "I think she would want us to get out of here while we can."

Katherine and the other Thane joined us at various intervals. Pushing through the door at ground level, we saw four fire trucks in front of the building. Casino customers were being escorted out. It was pandemonium. No one noticed our ragtag group crossing the street.

When we found a bench to sit on, Spencer set Ian down, and asked, "Can someone please explain what just happened? I was in the middle of smashing a Truss in the face when he turned and ran away. I know I look tough, but I expected him to put up a fight, at least."

"Pretty much the same thing happened to me," a man

who'd joined us on the stairs said.

The others nodded their heads like they'd had similar experiences.

I watched Ian as they talked. He was soaked from the sprinklers. His hair was covered in ash, and his face was streaked with it, but he was alive. I was alive. When he looked up at me, I could almost read his mind. He was thinking, *Told you we could do it*—or something very much like that.

Spencer and Lillian were still trying to figure out why the Truss had run out of the casino like crazy people.

"I cloaked a thought," I said to put the matter to rest. "I told them I'd escaped the casino and that Sebastian ordered them to go after me."

Chapter Twenty-Four

When we got back to Ian's house, I called home. Alex answered. "Hey, Alison. What's up?"

"Nothing much," I lied. "What's up with you?"

"I'm doing my homework and hoping I don't throw up dinner. We had bean burgers tonight."

I smiled and leaned my head back in the sofa. It was good to know some things never changed. "How are Mom and Dad? Everything is okay with them, right?"

"Yeah," he replied in bored tones. "Mom's on the computer. Dad's watching the news."

"Sounds like a typically boring night at our house."

"Pretty much. This afternoon was exciting, though. Your weird boss showed up at my school."

I glanced toward the dining room table where Lillian

was sitting. "She did?"

"She tackled some guy in the parking lot during my lunch hour. For an old chick, she's got some wicked tae kwon do skills."

"That's super weird."

"Tell me about it."

"Well, I'll be heading home soon," I said. "Tell Mom, will you?"

"Yep," he replied.

"I love you, Alex," I said before he could hang up.

"You keep saying that," he replied, unimpressed.

I ended the call and asked Lillian, "What happened at Alex's school today?"

"Oh, that," she replied. "I stopped a Truss from taking him. I didn't want to be so public about it, but the guy didn't give me a choice."

"Alex said you tae kwon do'd him."

"I just punched him in the neck," she said with a shrug.

We all stared at her. "Well, thanks," I said with a blink.

There was a moment of quiet after that. We'd all used our essences and we were hurting on different levels. Ian was the worst off by far. Katherine had tucked him under a blanket to help with the reverse heating thing, but he was pale and his eyes kept losing focus. I slid closer to him, so he could lean on me a little.

"How did Luke get to you guys so fast?" I asked.

"Luke," Katherine said. "We haven't seen Luke since he left town."

"He wasn't the mole," I said. "Sebastian had him locked

up in the casino with me. After Ian took the guards out, we sent him to find Lillian."

"I never saw Luke," Lillian said. "When Spencer and Katherine got back into town, I told them what the three of you were doing, and they started feeling out your location. Thankfully, it didn't take long to find you."

"We knew we were outnumbered," Spencer said, "but I wasn't going to wait for more help."

"You wouldn't have gotten very far if the thoughtmaker hadn't done her cloaking thing," Ian said in a cracked voice. "That was amazing."

I smiled over at him.

"Why are you dressed like that?" Katherine asked me.

"This is my wedding dress," I said, still grossed out. Everyone but Ian was stunned. "Sebastian wanted me to choose to likeness with him, so the two of us could rule the world together."

"Choose to likeness," Lillian repeated with disgust. "Even if you wanted to likeness with him, you couldn't make it happen."

"Maybe she can," Ian replied.

"Sebastian was half human," I explained. "He said being that way meant he could choose his own likeness."

"That's just ridiculous," Spencer said. "Aside from the fact that neither human nor dewing are attracted to each other after a certain point, a pairing between our species wouldn't produce viable offspring. We've done tests to prove it."

"Whatever your test results," I said, "it's possible.

Sebastian was part human. He tried to hide it, but I can tell the difference between human thoughts and dewing thoughts now. His were definitely human. Because we had that in common, he thought we could choose our likeness."

"He can't have been half human," Katherine said disbelievingly. "Maybe he'd just been raised by humans like you."

I shook my head in denial. "What happens to a dewing when they lose a leg or an arm?"

Spencer thought about it. "It takes some time, but it would grow back."

"Well, Sebastian was missing a leg. That's what my mother did to him when they fought. She must have cut his leg off and it never grew back. That's why he was so reclusive. He couldn't let anyone see him that way, because they'd know he wasn't really dewing. Not entirely, anyway."

"Whatever Sebastian was," Ian said, "his energy was stronger than I'd ever dreamed. I was half dead during whatever Alison did to him."

Lillian watched me, expecting the details I'd promised her, but I didn't want to explain everything about my fight with Sebastian Truss. Not yet, anyway. He'd called me a conduit, and I knew what that meant. All the energies around me back in his office had been the energies of the dewing he'd killed. I was just the gate they'd come through. The problem was, I didn't know how or if I could ever open the gate again.

Feeling too tired to explain it all, I said, "Sebastian was weak after his fight with Brandy and Ian. Ian was in bad shape, and I needed to get Sebastian to direct his attention to me. His main goal was to get me to likeness to him, so I used thoughtmaking to get him to believe I'd already likenessed to Ian. That really pissed him off, but it confused him, too. That's when my essence rose, and I crushed his mind."

It was an anticlimactic explanation, and I knew Ian suspected I was holding back. It was good enough for Lillian, though. "You finished him, right?" she asked me.

"I didn't have to. He was on fire when the ceiling collapsed on him."

"Hmm," Lillian said. "I would sure like to have been there when he died."

Silence settled for a moment. "What are we going to do for Brandy?" I asked quietly. "I hate that we had to leave her...body behind."

Ian studied his hands, and Katherine wiped her eyes. "We don't hold funerals," Spencer said. "But maybe in this case we could have a memorial or something."

"Yes," Katherine said. "That's what we'll do."

"So what now?" Lillian asked.

"I get to go home," I said, with a tear falling. It was the first time I'd let any out in years. "I'll go back to school and maybe even college."

"We'll be around for a while, too," Spencer said smiling. "Katherine and I have decided to stay in Vegas for a while. Ian wants to continue at Fillmore, so the three of us will be around to help you learn more about your heritage and abilities."

I'd expected that the Thanes would go back to their lives as soon as our business with Sebastian was finished. They'd changed their plans to help me. I took a deep breath as I looked at them. "Thank you," I said.

After that, Spencer and Katherine walked Lillian out. When Ian and I were alone, I looked inside my backpack, where I'd put Brandy's letter. I pulled it out and unfolded it. "Brandy gave me this," I said. "She told me not to read it until the fight was over. I think she meant for you to read it, too."

Ian looked over my shoulder as I read. *Dear Alison, If you're reading this, you lived. I can't tell you how happy that thought makes me. I want to say thank you for helping us carry out our crazy plan to fight Sebastian Truss tonight. If we were successful in our work, the world will be a better place tomorrow. If we weren't successful, you are part of a different puzzle with different players that will one day defeat him. You are truly gifted among us. No other dewing could have learned so much so fast. I know you were abandoned and hurt when you were young. I can't begin to understand why destiny placed you in such a position, but I hope in the end you won't turn away from those who care about you. Please tell the Golden One I never thought of him as an imitation of his father or Jack. He has always been the real thing. Remember your promise to me and be happy. Love, Brandy.*

I closed the note, wiped my tears away and leaned my head against Ian's shoulder. "Wherever she is now, I know she's happy," I said.

"Me, too," he agreed.

Looking down at my clothing, I said, "We need to have a bonfire in your backyard, so I can burn this dress."

I went home to find my parents cuddled up on the sofa again. Seeing me standing in the doorway, Mom asked, "How did it go today?"

Well, I'd been drugged, kidnapped, and almost killed. As usual, it was the almost that really mattered. "Same as always," I said, coming in.

"Where did you get those clothes?" she asked.

I had no idea what Sebastian's people had done with my clothes. I'd borrowed a shirt and pants from Katherine. The pants were about four inches too short. "Ah…I borrowed them from Ian's mom. I spilled something at dinner."

Mom got up. She touched my hair and kissed my cheek. "You're such a pretty girl," she said, "and almost all grown-up. You'll be at college this time next year. I can hardly believe it."

"Don't worry," I said. "We'll make the most of the time we've got until then."

I said good night to my parents and hauled my tired, sore self up to bed.

The next morning I sat up slowly, testing my muscles. As expected, I was stiff, but I could still move, which was saying a lot since I hadn't been able to walk after the tiger attacked me. The white-hot energy that had flowed through me last night must have had some kind of healing power.

Pulling back the covers, I saw Brandy's letter lying haphazardly on my nightstand. I'd been too tired to know what to do with it the night before. Picking it up, I ran my fingers over the creases in the paper. Brandy's fingers had folded the paper just a day before…now she was gone. She hadn't wanted me think of her death as a tragedy. To her it was an evolution. I would try to see it that way, too. But I would miss her.

I opened the top drawer of my nightstand and put her note between the pages of my dog-eared copy of *Dragonsong*. I wondered if she had ever read the book. I thought she would have liked it.

Mom was sipping a cup of herbal tea at the table when I went to the kitchen. She looked me up and down. "You love me, don't you, Alison?" she asked.

I poured myself some cereal. "Of course I love you, Mom."

"Then for the love of all that is holy, will you please let me buy you some clothes with color in them?"

I chuckled. I'd actually been considering a wardrobe update. "How about we go to the mall this Saturday?" I suggested.

Mom sighed deeply. "Finally," she muttered.

Alex came in looking upset. "Have you guys seen my rocks?" he asked.

I gave him a blank look.

"Two of my favorite rocks are missing from my collection," he said, sitting down.

"You have a million rocks in your collection. How can you know if two of them are missing?" I asked

"I really like my rocks," he replied. "I just know."

"What would your friends say if they knew how much you liked your rocks?" I asked.

"Nothing. Ben collects yo-yos. Mike likes old Hot Wheels. I like my rocks. What's the big deal?"

I hid my smile behind a glass of orange juice. "If I come across them, I'll let you know," I assured him.

At school, I stopped in the north hall to flip through my locker combination. I opened the door and moved things around, but about halfway through the process, I realized it wasn't necessary anymore. The hunt for thoughtmakers had ended with Sebastian Truss. I unloaded about half the book weight from my backpack into the locker. Then I tossed the notebooks I never used in the trash can across the hall. An enormous weight had been removed from my back, literally.

On my way down the stairs, I found the kissing couple clogging the way again. The dark space was just too inviting for a couple like Nate and Melissa to stay away from. In a replay of the past, I tapped Nate Hopkins on the shoulder. He mumbled, "Go away," but instead of using thought transference to remedy the situation, I leaned in close to his ear and yelled, "Move, please!"

He jumped backward about a foot.

"Thank you," I said sweetly as I scooted between the pair.

Connor was laughing when I got to class. His shellacked hair was perfectly arranged as usual. Instead of avoiding him, I slid into the desk next to him. "Hey, Alison," he said when I sat. "Where are Brandy and Ian?"

I'd been expecting the question. Everyone liked Brandy.

Connor's question was just the beginning of many to come. I worked hard to keep my voice steady when I responded. "She's going to live with her grandma in Rhode Island. She'd been thinking about it for a while. I guess the timing seemed right to her. She's leaving this morning."

Connor's face fell. He'd really identified with Brandy. "I wish she'd said something about it," he muttered. "But hey, there's always Skype, right?"

I wasn't sure how Ian and I were going to deal with the Skype issue. We'd have to figure something out. "Is Ian coming, then?" Connor asked.

"I'm not sure. He went with his parents and Brandy to the airport."

During class, my eyes kept moving to Brandy's empty chair. Once I thought I caught a glimpse of her sitting there. In the illusion, her black eyes sparkled, and she smiled like she'd never been happier. When I blinked, the phantom was gone.

I was feeling pretty low when the bell for lunch rang. I thought about going for a drive, but then I remembered Brandy and her table in the cafeteria. Her friends would want to know where she was. Connor could tell them, but she would have wanted me to do it. I changed direction and walked toward the cafeteria. After filling my tray with food, I headed to the table at the back of the room. Some of her friends were already there. Felicity Nathanson, the girl I'd talked with at the party, waved me toward her. Everyone welcomed me in like I was a part of their group. Brandy had left me with a ready-made group of friends. Another gift.

After the last bell, I felt Ian's vibration. I couldn't see him, but I knew he was nearby. I couldn't keep a smile off my face.

I found him standing with his shoulder against my locker. He still looked tired, and by the way he shifted his weight, I knew he was sore, too. My breath caught when he smiled at me. Whether I liked it or not, I was half in love with him.

"You don't look so good," I said, mocking him.

"You've never looked better to me."

"I suppose we both look better alive than dead." I opened my locker and exchanged a few books, keeping only the necessities in my backpack.

"I see you're moving on," Ian observed. "I think that's great."

I closed my locker door and spun the lock. "I didn't sense you around today. When did you get here?"

"Mom let me sleep late. They've been busy trying to clean up what we did yesterday. I just dropped by to make sure you were okay."

"I'm good. Except it's been hard explaining to everyone why Brandy won't be coming back to school."

"I'm kind of glad you took care of that. I doubt I'll be up to talking much about her for a while." Ian looked at me as we walked out of the school. "My interfering father has been taking credit for killing Sebastian. According to his version of events, he did it with one arm tied behind his back. He thinks telling everyone that will bring less attention to the situation, so you can remain relatively anonymous while you finish your time here."

I laughed. "I'm fine with it. What about you? Don't you want some of the credit?"

"Nope. I want to forget about it altogether, but that will never happen. There's something I need to tell you."

His tone indicated it wasn't good. "What is it?"

"Nikki Dawning has been missing since the day before yesterday. No one has a clue where she is."

I'd never liked or trusted Nikki, but the news was still upsetting. "What do you think happened?" I asked.

"I really don't know. Bruce and Amelia are doing everything they can to find her."

"And Luke, what about him?"

"My parents found him cowering at home. They had a tech check through all his emails and texts while they drilled him with questions to be certain he wasn't the mole. You were right. He had nothing to do with Sebastian. But Nikki did. She'd been sending emails from Luke's computer to his assistant, Maxwell. It seems they'd become friends somehow. She knew a lot about the clan meetings because her parents went to them. She mentioned her suspicions about you, too."

"I was right about her all along."

"It seems so."

"Do the Truss know Sebastian is dead?"

"My dad made sure of it. His tech hacked into the police department photos of the burned suite at the casino. There were a few gruesome one showing Sebastian's charred remains. Dad had them sent anonymously to some Truss higher-up on the food chain. It's still too soon to know if relations between the Truss and the rest of the clans will improve, but we did our part."

I sighed. "Yes, we did."

"I never doubted we would."

"Never?"

"Okay, maybe once or twice. But my doubt never lasted long. I knew we'd win."

His easy confidence was contagious. I was starting to see that if I could face Sebastian Truss head-on, I could do just about anything. Without thinking about it, I reached up and gently touched the worry line near Ian's eye. "I wish this would go away," I said.

"Is it that bad?" he asked, reaching up to touch it, too.

"No one notices it but me. I hate that you're marked for what you did for me, though."

He smiled. "I'm not."

We stopped at my car, and I put my fingers on the handle to open the door. Ian stopped me. He raised his hand to the side of my face. Then he rubbed my cheekbone with his thumb. I closed my eyes in response, and he rested his forehead on mine. "We make quite a team," he said.

I leaned into him, enjoying the warmth of his breath on my cheek. In spite of my best efforts, this boy I hadn't wanted in my life was now very important to me. I slowly moved away from him. "I have to go in to work," I said. "But if you're feeling up to it, we could go to dinner afterward."

His eyes lit up. "Okay, but you'll be paying. I just won our bet. You asked me to dinner."

"Hey, I didn't accept the terms of that bet."

He laughed. "Fine, but you have to admit I'm pretty irresistible."

I shook my head and laughed. I wouldn't say it out loud, but he was.

Acknowledgments

My sincerest thanks to the amazing Liz Pelletier at Entangled Publishing for being my editor and fierce supporter. So much thanks to Deb Shapiro and Heather Ricco for handling publicity on *Atlantis Rising*. Big thankyou to Meredith Johnson for tying loose ends. Thanks to Laura Ann Gilman and Stacy Abrams for their thoughts on the story. Thanks to Steven Parke for the lovely cover art. Genuine thanks to Madison Pelletier for her thoughts and ideas. And to all the other great people at Entangled who helped turn this dream into reality, I appreciate it more than I can say.

Much thanks to my sister, Jennifer, my beta reader and cheerleader. Thanks to my husband, Mark, for encouraging me to be patient and for taking care of things when I went into writing mode. And lastly, thanks to Ashlee, Alison, Amanda, and Ann, my little ones, for being my inspiration and for understanding when I have to shut the door for writing time.

BY PINTIP DUNN

Imagine a world where your destiny has already been decided...by your future self.

It's Callie's seventeenth birthday and, like everyone else, she's eagerly awaiting her vision—a memory sent back in time to sculpt each citizen into the person they're meant to be. A world-class swimmer. A renowned scientist.

Or in Callie's case, a criminal.

In her vision, she sees herself murdering her gifted younger sister. Before she can process what it means, Callie is arrested and placed in Limbo—a prison for those destined to break the law. With the help of her childhood crush, Logan, a boy she hasn't spoken to in five years, she escapes the hellish prison.

But on the run from her future, as well as the government, Callie sets in motion a chain of events that she hopes will change her fate. If not, she must figure out how to protect her sister from the biggest threat of all—Callie, herself.

Read on for a sneak peek!

1

"THE NEXT LEAF THAT FALLS will be red," my six-year-old sister Jessa announces. An instant later, a crimson leaf flutters through the air like the tail feather of a cardinal.

Jessa grabs it and tucks it into the pocket of her school uniform, a silver mesh jumpsuit that is a smaller version of mine. Crunchy leaves blanket the square, the only burst of color in Eden City's landscape. Behind our patch of a park, bullet trains shoot by in electromagnetic vacuum tubes, and metal and glass buildings vie for every inch of pavement. Their gleaming spirals do more than scrape the sky—they punch right through it.

"Now orange," Jessa says. A leaf the color of overripe squash tumbles from the tree. "Brown." Sure enough, brown as mud and just as dead.

"You going for some kind of record?" I ask.

She turns to me and grins, and I forget all about tomorrow and what is about to happen. My senses fill with my sister. The voice that lilts like music. The way her hair curves around her chin. Her eyes as warm and irresistible as roasted chestnuts.

I can almost feel the patches of dry skin on her elbows, where she refuses to apply lotion. And then, the moment passes. Knowledge seeps through me, the way a person gains consciousness after a dream. Tomorrow, I turn seventeen. I will become, by the ComA's decree, an official adult. I will receive my memory from the future.

Sometimes, I feel as if I've been waiting all my life to turn seventeen. I measure my days not by my experiences but by the time remaining until I receive my memory, the memory, the one that's supposed to give meaning to my life.

They tell me I won't feel so alone then. I'll know, without a shred of doubt, that somewhere in another spacetime exists a future version of me, one who turns out all right. I'll know who I'm supposed to be. And I'll never feel lost again.

Too bad I had to live through seventeen years of filler first.

"Yellow." Jessa returns to her game, and a yellow leaf detaches from a branch. "Orange."

Ten times, fifteen times, twenty, she correctly predicts the color of the next leaf to fall. I clap and cheer, even though I've seen this show, or something like it, dozens of times before.

And then I notice him. A guy wearing my school's uniform, sitting on a curved metal bench thirty feet away. Watching us.

The back of my neck prickles. He can't possibly hear us. He's too far away. But he's looking. Why is he looking? Maybe he has super-sensitive hearing. Maybe the wind has picked up our words and carried them to him.

How could I be so stupid? I never let Jessa stop in the park. I always march her straight home after school, just like my mother orders. But today, I wanted—I needed—the sun, if only for a few minutes.

I place a hand on my sister's arm, and she stills. "We need to leave. Now." My tone implies the rest of the sentence: before the guy reports your psychic abilities to the authorities.

Jessa doesn't even nod. She knows the drill. She drops into step beside me, and we head for the train station on the other side of the square. Out of the corner of my eye, I see him stand up and follow us. I bite my lip so hard I taste blood. What now?

Make a run for it? Talk to him and attempt damage control?

His face comes into view. He has closely cropped blond hair and a ridiculously charming grin, but that's not why my knees go weak.

It's my classmate, Logan Russell, swim team captain and owner of what my best friend Marisa calls the best pecs in this spacetime. Harmless. Sure, he has the nerve to smile at me after ignoring me for five years, but he's no threat to Jessa's well-being.

When we were kids, his brother Mikey made a racquetball hover above the court. Without touching it. ComA whisked him away, and he hasn't been seen since. Logan's not about to report my sister to anyone.

"Calla, wait up," he says, as if it's been days instead of years since we sat next to each other in the T-minus five classroom.

I stop walking, and Jessa clutches my hand. I give her three squeezes to let her know we're safe. "My friends call me 'Callie,'" I tell Logan. "But if you don't already know that, maybe you should use my birthday."

"All right, then." Coming to a stop in front of us, he jams his hands in his pockets. "You must be nervous, October Twenty-eight. About tomorrow, I mean."

I lift my eyebrow. "How would you have the first clue what my feelings are?"

"We used to be friends."

"Right," I say. "I still remember the time you peed your pants on our way to the Outdoor Core."

He meets my gaze head on. "Ditto for the part where you splashed us both with water from the fountain so no one else would know."

He remembers? I look away, but it's too late. I can smell the protein pellets we made a pact never to eat, feel the touch on my shoulder when Amy Willows compared my hair to straw.

"Forget her," the twelve-year-old Logan had whispered, as the credits rolled on the documentary on farming methods before the Technology Boom. "Scarecrows are the coolest ever."

I had gone home and daydreamed I'd received the memory from my future self, and in it Logan Russell was my husband. Of course, that was before I learned the older girls waited until a boy received his future memory before deciding if he was a good match. Who cares if Logan has dimples, if his future doesn't show sufficient credits to provide for his family? He may have a swimmer's physique today, but it might very well melt into fat twenty years from now.

By the time I figured out my crush was premature, it didn't matter. The boy of my dreams had already stopped talking to me.

I cross my arms. "What do you want, October Twenty-six?"

Instead of responding, he moves behind Jessa. She's taken the leaves from her jumpsuit and is twisting them around each other to make them look like the petals of a flower. Logan sinks down beside her, helping her tie off the "bud" with a sturdy stem.

Jessa beams as if he's given her a rainbow on a plate. So he makes my sister smile. It's going to take more than a measly stem to compensate for five years of silence.

They fool around with the leaves—making more "roses," combining them into a bouquet—for what seems like forever. And then Logan holds one of the roses up to me. "I got my memory yesterday."

My arms and mouth drop at the same time. Of course he did. I'd just used his school name. How could I forget?

Logan's birthday is two days before mine. It's why we sat next to each other all those years. That's how the school orders us—not by last name or height or grades, but by the time remaining until we receive our future memory.

I notice the hourglass insignia, half an inch wide, tattooed on the inside of his wrist. Everyone who's received a future memory has one. Underneath the tattoo, a computer chip containing your future memory is implanted, where it can be scanned by prospective employers, loan officers, even would-be parents-in-law.

In Eden City, your future memory is your biggest recommendation. More than your grades, more than your credit history. Because your memory is more than a predictor. It's a guarantee.

"Congratulations," I say. "To whom am I speaking? A future ComA official? Professional swimmer? Maybe I should get your autograph now, while I still have the chance."

Logan gets to his feet and brushes the dirt from his pants. "I did see myself as a gold-star swimmer. But there was something else, too. Something…unexpected."

"What do you mean?"

He takes a step closer. I'd forgotten his eyes are green. They're the green of grass before summer, a sheen caught somewhere between vibrant and dull, as if the color can't decide whether to thrive in the sun or wither in its heat.

"It wasn't like how we were taught, Callie. My memory didn't answer my questions. I don't feel at peace or aligned with the world. I just feel confused."

I lick my lips. "Maybe you didn't follow the rules. Maybe your future self messed up and sent the wrong memory."

I can't believe I said that. We spend our entire childhood learning how to choose the proper memory, one that will get us through the difficult times. And here I am, telling another person he screwed up the only test that matters. I didn't think I had it in me.

"Maybe," he says, but we both know it's not true. Logan is

smart, too smart to be beat by me in the T-minus seven spelling bee, and too smart to mess this up.

And then I get it. "You're kidding. In the future, you're the best swimmer the country has ever seen. Right?"

Something I can't identify passes over his face. And then he says, "Right. I have so many medals, I need to build an addition to my house in order to display them."

He wasn't kidding, something inside me yells. He's trying to tell you something.

But if Logan's one of the anomalies I've heard rumors about—the ones who receive a bad memory, or worse, no memory at all—I don't want to know about it. We haven't been friends for half a decade. I'm not going to worry about him just because he's deemed me worthy of his attention again.

Suddenly, I can't wait for the conversation to end. I reach for Jessa's hand and connect with her elbow. "Sorry," I say to Logan, "but we need to get going."

Jessa hands him the bouquet of leaves, and I tug her away. We are almost out of earshot when he calls, "Callie? Happy Memory's Eve. May the joy of the future sustain you through the trials of the present."

It's the standard salutation, spoken the day before everyone's seventeenth birthday. In the past, Logan's address would have filled my cheeks with warmth, but this time his words only send the chill creeping up my spine.

WE WALK INTO THE HOUSE to the smell of chocolate cake. My mother's in the eating area, her dark brown hair twisted into a bun, still wearing her uniform with the ComA insignia stitched across the pocket. She's a bot supervisor at one of the agencies, but she gets paid by the Committee of Agencies, or ComA, the governmental entity who runs our nation.

We drop our school bags and run. I hug my mother from behind as Jessa attacks her legs. "Mom! You're home!"

My mother turns. Powdered sugar clings to her cheek, and chocolate frosting darkens one eyebrow. The red light that normally blinks on our Meal Assembler is off. Actual ingredients—packets of flour, a small carton of milk, real eggs—lay strewn across the eating table.

I raise my eyebrows. "Mom, are you cooking? Manually?"

"It's not every day my daughter turns seventeen. I thought I'd try making a cake, in honor of my future Manual Chef."

"But how did you…" My voice trails off as I spot the small rectangular machine on the floor. It has a glass door with knobs along one side, two metal racks, and a coil that turns red when it's hot.

An oven. My mother bought me a functioning oven.

My hand shoots to my mouth. "Mom, this must have cost a hundred credits! What if…what if my memory doesn't show me as a successful chef?"

"It wasn't easy to find, I'll give you that." She takes off the rag around her waist and shakes it. A cloud of flour puffs into the air. "But I have complete faith in you. Happy Memory's Eve, dear heart."

She hoists Jessa onto her hip and pulls me into a hug so that we are in a circle of her arms, the way it's always been. Just the three of us.

I have few memories of my father. He is not so much a gaping hole in my life as he is a shadow who lurks around the corner, just out of reach. I used to pester my mom for details, but tonight, on the eve of my seventeenth birthday, the heavy knowledge of him is enough.

My mother begins to clear the ingredients off the table, the bare, gleaming skin of her wrist catching the light that emanates from the walls. She doesn't have a tattoo. Future memories didn't arrive systematically until a few years ago, and my mother wasn't lucky enough to receive one.

Maybe if she had, she wouldn't have lost her job. My mother used to be a medical aide, but as more and more applicants came with memory chips showing futures as competent diagnosticians, it had only been a matter of time before she got downgraded to bot supervisor. "You can hardly blame them," she had said with a shrug. "Why take a risk when you can bet on a sure thing?"

We sit down to a dinner usually reserved for the New Year. Everything has the slightly plastic taste of food prepared in the Meal Assembler, but the spread itself is unrivaled by the best manual cooking establishments. A whole roast chicken, its skin golden brown and crispy. Mashed potatoes fluffy with butter. Sugar snap peas sautéed with cloves of garlic.

We don't talk through most of dinner—can't talk, our mouths are so full. Jessa savors the snap peas like they are candy, nibbling at the ends and rolling them around her mouth before sucking the entire pods down.

"We should have invited that boy to dinner," she says, a snap pea dangling from her mouth. "We've got so much food."

Mom's hand stills on the serving spoon. "What boy?" she pries.

"Just one of my classmates." I feel my cheeks growing red and then remind myself that I have no reason to be embarrassed. I don't like Logan anymore. I help myself to more dark meat. "We ran into him at the park. It was no big deal."

"Why were you even there in the first place?"

The chicken suddenly feels dry in my mouth. I messed up. I know that. But I couldn't bear to be stuck inside today. I needed to feel the sun's warmth on my face, to look at the leaves and imagine my future.

"We only talked to him for a minute, Mom. Jessa was calling out the color of the leaves before they fell, and I wanted to make sure he didn't hear—"

"Wait a minute. She was doing what?"

Uh oh. Wrong answer. "It's no big deal—"

"How many times?"

"About twenty," I admit.

My mother pulls the necklace from under her shirt, where it normally resides, and rubs the cross between her fingers. We're not supposed to wear religious symbols in public. It's not that religion is illegal. Just…unnecessary. The traditions of the pre-Boom era gave their believers comfort, hope, and reassurance—in short, everything that future memory provides us now. The only difference is we actually have proof that the future exists. When we do pray, it's not to any god, but to Fate herself and the predetermined course she's set.

But my mom can be excused for clinging to one of the old faiths. She never got her glimpse of the future, after all.

"Calla Ann Stone." She grips the cross. "I depend on you to keep your sister safe. That means you do not allow her to speak to strangers. You do not stop in a park on your way home from school. And you do not display her abilities for anyone to see."

I look at my hands. "I'm sorry, Mom. It was just this once. Jessa is safe, I promise. Logan's own brother was taken by ComA. He would never tell on her."

At least, I don't think he would. Why did he talk to me

today? For all I know, he was spying on Jessa. Maybe he's working for ComA now. Maybe his report will be the one that sends my sister away.

Or maybe it has nothing to do with Jessa. Maybe the falling leaves reminded him of another time, when we used to be friends. My mind drifts to an old book of poems Mom gave me for my twelfth birthday. Pressed in between the pages, next to a poem by Emily Brontë, is a crumbling red leaf. The first leaf Logan ever gave me. A small piece of my heart, one I didn't even know still existed, knocks against my chest.

"You were lucky." My mother strides to the counter and snaps up the cake stand. "Next time might not work out so well."

She plunks the stand on the eating table and lifts the dome. The chocolate cake is higher on one side than the other, the frosting glopped on and messy. Each mark of the handmade-ness reproaches me. See how hard your mother worked? This is how you repay her?

"There's not going to be a next time," I say. "I'm sorry."

"Don't apologize to me. Think how you would feel if you never saw your sister again."

The chocolate cake swims before my eyes. This is so unfair. I would never let them take Jessa away from us. My mother knows this. I just wanted to see the sun. The world is not over.

"That's not going to happen," I say.

"You don't know that."

"I will! You'll see. I'll get my memory tomorrow, and in it we'll be happy and safe and together forever. Then you won't be able to yell at me anymore!" I leap to my feet, and my arm knocks the stand. It tips onto the floor, breaking the cake into a hundred different pieces.

Jessa cries out and runs from the room. I'd forgotten she was still here.

My mom sighs and moves around the table to put her hand on my shoulder. The tension melts away, leaving behind our shared guilt for arguing in front of Jessa.

"Which do you want? Clean up this mess, or talk to your sister?"

"I'll talk to Jessa." I usually leave the hard stuff to Mom, but I can't bear to sift through the chocolate cake, hunting for the few parts I can salvage.

Mom squeezes my shoulder. "Okay."

I turn to leave and see the eating table with its empty plates and balled-up napkins, crumbs layering the floor like an overturned flowerbox. "I'm sorry about the cake, Mom."

"I love you, dear heart," my mother says, which isn't a reply but answers everything that matters.

JESSA IS CURLED ON THE bed, her purple stuffed dog, Princess, tucked under her chin. Her walls have been dimmed, so the only illumination comes from the moonlight slithering through the blinds.

"Knock, knock," I say at the door.

She mumbles something, and I walk into the room. Sitting on the bed, I rub her back between the shoulder blades. Where do I start? Mom's so much better at this than me, but since she took an extra shift at work, I've had to pinch hit for her more and more.

I used to worry I wouldn't say the right thing. When I told Mom, she blew the bangs off her forehead. "You think I know what I'm doing? I make it up as I go along."

So I gave my sister a bowl of ice cream when Alice Bitterman told her they were no longer friends. And when Jessa said she was afraid of the monsters under her bed? I gave her a toy Taser and told her to shoot them.

Maybe it's not the best parenting in the world, but I'm not a parent.

Jessa turns her head, and in the glow of the walls, I see tears in her eyes. My heart twists. I would give up every bite of my dinner to take the sadness away. But it's too late. The food lodges in my stomach, heavy and dense.

"I don't want to leave," she says. "I want to stay here, with you and Mom."

I gather her in my arms. Her knees poke into my ribs, and her head doesn't quite fit under my chin. Princess tumbles to the floor. "You're not going anywhere. I promise."

"But Mom said—"

"She's scared. People say all kinds of things when they're scared."

She sticks a knuckle into her mouth and gnaws. We weaned her from the thumb-sucking years ago, but old habits die hard. "You don't get scared."

If she only knew. I'm scared of everything. Heights. Small, enclosed places. I'm scared no one will ever love me the way my father loved my mother. I'm scared tomorrow won't give me the answers I've been waiting for.

"That's not true," I say out loud. "I'm scared of one thing."

"What?"

"The tickle monster!" I attack. She shrieks and squirms away, her head flinging out. I wince as her face almost smacks the metal headboard. But this is what I want. A laugh that jerks her entire body. Screams that come from the pit of her belly.

After a full twenty seconds, I stop. Jessa flops across her pillow, her arms dangling over the edge. If only I could wipe out the topic so easily.

"What do they want me for?" she says, when her breathing slows. "I'm only six."

I sigh. Should've tickled her longer. "I'm not sure. The scientists think psychic abilities are the cutting edge of technology. They want to study them so they can learn."

She sits up and swings her legs over the bed. "Learn what?"

"Learn more, I guess."

I look at her scrawny legs, the knees scabbed over from falling off her hovercraft. She's right. This is ridiculous. Jessa's talent is a parlor trick, nothing more. She can see a couple minutes into the future, but she's never been able to tell me anything really important—how I'll do on a big test, say, or when I'll get my first kiss.

Jessa's frown relaxes as she snuggles into her pillow. "Well, tell them, okay? Tell them I don't know anything, and then they'll leave us alone."

"Sure thing, Jessa."

She closes her eyes, and a few minutes later I hear her slow, even breathing. Standing up, I'm about to slip out when she calls, "Callie?"

I turn around. "Yes?"

"Can you stay with me? Not until I fall asleep. Can you stay with me all night long?"

It's the eve of my seventeenth birthday. I need to call Marisa, speculate with her one last time what my memory will be—if I'll see myself as a Manual Chef or have a different profession altogether.

It's been known to happen. Look at Rita Richards, in the

class ahead of me. Never touched a keyboard in her life, but her memory showed her as an accomplished concert pianist. Now, she's off studying at the conservatory, all expenses paid.

And earlier this year, Tiana Rae showed up to school with bloodshot eyes when her memory revealed a future career as a teacher instead of a professional singer. Still, we all agreed it was better to find out now that it wasn't meant to be, rather than spend an entire life trying and failing.

Whatever the possibilities, one thing is clear: I need to be in my own bed tonight, alone with my thoughts. But Jessa won't notice if I leave ten minutes after she falls asleep. And tomorrow, she won't remember she asked me to stay.

"Okay." I cross back to her bed.

"Promise me you won't leave. Promise you'll stay forever."

"I promise." It's a lie, but a small one, so white it's practically translucent. I can't be concerned. This is it. The moment I've been waiting for all my life.

Tomorrow, everything changes.